BY ERIC CLARK

BLACK GAMBIT   (1978)

THE SLEEPER   (1980)

THE SLEEPER

THE
SLEEPER

ERIC CLARK

NEW YORK ATHENEUM 1980

Library of Congress Cataloging in Publication Data
Clark, Eric, fl. 1969–
    The sleeper.

    I. Title.
PZ4.C59242S1 1980   [PR6053.L295]   823'.9'14   79–5569
    ISBN 0–689–11032–4

Composition by American Stratford Graphic Services,
Brattleboro, Vermont
Printed and bound by R. R. Donnelley & Sons Co.,
Crawfordsville, Indiana

Designed by Kathleen Carey
First American Edition

For
IAN,
my godson

No great country was ever saved by good men because good men will not go to the lengths that may be necessary.

HORACE WALPOLE

ACKNOWLEDGMENTS

Many people helped me in researching the background to this book.

Some—like D., who first guided me when I was writing about Soviet Intelligence for a book on world diplomacy—have to remain nameless.

As does the equally anonymous G., who knows all the things detailed in this book. But of those I can name I would like to thank especially:

Margaret Clark
Raymond Hawkey
Iain and Elisabeth Elliot
George Schöpflin
Dr. A. G. Marshall
The late Dr. Julius Unsdorfer
and above all, and as always, Marcelle

THE SLEEPER

PROLOGUE

Hungary, November 1956

It was just after ten when she returned to the room.

He was lying on the makeshift bed where he had slept brokenly for the past three nights.

"It's time to go," she said. "Any longer and you might be too late."

From outside the rattle of submachine fire and the thud of artillery penetrated the room. Fenn heaved himself up. The walls of the room were bare except for a print of Montgomery Clift from a film the girl would never see; her bed, unmade, lay a few feet away. In the corner a shabby, one-eyed teddy bear sat propped against the door of a cupboard. Inside the cupboard, under a pile of clothes, lay a World War II tommy gun. Fenn knew because two days before he had seen her use it to shoot two Soviet soldiers.

He looked up. The girl was holding out a handful of papers. With her slight build, she looked even younger than seventeen.

"It seems all right," said Fenn, focusing on the exit permit.

"I just hope it looks as good to someone who has seen the real thing."

"It'll get by," she said. She spoke in German, their communicating language. Fenn struggled to translate the sentence, painfully trying to remember lessons from schooldays.

He was already dressed, and pulled himself onto his feet, his clothes hanging loosely on his body. He was well over six feet tall and extremely thin. The clothes were incongruous: city wear—a dark blue suit, a once-white shirt, a dark-red tie which hung unknotted.

"How bad?" he asked.

She shrugged. "The bastards won't even let us through to the cemetery to bury our dead."

It was just over a fortnight since the Hungarian Revolution had begun, only forty-eight hours since it had become obvious that it was all over. The last frontier post was now closed. There was no safe way out unless you had a visa.

"What will you do?"

"I'll stay. I'll be all right."

Fenn struggled into his overcoat and found himself trying to work out how long it had been since he had crossed the border from a peaceful Austria.

He paused at the door, wanting to hug her but embarrassed by his youth and his Englishness. She solved his dilemma by standing well away. "Tell them what it's like," she said.

At the street exit, a body lay across the pavement. Someone had placed a handkerchief over its face. On the wall opposite was scrawled a crudely painted slogan: *Ruszkik haza*—Russians Go Home.

Smoke hung over the city. Budapest, Fenn knew, was a battered wreck from end to end.

He walked warily, despite his exit visa and British passport, his eyes continually scanning the street. Suddenly he heard the sounds of raucous laughter and smashing glass, and, turning, began a detour through the side streets. Probably Russian troops looting a store. Intruding on them was a sure way of joining the thousands of Hungarians already being transported to Siberia.

Fenn cradled his small case in his arms—the classic pose of a refugee. Snow began to fall, but turned to slush almost immediately on the wet pavements. A Russian plane swooped low, but none of the few people on the street bothered to gaze upward.

He checked his watch. The face was cracked, but it still worked. November eighth—seventeen days since he had crossed into Hungary, an enthusiastic young journalist, not yet twenty-two, determined to be where the action was when it came.

Fenn was about halfway to the station when he saw the checkpoint. There was no use trying to avoid it; his papers had to be tested sometime. He was about forty yards away, however, when the shots began, followed by a scream—one of the Russians had been hit. People began running for cover, and almost immediately Soviet machine guns began raking windows all around him.

Instinctively, Fenn hurled himself through a gaping hole into a shell-battered house, feeling his fall cushioned by something cold and yielding. Struggling to his feet, he looked down, but he already knew what it was. A body. The man lay on his back, his chest and stomach brown with dried blood. A fortnight before, Fenn would have been sick. Now he had seen worse.

More firing outside. Fenn knew he had to get out—the tanks would be here soon. Looking up, he saw the rear wall of the house had been left intact and a door stood in the center. Fenn opened it, expecting to enter another room, but there was nothing; the whole of the back of the building had been destroyed. He stepped onto rubble and into the open air and hesitated for a moment, undecided.

A shape moved a few yards ahead and Fenn turned to retreat, when he saw it beckoning to him, yelling in Hungarian. The words meant nothing, but the meaning was clear: Follow me. The man began to run, a rifle in his left hand, and Fenn stumbled behind, negotiating the piles of broken brick.

They reached a street. A Hungarian police jeep stood parked in front of him, and Fenn turned hurriedly, but a hand grasped him. *"Nem! Nem!"* No! No! The face was friendly.

Fenn understood at once. The freedom fighters were being helped by police sympathizers.

"Hova mész?" Where are you heading?

He understood and answered in crude Hungarian, "A *pályaudvar*." The railway station.

The accent, coupled with his features, betrayed him.

"You are American?" The words, spoken haltingly, were in English, the first he had heard for over a week.

"English."

His arm was pulled. "Come."

They sat in the back, squashed between two men in police uniforms. Fenn's companion spoke to the driver. They argued, and then the jeep pulled away.

"It's all right," said the man. "He'll take you. Nothing personal. He doesn't like foreigners at the moment."

Fenn understood. The driver, like many Hungarians, felt the Western nations should have intervened. He had given up apologizing. He shrugged and slumped down in his seat.

He remained like that until they had stopped. As he climbed out, his companion pointed. "That way. You're almost there. There'll be a check, but you have papers?"

The jeep pulled away immediately and was out of sight before Fenn realized that he had not said thank you.

His papers had their first test at the station. The soldier who examined them ordered him to wait and fetched a Russian civilian who studied Fenn's visa, his face and the suitcase with its hotel stickers. As he stared into Fenn's eyes, there seemed to be recognition. He handed back the papers, nodded, and Fenn was through.

After an hour's wait, a train came, and Fenn found himself wedged into the corner of a corridor, held upright by a mass of people. A bottle of *barack* was handed around, and Fenn drank deeply. Since he hadn't eaten in twelve hours, the drink took immediate effect, and he slipped into a restless half sleep.

Shouting awakened him. They were at Györ, halfway between Budapest and Vienna. Fenn was lucky—minutes more and the train would have moved on, past his destination. He fought his way toward a door; a man tried to hold him back, obviously concerned that Fenn did not know they were still over thirty miles from the frontier, but Fenn shrugged him off and managed to get out.

Outside the station, the snow had turned to sleet. Fenn found a restaurant, ordered by pointing and ate with concentration. It would be a long time before he ate again. He found himself thinking again how easy it would have been to have gone to the British legation to wait with the others until the Soviets allowed safe conduct out of the country. As he had before, though, he dismissed the thought. That was no way to create an impact. When he reached freedom, he wanted newspapers clamoring for him and his story.

That was why he had not remained on the train longer. Here in Györ the battered Volkswagen he had bought before crossing into Hungary waited for him. During the first ten days, despite the increasing problems of obtaining fuel, it had twice taken him to the border, where he had handed over his stories to the news agency. Almost a week before, he had left the car hidden in a yard in Györ, afraid if he took it to Budapest it would be seized. With luck, it would still be there, the rolls of film taped under the seat.

He made two telephone calls from the restaurant. Takács answered the second one almost immediately.

"I'm back. Is it safe?"

"I'm not alone, but they're friends."

Fenn was not surprised. "I'll be about half an hour."

It was an hour, though, before he reached the house, after taking several wrong turns in the darkness. Takács pushed a drink into his hand. "They're beginning to search the houses," he said. "You should leave soon."

Through an open doorway Fenn could see half a dozen men sitting huddled and silent in an adjoining room.

"What about them?"

"They should have left two hours age. Been collected. Something may have gone wrong."

"Are they wanted?"

Takács nodded. "They're all on the list."

Fenn finished his drink. He had not removed his coat. "I'll take them."

Takács showed his surprise. "Why? If you want to get film through, you've already got enough problems. Get caught with them and. . . ." He made a gun with his hand and mouthed *bang*.

Fenn turned to look at the men again. They had begun whispering together.

"A gesture," he replied. "God knows we owe it."

"All right," said Takács, "but I hope you know what you're doing."

They spent the next fifteen minutes huddled over a map, discussing possibilities. Finally, they agreed. Fenn should drive to Sopron. The border there had been the last to close, just two days before.

"It's crazy to plan beyond that," said Fenn. "We don't know what we'll meet."

Takács stabbed the map with a finger. "It may have to be the lake."

"We'll see."

Tanks and armored cars were patrolling the streets as Fenn drove to join Road I toward Vienna, but no one stopped the Volkswagen—the checks would be concentrated closer to the border, Fenn knew. He crossed the Rába Bridge and turned onto Road 85. They were in open country now, mist billowing over the fields. No one spoke and Fenn drove mechanically. His immediate worry was fuel. Sopron was less than ninety kilometers away, but Fenn doubted there was more than five liters left in the tank. Takács, unable to supply any, had thought Fenn might get some at Kapuvár on the way, and had given Fenn an address.

The car did not make it. As the engine coughed to a halt,

Fenn pulled off the road, still three to four kilometers away from Kapuvár. Two of his passengers spoke German and he asked one to go with him. The man was small, middle-aged, enveloped in an overcoat too large for him. Under the coat, he clutched an automatic pistol.

Sleet drove into their faces as they walked and soon both were soaked and numbed with cold. Twice they saw the lights of approaching vehicles and huddled back from the roadside. Finally there were other lights. Fenn's companion knew the town, and they found their way to the address Takács had given, a small café on the outskirts. A hand-operated fuel pump stood outside. The café was closed, but a crack of light shone between the curtains.

The old woman who answered Fenn's knock was wary, her eyes darting from side to side; there was no mistaking her fear. Fenn's companion spoke quickly, urgency in his tone.

The woman opened the door wider. "*Gyorsan. Gyorsan.*" Quickly. Quickly.

Inside the hallway, she spoke in a high, nervous voice. Fenn's companion translated. "She says she will give us two cans. Then we must go. There is supposed to be no fuel."

She disappeared, gesturing them not to move. It was warm and an inviting smell of soup came from the kitchen. When she returned with the cans, she started to urge them to leave. Fenn's companion stood firm, and began to fire questions. Fenn watched the man's face; he could not understand the replies, but it was obvious that things were not good.

Suddenly the old woman relented, led them into the living room, fetched cups of soup.

Fenn looked questioningly at his companion. "Bad news?"

"She says Sopron's not safe. Swarming with Russians."

Fenn put down his cup. He had expected it. There was a telephone in the hallway, and he pointed toward it. The woman nodded: it was still working.

Fenn dialed the number he had called before, upon his arrival in Győr. It was answered immediately. "Fenn," he said.

The one word was enough. He listened, then spoke briefly and quietly. When he returned, his companion stared at him but said nothing.

It was midnight before they arrived back at the car. While the fuel was being poured, Fenn produced a tattered map and pointed at Neusiedler See, the strange, giant lake that lay part in Hungary, part in Austria. Fenn's companion translated. "Tell them I think we're within an hour of where we could cross."

The men held a whispered discussion outside the car. Finally the leader returned to Fenn and raised one thumb in a sign of agreement.

Fenn drove for just over an hour before he judged they were as close to the lake as was safe, then they abandoned the car and set off in the darkness. The sleet had stopped, but the wind was icy. Finally, they reached the reeds at the lakeside and paused. As they did, a star shell exploded in the distance, illuminating the water, followed soon afterward by the crackle of gunfire.

No one talked. They all knew what it was—Russian troops and Hungarian secret police searching for men like them.

Fenn's watch said three A.M. They must move. He knew the lake, the remainder of a prehistoric sea, was rarely more than waist deep—that it could be walked—but its black eeriness held him back. He contented himself with checking the rolls of film, wrapped in waterproof material, in his pocket. Still there . . . but the case could be left—why had he ever carried it?

Another burst of gunfire—far away, but it was the spur Fenn needed. He eased himself into the water, which reached up just above his knees. Even though he was already wet through and cold, it made him gasp. Then, without looking back, he began to wade unsteadily out into the lake, not even caring now if the others followed.

The men walked until dawn, every step an effort. Twice they found ground where the water was only inches deep and they rested briefly, as the bursts of gunfire punctuated the night. Once they thought they heard a patrol and stood motionless, turning toward each other so that their faces would not glow in the light of a shell. Even then, Fenn felt no fear—the simple effort of moving absorbed every thought and feeling.

Dawn came and the men began to feel even more vulnerable in the early light. Then came the sound. One of the Hungarians heard it first and lifted a hand to halt the others. Then Fenn heard it. He stood motionless, ears strained, trying to locate the direction. It could have been a bird or a young animal.

But it was not. The sound was unmistakable.

A baby's cry.

The Hungarian pointed and the men moved. Gradually the crying grew louder and, suddenly, the men came upon a patch of high ground screened by reeds.

The corpses within the reeds were huddled together: seven bodies, five men, two women. All had been machine-gunned, although there was no sign of blood until the men were very close. The only living thing was the baby.

It lay tightly wrapped in oilskin, packed with what looked like a piece of eiderdown, and strapped onto a man's chest. Only its head was visible; the body below kept it from the water—the man's dying act of protection.

Several of the men struggled to untie the straps, but the baby's head began rolling madly from side to side until one of them reached under the oilskin and produced what he had suspected might be there: bottles of baby milk.

The man held out his arms, took the baby and then, remembering his own children, began to feed the child. The men stared—hushed, smiles on their drawn faces. At last the baby was silent. Fenn took it, strapped it around his own waist, and began striding forward, full of renewed vigor.

The baby remained quiet, and from time to time the men stopped to peer at it, to touch its cheeks, to listen to its breathing, to will it to stay alive.

"Two months old, I'd say," said the man who had fed it. Another nodded agreement.

Fenn's elation began to yield to nervousness as the light

strengthened and still there was no sign of the Austrian side of
the lake . . . and then suddenly it was there: ground—and a
red and white Austrian flag.

Half an hour later the photographer found them. He had
been waiting for thirteen hours. Backing, he used up two rolls
of film. The best shots showed Fenn at the front of the straggly
column, the baby clutched to his chest. Soon the pictures
would be reproduced in newspapers and magazines throughout
the world.

Fenn slept in the hospital for seventeen hours before pains-
takingly dictating the story of his experiences. The agency rep-
resenting him auctioned it this time. A day later they nego-
tiated the writing of an "instant" book.

The offers of employment began within the week. The best,
financially, was from an American wire service. Fenn delayed
making a decision until he had received guidance, then he
signed a contract with the right-wing British *Daily Telegraph*.

This, it was thought, would help his access to the bureaucrats
and the diplomats throughout the West and would also reinforce his anti-Soviet and anti-Communist credentials. That
was especially important, because Fenn's father was a dedicated
Marxist and he had brought up his son to be one, too.

It was crucial that Fenn's conversion be seen to be complete.
For Fenn *was* a believer. Despite everything he had seen in
Hungary, he remained convinced that the Russians had done
only what was necessary. His escape had had to contain some
risk. Everything possible, however, had been done to minimize
it. After his telephone call from the café, Russian patrols on
the lake would have been instructed to shoot wide.

The main thing was to establish him in a position of future
usefulness which, as the correspondent of a respected, major
newspaper, is exactly where he would be. At the same time,
hundreds of other pro-Soviet Hungarians were being planted.
It was, after all, an opportunity too good to be missed.

Five weeks after his return, Fenn met his contact, Vladimir, in an apartment off the King's Road, Chelsea. The congratulations were fulsome. Fenn, though, was disappointed by his instructions: "Lie low, wait, do nothing until you hear from us. First you must establish yourself."

A week later Fenn was in the Middle East, reporting on the withdrawal of the Israeli forces from the Sinai Strait.

Lying on his bed, guzzling whiskey from a flask, waiting for a telephone connection to London, he read through a three-day-old *New York Times* passed on by an American colleague.

One item seized his attention—a picture of a small baby being held by a man and a woman. "Child of Revolution Meets New Parents," read the caption.

Fenn scanned the story. The baby he had carried out of Hungary had been adopted in Britain. He stared at the photograph for a long time. The finding of the child and its rescue had not been planned; in fact, it had been the only truthful thing in the whole "escape." Vladimir had called it a welcome bonus.

Now, staring at the newspaper, Fenn found himself hoping the child would be happy. The name of the couple adopting it was vaguely familiar, but no more: Joseph Banks and his Hungarian-born wife. He was a very rich academic. They had no children.

The telephone beside Fenn's bed rang and he lifted the receiver. "Your call to London."

Fenn reached for his notebook, dismissed the newspaper report from his thoughts, and began to dictate his story.

CHAPTER 1

WEST GERMANY, MAY 198–

The sound of sirens wailed outside—an exercise to test the camp's preparedness for a Soviet attack on Western Europe. The time was nine P.M.

Inside, in a guarded, windowless hut in a remote and restricted corner of the U.S. Army camp, four men were watching three others through a one-way glass mirror. One of the three men was in a chair, picked out in a pool of dazzling light from a spotlight above. Another was perched on a table, less than two feet away from him. The third was standing, and it was his voice, American Midwestern and distorted by the loudspeakers, which the four observers could hear.

"Shit. Nothing but shit." His expression was exasperated, his patience obviously exhausted. He turned away from the man seated and faced his colleague perched on the table's edge.

"It's all shit. He's got nothing. I don't know why we're wasting our time. God, Ed, he's lying and you and me have to stay here and listen to this crap day after day, night after night."

With a sudden movement he turned and grasped the hair of the man in the chair. The man was big, perhaps 200 pounds, but he was too tired to struggle. His head was yanked back. "Why did they send you? Who was it? Who briefed you?"

He yanked again and the man on the chair, who was called Vitali Suslov and who for almost a month had been protesting that all he wanted to do was defect and give information, fell sideways and then, ridiculously, keeled over on to the floor.

"I don't like this," said one of the observers. His accent was upper-class English.

"It'll be over soon. He's had enough for now." The speaker was American. He leaned forward and pushed a button on a small control panel. In the room one of the interrogators felt a brief stab of pain as the tiny electrical charge from the disk taped to his side was activated. He nodded to his partner and with feigned resignation they dragged the Russian out of the door.

The American who had pushed the button flicked a switch on the same control panel. A picture of Suslov being heaved into a tiny cell appeared on one of the two television monitors.

The interrogators lifted him on to the camp bed, the sole piece of furniture. Suslov did not move when they left, but the observers could hear the trembling of his breathing—magnified by the sensitive microphones planted to pick up anything he uttered in his sleep.

"Come on," said the second American, who had remained silent most of the half hour the two Englishmen had spent in the observation room, "I'll buy you a drink. I know this stuff is necessary, but I feel like you—it gives me the creeps."

The "bar" was in another part of the same building—a table with a few bottles and glasses. Furniture was kept to the minimum to facilitate the daily physical and electronic sweeps for bugging devices.

The American, whose name was Hunter, was in his midthirties, and had cropped hair and a tan that had obviously taken a lot of work. He poured drinks and handed them around before speaking.

His tone was apologetic. "We call it 'hostile interrogation,'" he volunteered. "It looks tough but no one gets really hurt. It's just to put over the message that they're being questioned for real. It's what they *think* might happen to them that's important."

The two Englishmen raised their glasses and caught each other's gaze. Ravensthorne, of the British Secret Intelligence Service, knew the remark was directed mainly at him—he was the one who had voiced his distaste during the interrogation—and his tone was conciliatory. "I know," he said. "Just me getting old."

Both he and Meadows, of the British Security Service, MI5, were taking it gently, allowing the Americans to dictate the pace.

The surprise invitation to the interrogation—and to read transcripts of earlier questioning—had come twenty-four hours earlier. Suslov had defected from the Soviet Mission to the United Nations in Geneva. *If* his defection, a month before, was genuine, it was an important one. If he was to be believed, he operated a clearing house for intelligence information collected from Western agents in Switzerland.

The Englishmen, though, were skeptical about his credentials —even though both knew that at least a third of the Russians working in Geneva were members of the KGB or of military intelligence, the GRU.

"He didn't bring much in the way of documents," Ravensthorne said. It was a statement, but in keeping with the gentle approach he voiced it like a question. His manner suited the tone—a rather effete-looking man, tall and stooping, dressed in good clothes that had been treated shabbily.

"That's right. That's one reason we worried a lot at first."

Suslov, as all of them were aware, would have known that his reception by the Americans would owe much to the paper he was able to take with him. Contrary to general belief, intelligence services were far from enthusiastic about defectors. If they were genuine, it was often better to persuade them to remain where they were and operate as agents. Quite often the information they wanted to give was already known. Once they fled, that material was compromised and its usefulness gone.

And, of course, there was always the chance that the defector was a plant. A man meant to spread disinformation or to find out from the questioning what the opposition knew and did not know.

Meadows thought all this, and said, "But you decided you wanted him?"

Hunter spread his hands. "If he was what he said he was—and we're now convinced he was telling the truth about that—then what he could *tell* us was worth what he's asking."

"Which is?" Meadows had wondered about the Russian's motive. Apart from the bare notification that they had Suslov, the CIA had volunteered nothing.

"Two things," said Hunter. "First, he says he was unappreciated, passed over for a top job that went to someone younger. You'll see that on the transcripts. The second you won't. He wants money for names: $200,000 down and $40,000 a year. Plus, of course, things like a new identity."

Meadows put down his glass. He was a square-built man, solid, dependable-looking. His method of working was to plod away, probing the same spot until he was satisfied.

"But he still didn't bring much in the way of papers."

Hunter shrugged; he didn't care what the Englishmen believed. Then he remembered his orders: Treat them with kid gloves.

"He says he planned to bring documents. Then after his meetings with us he suspected they were on to him and had to run, grabbing what little he could get his hands on quickly."

Ravensthorne decided to intervene. "How would you assess him now?"

The CIA man swirled his drink. "Still early, but I'd say maybe sixty-five to thirty-five genuine."

Ravensthorne's tone conveyed his skepticism. "As high as that? Already?"

He put down his drink unfinished. His brief, given before leaving London, had been simple: Listen, but don't be anything but noncommittal.

He looked at his watch. 9:57. He was tired, but the important thing was to impress on the CIA how London felt—he had to display gratitude but show he was not convinced, be thankful but at the same time be a little patronizing.

"Perhaps we could read the transcripts," he said.

The American put down his glass.

"I thought maybe you'd say that," he replied, smiling.

He gestured toward a door.

"They're all waiting."

The two Englishmen read until after three o'clock the following morning. There were a month's transcripts—raw, unedited.

They said little to each other, and even that was small talk—they knew that the Americans were certainly monitoring them.

Both, though, noted the same three items of information: (1) the date that the Soviet Mission in Geneva had known of the secret agreement between the United States and Israel; (2) the reference to Suslov being instructed to cease to find out the United Kingdom's current attitude toward neutron weapons; and, above all, (3) the Soviet Union's detailed knowledge of the secret transfer of American Cruise missile technology to the British—information not known even by Britain's NATO partners.

At the end of the reading the two men looked at each other.

"Christ, I'm tired," said Meadows.

"I think we should turn in," said Ravensthorne.

They would have liked to talk. Both knew what the other must be thinking.

Banks. Sir Joseph Banks. Friend and adviser to the man who might just be the next British prime minister.

And a man who as far as the Americans were concerned was a high-priority target. To their mind, a spy and a traitor. The man who, they thought, had given the Soviet Union the highly sensitive material that Suslov had detailed.

CHAPTER 2

The helicopter pilot's voice crackled over the cabin loud-speaker. "Coming into view now, sir."

Although the cabin normally held seats for eight people, the inside had been stripped to provide working and resting area for just one man. Richard Stanley Godwin, former British Defence Minister, and, he firmly believed, the country's next Prime Minister.

Godwin heard, but continued reading until he had finished the sheet in front of him, then he carefully packed his papers into his briefcase before looking out of the window.

He saw the spire of the church and then, perhaps a mile away from it, the house—golden limestone set in lush, green fields. He shivered. The sight moved him. England, his England.

The landing strip had been marked out in a paddock, and Godwin could now see the house's owner and his friend and supporter, Sir Joseph Banks, waiting to greet him. It was typical of the man, thought Godwin. Banks must have asked that a watch be kept for the helicopter, and then the moment it had been seen he had dropped everything so that he would be there.

The helicopter trembled as the pilot held it against the

strong wind and then gently the Bell twin turbine 222 set down.

The moment Godwin emerged, Banks stepped forward to greet him, the tufts of white hair on the sides of his otherwise bald head blown into shapes vaguely like horns by the helicopter blades.

It gave him an even more bizarre appearance than usual. At best, he was a man whose looks attracted attention—not only was his body immensely fat, but all his features were larger than life: a huge nose, thick lips, a fold of surplus skin under his eyes. His stomach and the rolls of fat under his chin spoke, accurately, of a man who overindulged. In contrast to this was the dandyishness of the dress—the lilac shirt with matching tie and pocket handkerchief, the gold fob watch, the pale tinted glasses.

When he spoke, his voice was deep—the voice that was sought after for conferences and after-dinner speeches—and Godwin forgot the grossness. Banks was not only rich, powerful and intellectually renowned, but also a great charmer.

As they walked to the house, Banks waved back toward the helicopter. "Proving useful, I hope."

"I could never have done so much without it."

The helicopter belonged to one of the companies controlled by the Banks family. Now it was being made available to Godwin for his election tour.

Godwin began talking about the campaign before they reached the house, his voice excited. Polling day was only ten days away. Banks smiled inwardly. Godwin's enthusiasm, his total conviction in himself, and his views (which in the main coincided with Banks's own) were among the reasons he backed the man with his money and with whatever influence he could bring to bear.

The room they entered was huge, a massive tapestry dominating one wall. Without having to be summoned, a boy appeared and poured champagne. Godwin knew, without looking, it would be from the Banks's family vineyards in Epernay.

He sipped and stared at the tapestry, although he had admired it many times before. It depicted Edward I's army facing the Scots at Falkirk at the end of the thirteenth century. The Scots were drawn up in an incredibly strong defense position—but they had not expected the new English weapon, the longbow.

"It must have been devastating," said Godwin as Banks moved beside him.

"It was. The Scots were slaughtered. As you say, devastating. Quite a weapon—fast, lethal, accurate to two hundred and fifty yards." His voice conveyed admiration.

"Careful," said Godwin, jokingly. "You don't sound like the man I hope will be my disarmament adviser."

Banks reached for more champagne. "Now don't goad me, Richard," he said. "You know I'm not against *just* war, only against us destroying ourselves or stocking up more weapons than we need to keep the military happy and the manufacturers rich."

It was a subject on which both men felt strongly. Although a passionate anti-Communist, Godwin was a firm advocate of arms control and disarmament. His convictions were forged by many things—not least, anger at the money arms took that could help finance some of his other plans. Mainly, though, his strong feelings had evolved from instinctive antagonism to the military and the military machine. The arms producers and their users, he believed, constituted a terrible mutual-benefit club. The warriors wanted arms; the manufacturers wanted to supply them. Together they conspired to keep each other powerful. As Defence Minister, he had tried to tackle them. Even with his talents, he had been hardly able to make a dent.

A major problem was getting information on what was really happening. The men who advised the politicians were part of the military machine—which was where Banks had come in. Both before and after World War II Banks had established himself as one of the world's leading academic thinkers on the subject. Godwin had needed Banks when he was only a back bench Member of Parliament; more when he was Minister of Defence. As Prime Minister . . .

The two men lunched outside in a small, white-walled patio. As always when they ate together, the portions were too large for Godwin. The politician wondered at the other's capacity for food and drink, and marveled at Banks's health in view of them. Banks had a reputation for working and playing to the limits. His work load was prodigious—and even though he was at the age when most men think of retirement, he seemed determined to add to his commitments, not shed them.

Despite his attempts to be abstemious, Godwin was slightly drunk after lunch. It was a good feeling. It was rare that he could relax, but he could with Banks, if only because he was the one man who genuinely wanted nothing from him.

A large bowl of strawberries and a jug of cream were placed on the table together with a third bottle of champagne.

Godwin served himself.

"You'll join me?" he asked.

Banks was already eating again. He paused, his spoon halfway to his mouth. He knew what Godwin meant: Would he advise on disarmament again?

"After last time?"

Godwin put down his spoon and brushed away a fly.

"I'm sorry about that, Joseph," he said. "It's just another indication of why I need you."

During Godwin's term as Minister of Defence, Security had suggested that Banks should be investigated. Nothing *really*, but there had been some leaks. . . .

Godwin had stamped on that firmly. Very firmly.

His official advisers did not want disarmament, no matter what they said. It followed that they did not want Banks with his views and influence. Hence, their rather unsubtle attempt to discredit him.

The meal finished, they walked, both still holding their glasses.

Banks led the way to the stables. A groom was checking the horses. Banks paused at one stall. "I've just bought this one for Jennifer," he said. "I hope she'll like it."

His voice was worried, not boastful. He really did hope she would like it.

"Is she here? I'd like to see her."

Banks finished his champagne in a gulp. "No. Away. Having a bit of a holiday." His tone did not invite further inquiry. Godwin suspected that she had gone off with a man again. He was not a man for gossip, but people kept him in touch. It was sometimes unpleasant, but necessary.

They began to walk back to the house, both men suddenly somber.

Godwin had feared asking the next question, anxious not to spoil the day's mood. But if he had to ask, this was the moment.

"Will I see Pip?"

Pip was Banks's wife, Hungarian, a woman he had met just after World War II in Austria. On the strength of his wartime secret service career in the Special Operations Executive in North Africa, he had been persuaded to take a short secondment at the Defector Reception Center in Vienna before his return to academic life. Pip—Piroska—had been an interpreter there. Their marriage had been idyllic for years. Their one big sadness—that they could not have children—had been removed by the adoption of Jennifer.

Without meaning to, Godwin found himself staring toward the extensions to the house. The new buildings, carefully constructed to match the rest, were, Godwin knew, sealed off by heavily locked doors.

"Not today, I fear," replied Banks, his voice emotionless. "I gather she had a bad night."

"Sorry to hear that," said Godwin. "Perhaps next time." One had to keep up pretenses.

Then he saw Banks's face, full of genuine hurt and sadness.

"Her voices returned," said Banks quietly.

Godwin found it impossible to say anything. Pip had developed schizophrenia late in life. Gradually she had withdrawn into a world full of fantasies. Banks refused to allow her to be confined to an institution even when her illness became chronic and her voices urged her to commit dangerous acts.

He had built the new extension after she had tried to set fire to the house. She lived there now with her two nurses.

Minutes passed. Banks was staring into the distance. "At least she's there," he said at last. "There are still days . . ." He turned to Godwin, embarrassing with the intensity of his gaze. "I don't know what I'd do if she wasn't there at all."

Godwin reached out to touch his arm, checked himself.

Banks shrugged with his hands, tried a smile. "Sorry," he said. English gentlemen do not parade their emotions, even to friends.

He started back toward the house, calling over his shoulder as he went.

"Some shop talk," he said. "A walk to the village, a drink in the pub, a good dinner, and a game of billiards. How do you fancy that?"

The future Prime Minister, hurrying to catch up, beamed, his embarrassment gone, his sadness submerged.

CHAPTER 3

Election day began with all the wrong omens for Godwin.

The weather forecast promised a fine, dry day—traditionally supposed to help the party in power. The latest polls gave his opponents a seven-point lead. And Ladbrokes, the bookmakers, were quoting odds against his victory of seven to four.

Godwin's wife, Georgina, watched him across the dining table as they breakfasted. She had seen what the polls said, sought his reaction, but would not ask.

Godwin sensed her gaze and looked up from his newspaper. "They'll look silly when the results come in," he said.

Georgina knew he was not saying it because confidence was what was wanted of a politician. Godwin believed it. Totally.

"They don't understand the people and what they want now," he continued. "They live in their ivory towers and have great liberal thoughts. But they don't know."

Georgina nodded. She believed too.

They spent the day in Godwin's constituency. His own victory to retain his Parliamentary seat—a victory never in doubt—was announced early.

By the late evening, when they traveled back to London, there had been nothing of real significance. The election could still go either way. Certainly no one was going to have a landslide victory.

Godwin's secretary, Merton, was still up when they walked past the small, waiting crowd into the house.

"I'm going to bed," announced Godwin. "I suggest you do too."

Merton, who was in his twenties, keen, and had only held the job for six months, could not hide his surprise.

Godwin smiled. The excitement of youth! "Nothing will happen for a few hours," he said. "And if it does, someone will wake me."

On his way to the bedroom he looked into the study to glance over the list of messages. Only two—from key party officials—could not wait. He phoned them. Then he decided he would return Joseph's call.

His wife looked in. "They're wrong, dear," she said. "I still believe they're wrong."

She was referring to something they had both sensed. Even Godwin's colleagues doubted he would win.

"Thank you." He kissed her good night, tenderly, brotherly on both cheeks. Sex, always forced and performed as a duty, had ceased between them years before. Now they channeled their energies into his political future—like celibate priests for their faith.

Banks answered quickly; he must have been sitting by the telephone. "Richard, I never expected you to call back—not tonight when you're so busy. It was only to say thank you."

"Thank you?" Godwin was puzzled.

"Yes, thank you. Because of those stupid pollsters, I got excellent odds on you at my bookmaker. I expect to make a fortune."

Godwin chuckled. It was good to have one's self-faith reaffirmed. Whether Banks had genuinely placed a bet or not did not matter. The reassurance was good—and at precisely the right time.

He slept, undisturbed until six, when the news was that his party had won two marginal seats.

His colleagues began to wonder, his opponents to fear, that he *might* win after all.

At 2:18 that afternoon the outgoing Prime Minister finally conceded defeat. It looked as though Godwin, against all odds, would have a majority of as many as thirty seats.

At his home, Godwin received a succession of notes and telephone calls, all congratulating him, all assuring him that the senders had never doubted his victory for a minute.

Godwin enjoyed the moment. A defeat could easily have meant he would have lost the leadership of the party too. He had insisted on leading the campaign personally, defining the main issues. If the tactics had proved wrong, no one else could have been blamed. But, of course, as *he* had always known, they had been right.

Within two hours the machine that organizes the change-over of prime ministers was fully in action. Barricades held back the crowds when he and Georgina arrived at No. 10 Downing Street. A brief word to reporters and then he was inside, with the frock-coated doorkeeper closing the door behind him.

He had been in the house many times, but this time was different. This time it was *his* house, *his* office. The private secretaries—calling him "Prime Minister"—were *his* private secretaries. . . .

He received his first briefing as the country's political leader, glanced at urgent cables, and then there was a whispered message and he was led away to accept the telephoned congratulations of the President of the United States.

Suddenly, wanting to be alone, he swept everyone away, and sat in the Cabinet Room. He took the Prime Minister's seat—the only one with arms—and turned and looked up at the portrait of Walpole above.

In a rare moment of almost boyish pleasure, he lifted his

feet and placed them on the Cabinet table. He kept them there for no more than a minute.

There were sounds from the adjoining private secretaries' rooms.

Time for action.

Godwin stood and went out. One of the assistant private secretaries was on the telephone. Godwin could not help hearing his end of the conversation.

"No, Sir Joseph, no. I'm afraid that the Prime Minister really is engaged."

Godwin took the receiver from him. His words were soon to carry around Whitehall, to be noted by all the bureaucrats.

"I'm always in to Sir Joseph," he said.

As the burdens of office grew, it was—inevitably—not to be so. But the point had been made.

It was inconceivable, surely, that such a man could be a traitor.

Both men shared that same thought as they set out to walk in the June afternoon drizzle followed at a discreet distance by their respective bodyguards. They huddled under an umbrella. Sir Edward Crimpton, director of SIS, and Sir Robert Hollen, his MI5 counterpart, had lunched together at one of Hollen's clubs, the Atheneum.

The meal had been arranged some days before in the light of a possible change of government. It did, after all, make sense for the two men to know the outline of the briefing which the other would give the new Prime Minister later in the week.

Now, however, their thoughts were on a subject they had agreed would not be in the briefing even though it was their major concern—the American claim that that Suslov's "evidence" was convincing additional proof of Banks's treachery.

They crossed the Mall and began a circuit of St. James's Park. Crimpton broke the silence. He was a tall, round-shouldered man with a head of silver hair that was too long for a man of his age.

"I suppose it is inevitable that Banks will be brought back," he said. "We're not getting into a flap about something that may never happen?"

Hollen slowed to light his pipe. He was shorter than Crimpton, and stout, his face white and moon-shaped, and he had a faint trace of a moustache as though he had never decided whether to grow one or not. His words were calm, considered, but were often belied by his mannerisms—nervous pulls on his collar or twitches of his neck.

Finally, after several matches, smoke began to billow in the breeze.

"No doubt, I'd say. Godwin's got a fixation about disarmament—his only left-of-center view. So has the party—not out of conviction but because they see some money saved. And it so happens that it's in line with what the Americans want, officially at least."

"And then, of course," Crimpton interjected, "there's Banks himself."

"Exactly. You know he's got a garden key?"

Crimpton mouthed astonishment. A garden key meant Banks could use the back entrance to No. 10 Downing Street—a privilege reserved for the Prime Minister and his family, the private secretaries and very close advisers.

Bent forward against the rain, the two men remained silent for several minutes, seemingly oblivious to anything but their own thoughts.

"Banks *is* superb at what he does, you have to admit that." Crimpton's tone conveyed his admiration. Banks's background was the kind that impressed him: an old family, wealth rejuvenated by eighteenth- and nineteenth-century adventuring. Banks himself held a large holding in the family's conglomerate of companies that ranged from property to timberland to plastics, but he played little part in the business administration, preferring to devote himself to intellectual pursuits. He had quickly established an international reputation, first in the United States before World War II and afterward at Oxford.

Furthermore, he went to the right tailor, bought his wine from the right wine merchants, belonged to the right clubs.

They reached the center of the park, paused and looked back at the Whitehall skyline—an Eastern-looking fairytale of roofs above the trees.

"But is he guilty?" insisted Hollen. "Isn't that the point?"

It was a question both men had first had to face three years before when the Americans had approached with "proof." The evidence offered had been circumstantial—Banks was not the only man with access to the material that the CIA had discovered had been leaked to the Soviet Union.

Such inquiries as could be mounted then had ceased when Godwin had left office on a change of government and Banks had lost access to highly sensitive material.

"You think he is?" asked Crimpton.

"I'm not sure. Certainly not enough evidence to convict a man in a court of law."

"But then we're not seeking a conviction, are we?" said Crimpton.

"No, but it will be even harder to persuade the Prime Minister than it would be a judge."

The rain stopped. Crimpton tested the air with his hand. Satisfied, he began to furl the umbrella.

"So?" he insisted.

Hollen was forced to commit himself. "I'd say not much *real* evidence, but enough suspicion to regret his having any access to important information."

They reached the end of the park and crossed into the calm of Green Park. Tourists huddled against the railings of Buckingham Palace despite a sign which "regretted" that the day's mounting of the guard had been canceled.

"I've tried to keep an open mind," volunteered Crimpton, who had been one of the men three years before who had thought Banks *not* guilty. "I'm damned, though, if I can see that this so-called new evidence adds much. A defector who may or may not be genuine produces a few more pieces of highly circumstantial evidence. That's all."

Both Crimpton and Hollen had received reports from their men who had witnessed Suslov's interrogation. They had been in agreement—an American-staged charade. The defector might be genuine, but this replies were either rehearsed or limited to what the CIA *wanted* British intelligence to hear. The point? To warn the British that their doubts about Banks were as great as ever. And that this time they expected action.

Crimpton stopped and turned to face Hollen. "I'm not sure we're not past the point of worrying about the nicety of his guilt or otherwise. Our American friends are beginning to lean on us *very* heavily."

"Us too."

"You mean apart from the stage show in Germany?"

Hollen nodded. "Yes, for two-three weeks now we've been suspecting material is being held back. Northern Ireland, for example—American feed-in on who is giving money and where arms are coming from has dwindled by about half."

Crimpton began to laugh, a forced, high-pitched sound. "We can't persude the Americans he's innocent and we'll never convince the Prime Minister he's guilty. What a beautiful situation to be in."

"Do we go to Godwin, though? Try again?"

The key question of the afternoon.

Crimpton had already considered it. "I don't see how we can. We tried three years ago. We've got little extra evidence now— nothing very convincing. Godwin threw us out then. Now he's Prime Minister."

"But you agree we must do something?"

The second key question.

"Yes. Yes. I don't see we have any alternative."

"Then if we feel we can't see the Prime Minister, we must go to Chambers."

Chambers—Sir Peter Chambers—was Secretary to the Cabinet, a man who had served six administrations. A power behind the throne. Governments came, were voted out of office, he went on, master of a vast army of changeless civil servants, holder of more secrets than probably any other man in Britain.

It was the only possibility and both men knew it.

Hollen shuddered. He had only another year to retirement. He did not want to take risks now.

If anything went wrong, he was placing his head neatly on the block.

CHAPTER 4

Sir Peter Chambers was practicing on the private croquet lawn in the grounds of his house.

Croquet was a passion. With his punishing working hours he had less time to indulge it than he would have wished. That was why he had built the private court—full size, larger than a tennis court, and floodlit so that he could play on autumn evenings. Fortunately, thanks to his American wife—and her late husband, a cable TV tycoon—he could afford the luxury.

Colleagues thought croquet was the perfect game for him. Despite its popular image, it was a game calling for great mental and physical skills, plus determination to win and great ruthlessness—characteristics Chambers had in full measure.

At eleven-thirty on Sunday morning Chambers managed to retain the look of a top civil servant despite the white trousers and leisure shirt. Even at home he carried a slight air of weariness—the look that told politicians of the weight of the problems on his shoulders.

Chambers knew his colleagues would begin arriving soon— Like him they were punctual men—but he did not return indoors. They could join him outside.

He looked back toward the house—after croquet, his other passion. The front overlooked the River Thames. The rear gardens, in which he now stood, were screened by high walls, and contained a small lake, lawns and a tree-studded area perfect for picnics.

The house itself had been built five hundred years before by a wealthy London merchant and then been ruined over the centuries by new owners determined to alter or modernize it. Chambers, with the seemingly bottomless resources of his wife's fortune, had restored it to its original glory.

The men Chambers was expecting were Hollen and Crimpton and the heads of three government departments—the Foreign Office, the Defence Ministry and the Treasury. He was about to seek their advice because of their years in power, their wisdom, and their positions in the machinery of real government.

Even though he had not told Hollen and Crimpton, the problem the two men had brought to him was not unknown. He had already received a similar approach from Sir Richard Fogarty, former head of both MI5 and SIS, and still the Cabinet's chief advisor on security although officially retired. Fogarty had been warned by the Americans, unofficially, that they were prepared to withhold even more information than the heads of the two security services realized.

There was a shout from the house—Chambers's wife letting him know that the first of his visitors had arrived. He waved for the newcomer, Defence, to join him.

Chambers had called his colleagues together with some reluctance—his training and instinct told him he should put his political masters first. The meeting, in itself, was a small betrayal of that, but he consoled himself with the example of predecessors who had been forced to rise to unusual situations—men like those who had passed secret information about Germany to Winston Churchill while he was in the wilderness before World War II.

Chambers waited until they were all gathered, drinks in

hand, before thanking them formally. "I asked you," he said, "because it concerns the Prime Minister fairly directly."

Chambers nodded at Hollen and the security chief began recounting the situation.

For two of the department heads, the story confirmed rumors they had heard three years earlier, before they had reached their present exalted positions. The third—Foreign Office—knew the background and shuddered at the ramifications of what they were being told.

"What we have to do, I feel," said Chambers, "is decide what if anything *we* should do."

The head of the Foreign Office picked up a spare mallet and began to hit balls. Chambers watched and winced. Foreign Office prided himself on being good at the game but he had a fairly common mistake that offended Chambers—he hit the ball with an exaggerated follow-through. It was intentional—meant to create top spin in the mistaken belief that this would help the ball through the hoop if the shot was not totally accurate.

Comments and questions began immediately.

Defence made the point that the Americans were reacting in a way that the Russians so often did: hardly a week passed by without the Russians being convinced that a Soviet official, frequently innocent, was passing information. Then, much to the amusement of the West, the official was transferred to a minor post or sent to a labor camp.

Treasury raised the question of interrogating Banks; surely the man could be made to confess if he was guilty. Immediately he had spoken he realized the stupidity of the suggestion.

Foreign Office asked a question: When, was it thought, might Banks have been recruited? Hollen answered. There were two possibilities. It might have been in the classic fashion during the thirties when many intellectuals had believed that Communism held the only answer to Fascism. Alternatively, Banks could have been approached during the war when, as an SOE operative, he would have had close links with Communist resistance groups.

"His wife's Hungarian." Defence.

Again Hollen replied. "Yes. We've looked at that. An obvious blackmail lever, of course—but as far as we can trace there are no family left there."

"And the daughter?" Again Defence.

Hollen shrugged. "We don't even know her real name, let alone her family, if they still exist."

Chambers's daughter brought fresh drinks. She was a tall, horsey-looking girl, the product of his first marriage with the daughter of an earl.

Treasury picked up a croquet mallet and began using it like a golf putter. "Who first put together the pieces and came up with the accusation of Banks?" he asked.

"The Americans," said Hollen.

"Wanting to pass the blame. Surely they resent the man and what he stands for. On arms he's *too* liberal."

Defence did not like Bank's views either, but he was forced to agree. "They think he's a bad influence—naive, a bit dangerous."

"Could the leaks have been American?" Treasury sent a ball through a hoop and allowed himself a smile.

"For most of the things we know, yes. But there are two instances that would seem to have needed access to Cabinet papers."

"And Banks is the common factor?"

"He could be."

Foreign Office returned to the Suslov defection. "How seriously do we take this new information?"

Crimpton looked at Hollen and Chambers before replying. "I think," he said carefully, "that we'd all agree that it adds something—but not very much. The key point is that it represents the Americans serving notice on us that they expect us to do something."

It was Foreign Office who fed Chambers with the question he had been waiting for. "What happens if we don't?"

Chambers's reply was blunt. "They're blackmailing us. That's our problem. Whether Banks is guilty or not."

He turned toward Hollen and Crimpton. "They're holding back intelligence material, as you know."

They nodded.

"They are also threatening to withhold defense research information. You all know what they would mean?"

Defence looked stunned. The Americans, with their vast resources of men, money and equipment, dominated research—but routinely passed much of it to the British whose defense contractors used it to lead their European rivals.

"They also," Chambers continued, "hint that they may withdraw commercial intelligence facilities."

This time Treasury looked visibly shocked. America, in common with other countries, intercepted commercial information as well as diplomatic and military. Again, most of this was passed to Britain, indirectly giving enormous advantage to British exporters.

Treasury spoke for them all. "We've no alternative, have we?"

Each of the men present sought the eyes of his companions.

"We agree?" asked Chambers. "Even without the Prime Minister's agreement—or even his knowledge?"

There was a long silence. Then Defence spoke. For all of them. "We owe it to the country."

Chambers walked a few yards away from the rest of them, conscious that they expected him to take the final decision, unofficial and illegal though it might be. He had been a bureaucrat all his working life. He was rich, but money did not concern him. He liked, above all, anonymous power. He was ambitious, but he was also an honorable man, according to his Establishment standards.

His creed was simple: Britain first. An ordered, democratic, free Britain.

He turned toward Hollen, conscious that the others were watching and waiting.

"My feeling," he said slowly, "and I hope others agree—but I alone am willing to take the responsibility—is that we must begin a new investigation."

Hollen bowed his head. No one else spoke. Hollen had to go through the ritual. "Without the P.M.'s permission?"

A jet airliner, beginning its descent to Heathrow Airport, filled the sky with noise. Chambers waited until there was silence. His voice when he spoke held no doubts.

"Without the Prime Minister's permission."

CHAPTER 5

Andrew Brighouse was kneeling on the floor of what was once the second bedroom and was now his aquarium.

Tanks lined the walls, providing a constant theater of color and beauty—silver, orange and black beacon fish, blood-red flame fish, gold and violet zebra fish, green, red and yellow swordfish. . . .

It was, Brighouse liked to think, the perfect contrast with the murkiness and grayness of his working life.

He finished checking that the new tank was perfectly clean and free from every trace of soap, then, with effort, he lifted it onto the already-waiting table.

Brighouse was in his mid-fifties and had a military look from his posture to his neatly trimmed moustache and short-cut silver hair. He was dressed in tweed trousers, a Viyella shirt, and a wine-colored cardigan, which he kept around the flat and wore constantly when he was indoors, winter or summer, hot or cold.

He began placing gravel in the tank, carefully tapering it from two inches deep at the back to an inch deep at the front.

It was Monday but Brighouse was beginning three days' leave—time owing after an assignment in Hong Kong.

He checked two rocks for sharp edges before adding them to the tank. At that moment the telephone rang—the loud, insistent ring that somehow says that the call is not going to be a welcome one.

Brighouse cursed, wiped his hands on an old piece of towel, and without hurrying made his way to the living room. The flat, in an old mansion in Bloomsbury, had only two bedrooms, a kitchen, a tiny bathroom and a living room, but they were separated from each other by huge, high corridors of a distant age.

The noise when Brighouse entered the living room was ear-splitting. Because of the distance between rooms and the thickness of the walls, Brighouse had had an extra loud bell installed.

He was not surprised by the voice he heard: Hollen's.

"Andrew, I'm *so* sorry to bother you at the beginning of a few days' hard-earned rest. . . ."

Brighouse knew immediately what Hollen wanted. "You'd like me to come in?"

"*Please*, Andrew." Brighouse could envisage the other, fidgeting with his pipe or nervously plucking the corner of his pocket handkerchief.

"Now?"

"Well, *if* that wouldn't be *too* awful. . . ."

They sat at the small conference table at one end of Hollen's room. The air was heavy with pipe smoke—security ordained that windows should remain closed, and the air conditioning was primitive.

Brighouse, looking more military than ever in his dark gray suit, read silently through the file, his face expressionless.

Hollen had chosen Brighouse to direct the operation because the man was not only good but safe. Someone who would not take risks, would not compromise the assignment. That morning, before telephoning Brighouse, Hollen had sent for the man's file and glanced through it even though he already knew everything he needed to know. But to see it in typescript was comforting. He lingered over a passage written shortly before Brighouse was recruited into the Security Service. The man, who was observing him as a possible recruit, wrote: "Not an innovator, but tell him to do something and it will be done, without wasted effort and moreover without unpleasant or embarrassing side-effects."

Although the statement contained much truth, Hollen now knew it failed to do Brighouse full justice. The man could, and did, innovate—but he did so with caution, only after considering every consequence, rather like a chess player reviewing his opponent's possible retaliations to his next move.

Brighouse finished reading and looked straight at Hollen. His eyes said, "Well?"

Hollen handed him a slimmer folder. "What you've read is past history," he said. "What we heard some time ago and what our investigations turned up—or rather didn't turn up. This is more recent. Very recent."

The file covered Suslov's defection, statements and the MI5 observer's comments. It was marked "No Copies"—the one Brighouse held was the only one in existence. That alone made his pulse quicken as he read, although his eyes still betrayed no emotion.

Hollen suddenly remembered that the file on Brighouse was still on his desk. He walked over and slipped it into a drawer. It would be bad form if Brighouse saw it there.

The junior man had been with the service ever since being recruited in the 1950s. He had quit the army, where he had been a major, together with a number of other officers in the general reduction of manpower decided upon by the government of the day. Brighouse had already been approached by MI5. The agency had noted his intelligence work in Kenya and Cyprus and his obvious aptitude for it.

Hollen heard a cough, turned and saw Brighouse had finished reading.

Brighouse took the initiative. "Are we planning to reopen the investigation?"

"As from now."

"Do I take it you'd like me to direct it?"

"You're so obviously the best man."

Brighouse waited. There had to be more. There were men in the organization better at that sort of probing if that was all that was involved.

At last Hollen told him about the decision to investigate without the Prime Minister's knowledge. All those involved would be acting "unofficially," he added. He did not need to spell out the risk. "In the circumstances, of course," Hollen continued. Brighouse swept aside the implied suggestion that, if he wished, he might refuse the assignment. Just as Hollen had known he would.

At heart Brighouse was still a soldier. His philosophy was simple: country first. And he believed, just as had his military ancestors, that generals were more likely to see that Britain did come first than the politicians.

Brighouse's room was on the fourth floor of the large, anonymous white and red brick MI5 building, two floors below Hollen.

He qualified for a fitted carpet, a hat stand and a painting of Westminster Bridge. He had added little himself—a regimental portrait, a silver cigarette box, out of which he smoked two cigarettes a day (one with morning coffee, one with afternoon tea), and another wine-colored cardigan, his office one.

He began work immediately. Like all good counterintelligence operators, he began by reading what was already known, but at the same time determined to reexamine every piece of information. He also started with the assumption that Banks *was* guilty. You had to believe that. All that was missing was the evidence. His job was to find it. This positive approach was, he knew, essential.

To keep it, he forced aside the likelihood that if the CIA genuinely believed Banks guilty, they would have investigated illegally—whatever MI5 had done. Obviously they had found nothing.

The first stage of the review had to be conducted with painstaking care. Every known or suspected leak of information had to be matched against the names of men who could have known those secrets.

Then, under the guise of renewing Banks's positive vetting, Brighouse ordered a new probe of Banks's background, family, friends, lifestyle.

Because of the Hungarian links—Banks's wife and adopted daughter—Brighouse enlisted the help of the service's Hungarian expert, Laszlo Rajk, whose family, despite his name, had left that country four generations before. He had made himself perhaps the leading expert, though, on the country's intelligence services and on dissident Hungarians in exile.

Checks were made on Banks's finances—the figures made Brighouse reel even though he had known the man was rich. His past traveling was probed—fortunately Banks had arranged much of it though one agency and had changed many of his bills to a credit card. The service had informants in both.

A researcher put together a detailed biography of Banks; the service's psychologists examined it in case they could suggest new areas to investigate.

After eight days, however, Brighouse had to confess that he had virtually nothing. The only new piece of information that had emerged could mean something or be totally worthless.

Banks had made an unscheduled stopover on his way back from a conference in Stockholm. Brighouse had in front of him a credit card file receipt for the overnight hotel bill. Would a man use a credit card if he was there for a clandestine purpose, such as a debriefing by his controller? He might. People were notoriously careless about the most obvious things. But Brighouse had to admit the reason for the stopover could be far

from sinister—a desire for a break, a wish for solitude. Even a
yen for an illicit weekend.

Before the end of June, Brighouse received Hollen's permission to put a surveillance team on to Banks. It was a difficult decision because it meant involving another eight men in
the operation and because there was always the possibility of
Banks spotting his tail.

In that unlikely event two cover stories were prepared: MI5
would suggest that the observation teams must be Soviet and
would promise investigation and action; alternatively, Hollen
would reveal an anonymous threat against Banks's life and
claim that the men were not following Banks but were there to
protect him.

Taps were also placed on Banks's telephones at his London
and country homes. Names of telephone callers—and of people
he called—were checked back to insure they really were who
they were supposed to be. Photographs of everyone he met were
compared against pictures and descriptions in intelligence files.

The paper mounted: reports, transcripts, surveillance forms—
filled in with timings of almost everything Banks did, and
boring in the extreme.

Of course, there were periods when they lost him, sometimes
for hours on end—private parties which they could not enter,
small gatherings it was impossible to infiltrate—but MI5 men
became art gallery visitors, waiters at banquets, window clean-
ers, and trainee taxi drivers.

And they found nothing.

Brighouse would have liked to search Banks's homes. He discussed it with Hollen, but both agreed, reluctantly, it was too
risky. Banks's country house was isolated and had a resident
staff who had been with him for years, as well as nurses nearby
and a farm manager who called frequently. London was just as
difficult in a different way. There were fewer people around—a
resident manservant and Banks's adopted daughter, who had a
self-contained apartment within the house. Banks or the man-

servant was there most of the time, however, and reports showed that security safeguards were good.

"What we need desperately," said Brighouse at one meeting with Hollen, "is someone close to him." For such a public man, Banks had surprisingly few friends. He had colleagues, acquaintances, and entertained at clubs and restaurants rather than at home.

Other ideas were considered—feeding false snippets of information to see if they reemerged via Soviet double agents, but that would have meant giving false material to the Prime Minister.

The more the absence of evidence against Banks, though, the greater became Brighouse's conviction in the man's guilt. It was not that Brighouse was an instinctive man. It was that Banks was *too* clean.

With Rajk's guidance, Brighouse extended inquiries to embrace the girl, Jennifer. There was a great deal of dirt—she was what Brighouse would have called, datedly, a jet-setter, a high liver. There was also evidence of instability—she had twice been admitted to a private clinic suffering from drug overdoses. On neither occasion, however, had the quantities she had taken been sufficiently large to kill. Brighouse sought psychiatric advice and received a detailed paper that linked the girl's problems with her mother's illness ("Subconsciously she probably feels that her mother has deserted her. . . .") and her father's preoccupation with work. Interesting, Brighouse decided, but nothing to help him or to add to the knowledge about Banks himself.

At the beginning of the second week of July the investigation was taking up a disproportionate amount of time. Only the American pressure kept it from being relaxed—pressure that was being increased in the light of a decision to renew arms and troop reduction talks in Vienna the coming October. Resumption of the talks, started seven years before and in abeyance for twelve months, would mean a flood of new defense assessments and research papers—most of which would find their way to Banks.

Saturday, July 12, however, saw two events that even without the forthcoming talks would have kept the investigation going.

The first was a "suggestion" by the Americans that if the British could not find enough evidence, perhaps they should consider alternative ways of dealing with Banks. For example, they would be happy to leak what material they had—suitably embellished, of course—to a European scandal magazine. The British did not believe that particular story: Banks would simply have claimed it was a Soviet plot to get rid of him because they feared him. They did, however, take the point.

The second event was the discovery that despite the earlier investigation Banks *had* managed to retain a secret. A major one.

CHAPTER 6

Every Saturday afternoon Sir Joseph Banks adopted the same ritual.

After spending the morning working at home, he took lunch in a gambling club in Curzon Street not far from the Hilton Hotel. Then for two hours, rarely longer, he indulged in his liking for gambling.

This weekly routine had been noted on the file during the earlier investigation. It was a comforting surprise to those following him this time that whatever else might have altered, this remained.

On Saturday, July 12, three men followed Banks—fewer than positively needed but more than could be afforded. Davidson, the senior man involved in the observation, took up a position in a wine store opposite the club.

At 2:35 he was hungry and bored. He did not see the new customer until too late. He was a man Davidson had worked with years before when they had both been in the police force.

"Hey, you old reprobate. What are *you* doing around here?"

Davidson began to reply, but the other was not interested.

"Come on, come on. It's been too long." The man gestured

toward the gambling club. "I handle security over there now. Come and have a drink."

Davidson was about to refuse when he realized it would provide the first chance for someone actually to observe Sir Joseph Banks inside the club. The problem with following a man into a gambling club was not so much that you had to be a member but that you had to gamble.

They drank in a large, almost empty bar. Davidson acted dumb. He had, he said, never been in a gambling club before. As he had expected, he was finally led through to the gambling room. There were only about a dozen people. None of them was Banks.

After a few minutes, the security man led Davidson out and up a sweeping staircase into the office section. Chandeliers and oil paintings gave way to functional rooms. The glitter had been left where it belonged, with the customers.

The security man poured drinks. Photographs on the wall showed him with famous visitors. Davidson showed that he was impressed. The time had come, he thought, to probe.

"Fascinating," he said, making a tour of the pictures. "I didn't realize you got all these incredible people."

The other said nothing.

"Funny," said Davidson. "When I was across the street, I could swear I saw someone I've seen on television a few times—that academic, supposed to be a millionaire, talks about war."

"Sir Joseph Banks," said the security man immediately.

"That's him." Davidson beamed. "I was sure I saw him, but I must have been mistaken."

The security man, still keen to impress his old colleague, poured fresh drinks. "Oh no," he said. "You got it right. Comes here every Saturday. Has a good lunch, goes into the gambling rooms, plays for fifteen minutes and then leaves through the back." He began to giggle. "You'd be surprised at the secrets you come across here."

Davidson tried to keep his voice steady. "But what's he do it for?"

"Oh, he comes back a couple of hours later and then out the

front again. God knows why. Must be paranoid, afraid someone's following him." For the first time the thought struck him. "You're not, are you?"

"Didn't even know this place existed until I stopped to buy a bottle of wine to take to my girlfriend's." He looked at his watch theatrically. "For which," he said, "I'm now too late to go."

"Never mind," said the security man. "She'll only appreciate you more. Come on, one more drink for the road."

Davidson held out his glass. He was trying to think how he could turn the conversation back to Banks and find out more without rearousing the security man's suspicions.

It was not necessary. The other's desire to impress triumphed again. He returned to the subject unprompted. "We're a front," he volunteered. "There's a mistress in a flat over the street. He walks over, lays her and comes back ninety minutes later. Just in time for another quick flutter. Lovely, isn't it, the way the rich live?"

Davidson wanted to leave, but he forced himself not to hurry. He might need to return.

Besides, he had almost an hour yet. An hour to go round to the back of the club, and keep a watch for Banks leaving a block of flats.

The second event which brought fresh life to the investigation resulted from further transcripts of Suslov's interrogation.

Among those who analyzed them was the Hungarian expert, Rajk, whom Brighouse had involved in the investigation early on.

The latest transcripts contained an interesting warning— according to Suslov, the Russians were experiencing problems in the wake of successful Western intelligence operations against agents. Because of this, numbers of "sleepers" were being reactivated in Europe.

The warning set off a trigger in Rajk's mind—although it was several hours before he began to remember.

Mid-afternoon he started burrowing through the archives. He could not recall the name, but the dating enabled him to find the file he wanted. All the time he was remembering Brighouse's frustration at not being able to place someone really close to Banks.

He opened the folder. The last entry was over two years old— no more than a note that the man still existed, was living in the same place, was still inactive.

Rajk flipped through the pages. The last time this particular Soviet recruit seemed to have done *anything* was ten years before.

"Inactive?" muttered Rajk. "This sleeper's not just dormant. He's dead." That's why, he suspected, no one had thought of him. Who remembered him now? Who cared? When the files were computerized, they had not even bothered to cross-reference him to Banks—too slender a connection.

Rajk signed for the file and made for Brighouse's office. He threw it on to the other's desk. "Take a look," he said. "I think you may find it interesting."

Brighouse turned the cover. A yellowing newspaper cutting fell out and Brighouse bent to retrieve it.

It showed a man, tall, young, grimy, exhausted, carrying a baby to safety out of Hungary.

CHAPTER 7

It was a small point, almost certainly meaningless—but nevertheless the sort of trivia that gets entered on surveillance reports just in case the total of the seemingly worthless adds up to something.

When Banks crossed the street from the rear entrance of the gambling club to his mistress's block of flats on July 19 he was carrying a newspaper—a *Daily Mail*. It was easy to see that because the newspaper had a distinctive front page, taken up almost entirely by a photograph of a riot.

When Banks left the block he was without the newspaper. Both the men watching Banks, one stationed at the rear of the club and one in the entrance hall of the apartments, made entries of the fact in their notebooks.

The following day another observer watched the mistress—by now identified as Stella Harding, aged thirty-four, former flower shop manager—cross the street and go into a coffee house.

She carried the same distinctive newspaper.

The watcher noted in his report that she left twenty-seven minutes later, carrying nothing.

The possibilities, of course, were almost endless—she had taken a day-old newspaper to read because she had nothing else readily at hand, or there was a particular article she wanted to finish . . . and then she had left it behind because she had no further use for it. But the watcher was trained to be suspicious about such things. He went into the coffee house and could not see a newspaper left on a table.

And even that probably meant nothing: someone else could have picked it up to read, a waitress taken it to throw it away. . . . It could, however, have been the woman passing on a message from Banks.

On the Monday morning when the surveillance reports were discussed, that was what Hollen preferred to suspect. Brighouse agreed. Both men were already suspicious about Banks's mistress in the light of the discovery that he had installed her in the flat four years before and paid all her bills—in return for just one visit a week.

"Unbelievable," Brighouse said.

"*Must* be something else behind it," Hollen had agreed. "It would make a good regular message box. Any other boyfriends—foreigners?" He laid a great deal of emphasis on the last word.

So far checks had yielded nothing useful. But there *had* to be something suspicious.

Sitting, examining the surveillance reports, Hollen came to a decision. "That idea we discussed after Rajk came to see you," he said.

"Getting his man near?" asked Brighouse.

"That's it. Let's try it."

Brighouse agreed. They had almost exhausted all avenues. "We'd need someone like Jardine or Mallahide to deal with it," he said.

"Jardine's engaged," said Hollen. "You can have Mallahide."

"Is he fit enough?"

"Ugly, but fit," replied Hollen. "And screaming to be back in action."

*   *   *

David Mallahide wiped the shaving soap from his face and carefully examined his reflection in the mirror.

The dark rings under his eyes were beginning to fade at last. None too soon, he thought. The plastic surgeon had warned him before the operation that rhinoplasty was unpredictable—in altering the nose, blood could seep under the skin causing temporary or even permanent discoloration, but he had hoped to look normal before now.

Not that it was a risk he could have avoided. Most of the plastic surgeon's patients had a choice—they were undergoing the operation for cosmetic purposes. Not so Mallahide. The bullet from the 7.65 mm Vz27 Czech-made pistol had removed half his nose. The surgeon had had to use cartilage taken from his ribs to rebuild it.

Mallahide walked through into the bedroom and began to dress. The shooting had been ironical. Operating undercover in Northern Ireland, Mallahide had feared exposure—and the consequences—daily. What he had never anticipated was that he would be shot by accident—stray bullets in a bar, aimed at someone else yards away. And yet he had been lucky. A second bullet had struck his skull, but at a tangent, producing a glancing blow. That fact, coupled with swift hospital treatment, had saved him.

He began to button his shirt, looked out of the window at the traffic below, and wondered what the day would bring. He was bored. Since the operation and a brief convalescence, he had been on light duties, much of the time involved in training operations for new recruits. Those, at least, were marginally less boring than updating files.

Mallahide had always worked with enthusiasm, reveling in his work. Now, at a time when there seemed nothing worthwhile he could do, he burned with a new conviction that made inactivity even worse.

His father, a policeman, had instilled in him a belief in the *status quo* and the necessity to defend that. In his early days in the service he had acted on that belief, but coldly, objectively, professionally. Now he *felt* it. Since the shooting, it was a personal, emotional thing. Behind men like those who shot him were the Communists, which really meant the Russians. He began cutting out quotes from magazines and newspapers and pasting them on the back of a cupboard door. The latest one read, "The Soviets have been at war for sixty years. They are waging war, subversively, economically, scientifically, technically."

He took to using a key ring he had bought as a curio years before—one with a clear plastic tab containing what was claimed to be a genuine piece of barbed wire from the Berlin Wall.

The bullets that had hit Mallahide had been Communist supplied. Czech-made, delivered to the IRA on Soviet orders.

His one desire now was to pay them back—to settle the score.

CHAPTER 8

Fenn was the first to wake. His head was heavy from the lunchtime drinking and he could not even guess the time he had been asleep.

It was difficult moving his left wrist or moving his head to see the time—his wife's head was on his shoulder, the two girls, his daughters, were huddled the other side of him.

It was 4:45. Outside the sun would be blistering, but inside it was cool and dark, thanks to the thickness of the stone wall and the heaviness of the curtains.

Gemma began to stir. Fenn was surprised that the two girls were sleeping so long, but it had been an exhausting morning —an early visit to Malta to check over the two apartments they owned before more holiday visitors arrived to rent them. Then the long birthday lunch, followed by the communal sleep.

They had celebrated at lunchtime so that the girls could join them—although like the Gozitans among whom they lived the children kept late evenings. Tonight he and Gemma would enjoy a simple meal alone together at one of the island's restaurants.

Downstairs, the telephone began to ring. Fenn cursed

silently but did not consider not answering it. A telephone call was a rare event.

He pulled himself loose, rolled on to the tiled floor. As he reached the door, pulling on his robe, Becky, the younger one, began to cry.

The telephone was in the only downstairs room, an area they had created by knocking all the original ground floor rooms into one. One end was dominated by a huge farmhouse table, the center of the house's activities. It was still laden with dirty plates and glasses.

Because it was his birthday and because his head was reeling, Fenn picked up the bottle of malt whiskey—his present from the girls—and drank before lifting the telephone receiver.

"James? I almost hung up. Thought you were out."

It was Best, another Englishman, who dabbed in property, though usually only on Malta itself. He and Fenn occasionally did business.

"Sorry. I was in the workroom."

Strange that he felt the need to apologize. Why couldn't he just say: It's my birthday, I'm forty-five today and we had this huge lunch and Gemma and I got a bit pissed and I've been sleeping it off?

"James, I've got quite a nice little one for you. That's if you're free tomorrow."

No need to check a diary. "Sure. No problem."

"It's some guy from Bradford. Quite young. Wants a holiday place. I tried to sell him here but he's set on Gozo, says he saw it a couple of years ago and fell. Has been thinking since. Just came into a little money."

"He's serious?" Gozo, like all holiday islands, drew people who, on the strength of a visit, vowed they had to live there. Then they went home and the dream evaporated or they found they could not afford it.

"Seems so."

"There's nothing I know of at the moment."

"I know. I told him. But he thought maybe if you could drive him around, explain things to him, he'd be able to make a quick decision if anything came up while he was back home."

Fenn leaned over the table, poured more whiskey and then changed his mind. He drank spirits rarely now. Better to take it easy. There was still the evening.

"James? James? Are you still there?" The telephone crackled. Lines were notoriously bad.

"Yes, yes. Okay, if you say so."

"Oh, and he'll pay for the ride. I explained that was only fair in case he changed his mind later. Told him you'd take it into account if he eventually bought."

"How much?"

"Forty."

"Maltese?"

"Sterling."

For the first time, Fenn permitted himself a grin. "He is serious."

He took details, thanked Best, made tea—a habit he had not been able to break after six years out of England—and carried it upstairs.

The girls had moved to their own room. Gemma was sitting up, partly covered by a single sheet. Her arms were folded under her breasts.

"Hey," he said, "I think I fancy you."

"Tea," she said. "Tonight, if you're good."

They sat side by side, sipping the tea.

"Who was it?"

"Charlie Best."

She wrinkled her face. "Oh, him!" She thought he was a man best avoided—one of those expatriates who lived on the fringes of the local underworld.

"No, it sounds all right this time." He told her.

"Forty. Forty sterling?"

"Yes. That'll keep us in wine for a few weeks."

Gemma began to laugh.

"What is it?" Not understanding.

She spoke through her laughter. "I was just thinking that

when we first met you'd spend that much on one business lunch. And then take a taxi back to the office."

Fenn arrived at Mgarr Harbor early, parked and strolled on to the dock to await the day's first ferry.

He had spoken to the man from Bradford at his hotel the previous evening and had been surprised the man planned to arrive so early—the first ferry left at seven-thirty A.M. and to catch it the man had to travel across the main island. But Fenn was pleased. It meant they should be finished early.

Fenn liked Mgarr. On quiet days he sometimes drove over just to stroll through the village or to sit on the dock watching visitors arrive and depart—Maltese salesmen in their black suits, tourists slung with cameras, guides ready to shepherd visitors into waiting coaches.

A local priest, hands clasped as though in prayer, nodded to him—on an island with a population of twenty-six thousand you soon got to know many of the other inhabitants by sight.

The day was warming and Fenn took off his cotton jacket, leaving himself dressed in T-shirt and jeans. He stood, arms folded, looking out to sea. A few Gozitans stared—he was a striking-looking man: tall, wiry, a hawklike face, deep brooding eyes. His forehead was high, but the hair, dark, was full at the sides and at the back.

He picked out his visitor immediately—medium height, early thirties, blue blazer, dark glasses, a shoulder bag. He watched for a while, and then approached from the side. "Mr. Mallahide?"

He was surprised at how fast the man turned, how taut his body seemed to go. Then as quickly as he had tightened, he relaxed.

"And you're James Fenn. Nice of you to meet me and show me around at such short notice."

Fenn led him to the car, five years old—new by Gozo standards.

"Breakfast?"

"A coffee and a roll or something would be welcome."

Fenn had expected a North Country accent, having been told the man came from Bradford. But why? He himself came from an area in the Midlands of England, which had one of the most pronounced of accents, but his own accent was placeless, classless. Like Mallahide's. Then he realized why he was puzzled—Mallahide must have volunteered that he came from Bradford. A strange thing to do. Most men, surely, would simply have said England. Then he realized he was still reacting the way he had once been trained to do. Stupid.

"Okay," he said. "We'll go to the capital. It's only two miles."

He began to drive inland, gestured with his left hand toward Fort Chambray, which dominated the port. He might as well begin the guided tour. "One of the old Knight Grand Cross forts," he said.

"What is it now? It looks occupied."

"A mental hospital."

"Even here," Mallahide muttered softly. "Even here."

Fenn was surprised by the other's tone, but hurried on with his briefing.

"I don't know how well you remember things," he said, "but you'll find Gozo's more spectacular than Malta—deeper valleys, steeper cliffs, even though it's only nine miles long, half that across." He went on to explain that it was also greener—but not now in summer when both islands looked like barren rock with only the occasional carob tree providing a patch of green.

"You've chosen a bad time to come," he added. "Many people try to get away when it's this hot." He grinned. "England's a favorite place."

"It was the only time I could manage."

The voice was flat, discouraging small talk.

They reached Rabat, the capital, parked, and took coffee outdoors. It was not yet eight but the city was already alive. It would rest at midday when the heat became too great.

As they drank, Mallahide explained that he wanted a small

house where he could holiday and which he could rent out at
other times.

"Why Gozo?"

"Who knows, really? I saw it when I was on a tour and
thought it was just the place. You must know the feeling.
Didn't I hear something similar happened to you?"

"It can be an island that gets you." Fenn did not elaborate
on the things he loved—the simplicity of the people, the
strength of their faith which he admired and envied, the
gentleness of change (even the language retained hundreds of
words that had fallen into disuse on Malta itself). Mallahide
only wanted a holiday home. These things would not concern
him.

Fenn outlined the situation—nothing for sale at the moment, but he was willing to look. He explained that this was
one of the many things he did, act as a go-between in house
deals. "I can advise if the price seems right—but you'd better
be warned that I try to be fair with both sides. The buyer
because I'm working for him, the seller because he's probably
Gozitan and I live here."

He expected Mallahide to probe further about how he
earned a living. Strangers usually did. But Mallahide seemed
anxious to begin the schedule Fenn had proposed—first, a
quick tour of the island, then a slightly more detailed look at
villages where Fenn thought houses might come up for sale.
Then over lunch he could answer any questions that remained. "I'd invite you home for a meal, but today's one of
the days my wife works—she teaches part-time at the secondary
school. And you don't want to risk my cooking. . . ."

In truth, he did not like taking strangers to their home—
a nervousness that remained from the past.

Back in the car, Fenn noted that even though the windows
were open, the smell of Mallahide's after-shave still clung. It
was a strangely cheap smell for such a man. Then Fenn placed
it: not after-shave—eau de cologne.

At Nadur, Fenn had to stop the car while a herd of goats
passed. Mallahide asked, "Isn't your house around here?"

Fenn pointed. "On that hill. It's an old farmhouse." On on one side it overlooked the town, on the other the sea. He made no move to invite Mallahide to take a closer look.

By noon Mallahide thought he had seen enough. "Let's lunch then."

They ate at the hilltop village of Xaghra—local food: fish soup, rabbit, peppered sheep's milk cheese.

While they ate, Mallahide probed: "You've been here for a few years. Obviously you must like it. Charlie Best said you used to be a journalist. Don't you miss the excitement? What's it like bringing up a family here?"

Fenn answered politely, but with the minimum of hard fact. It was not that he had anything to hide, but he was not a man to share personal detail with a stranger.

Why should' he, how could he, describe how he had begun to change after his first wife had died? And then what meeting and marrying Gemma had meant? How they had first visited Gozo when she was pregnant with Kate, his elder daughter, now six. How, when his newspaper was reducing staff and offering severance pay, he had left at the age of thirty-eight. How, a year later, in a moment of apparent madness, they had sold up in England and moved.

"Look," Mallahide went on, "if it's rude don't answer, but I must admit I'm curious. Can you earn a living doing this?" He meant helping people like him find a house.

Fenn did find it rude, but he answered briefly. "We had savings. Life's quite cheap here. We have a couple of places we rent out. I keep an eye on a few holiday homes while their owners are away. That takes care of the overhead. People like you are the occasional butter."

He also, though he did not volunteer more information, wrote a little. And Gemma worked.

He checked the time. "If you want to catch the one-thirty ferry, we'll need to move."

"Look," said Mallahide, "it's such a good day, why don't you drop me there? I'll wander and catch the next one."

"All right."

Fenn drove him to the harbor, pleased that he did not have to spend the afternoon with the man. He did not dislike him, but he had not warmed to him . . . and he felt some distrust. Of course, he was reading too much into things—he saw too few strangers. But take lunch, for instance. Mallahide had eaten each course as soon as it arrived without pause. And between mouthfuls he had not put down his cutlery. He ate as though no time should be wasted.

It wasn't greed; it was more the action of a man who knows he may be called away any moment, so he must eat when he can. Fenn had seen it before. Detectives did it. So did reporters on tight assignments. And soldiers in battle zones.

Back at the harbor Fenn switched off the engine and wondered whether he would have to ask for payment or whether Mallahide would produce the money.

Mallahide looked at his watch. "What time is it now?" he asked.

Fenn told him.

Mallahide adjusted the hands. "My watch are fast," he said.

Fenn glanced at him, but Mallahide seemed to have noticed nothing strange in his reply.

Mallahide pointed toward the sea. "That's Comino out there, isn't it?"

"Yes. The little islet you see next to it is Cominotto. Uninhabited."

"How long to get there?"

"On a good day like today? In a small boat? Twenty minutes maybe. Why? You don't want a house there."

"Could you get a boat? Take me out?"

"Now? You'd roast." The temperature was well into the nineties.

"I like the sun."

Fenn was still wondering how serious Mallahide was when the other removed his dark glasses for the first time. As Fenn had guessed from the puffiness near the cheek bones, Mallahide's eyes were dark and bruised. Plastic surgery, he guessed. A nose job.

"Perhaps," Mallahide said, "I'd better come clean. Charlie Best wasn't the first person to suggest I contact you. Josef's second cousin, Leonid, insisted I should seek you out to say hello."

Fenn felt the blood drain from his face. Even in the heat he went cold.

After ten years, ten long years, what he had always feared but refused to think about had happened.

His spy masters in Moscow had decided to call him back into action.

CHAPTER 9

Fenn borrowed a small motorboat. It was not difficult. He was known, and no one wanted to go out to sea at this time of day.

"Some fool visitor," explained Fenn to the hotelkeeper who owned the boat. "Impatient to see everything."

The man smiled and nodded. He understood. Furthermore, he could let Fenn see that he did. The Englishman had been on the island long enough to be treated as a permanent resident. Besides, the hotelkeeper knew, as did many other Gozitans, that although Fenn and his wife were not believers, they respected and they gave to the Church. That mattered a great deal.

There was no cover on the boat. Both Fenn and Mallahide were bareheaded. The visitor, Fenn was certain, would burn, whatever he had said. That, Fenn decided, was the other's problem. Fenn did not like the sun at this time of day. Like the islanders, he preferred to be indoors until later. But his skin, though pale for someone living on Gozo, would not burn. He was acclimatized. He pulled the starter and pointed out into the sea.

Minutes out and the boat began to pitch. Fenn looked at Mallahide. He was sitting, gazing forward, obviously relaxed.

Fenn's mind was reeling.

Two things suddenly made sense. Mallahide's smell—cheap eau de cologne. He remembered it now. A common smell in Russia.

And that strange phrase. "My watch *are* fast."

Again it made sense. Again Russian. There is no Russian word for watch. Literally the word used is "hours." Mallahide —or whatever his real name was—would have had to translate "the hours are slow." Hence the wrong verb.

He began asking himself questions.

Why after all this time? Except for occasional bad moments when he woke early and his mind flooded with fears, he had come to convince himself that the Russians had written him off, even forgotten him. After all, what use was he now? What access did he have? He was not a foreign correspondent for a well-known newspaper, nor had he been for a very long time.

Why would they want him? To keep an eye on the Chinese or the Libyans so active in Malta now? He supposed he could get low-grade information, but there must be others better placed. As an Englishman, he was naturally suspect.

He realized he would soon know.

"Can we anchor here?"

They were in the narrow, shallow strait between Comino and the islet.

Fenn, Gemma and the girls had been here often. He dropped the anchor, gazed down at the clear, white sand beneath the bright blue water. He and Gemma loved diving here. There were caverns, silver and green, to be explored.

"I'm sorry I had to do it that way," said Mallahide almost immediately. "I wanted to spend a little time with you before I let you know what I really wanted, and I couldn't think of another way."

He smiled—or at least his mouth did. Mallahide had replaced his glasses and Fenn could not see his eyes. "One thing I was asked to say especially was that Vladimir sends his best regards and says that he has thought of you often and hopes one day you will meet again."

Vladimir—Fenn's first controller . . . a long time ago when he had really believed.

"You know I'm out of things now?"

There was no answer, so he rushed on: "I mean, I've no access, haven't much opportunity to carry. . . ."

"We didn't ask much when you had."

That was true. After the initial assignments, and none had been major, he had been put to sleep. To wait. To wait for the big one?

"So what good am I now?"

He realized he was pleading.

"We want you back in England. There's a job there. You remember Sir Joseph Banks?"

Fenn did. He still saw the man's name regularly in the *Times of Malta.*

"We need someone close to him. For you, it should be relatively easy. Normally he's a hard man to get near."

"What about this?" Fenn gestured back toward Gozo.

"It need take no more than two months. We'll supply a good cover story. Then you can come back." He smiled, a huge smile. "And who knows, I may even buy a house from you."

Fenn arrived home before Gemma. He remembered that she was taking the girls to a birthday party given for one of Kate's friends. It was nearly five. He doubted that they would return for at least another hour and a half.

He made strong black coffee and carried it across the courtyard to the outbuilding that they had converted into a study. It was a plain, square room, whitewashed inside and with shelves covering one whole wall. There was a sofa which converted into a bed for visitors, a drawerless desk, and a bright red filing cabinet that they had brought with them all those years before.

There was only one painting—a large abstract, painted by his first wife. It was the only work—apart from a sketch of him that was filed away—that he had kept.

He sat, sipped the coffee, fought the desire for a drink and thought about what Mallahide had said.

They wanted a watch kept on Banks. It had not been spelled out, but the inference was that they were assessing the possibility of recruiting him. They needed information, perhaps leads as to how to blackmail him.

It had been taken for granted that Fenn would agree.

There was a simple cover story to account for his absence. Within a few days he would receive a letter purporting to come from a newspaper for which he had once worked. It would ask if he would take part in an investigation being conducted by that newspaper, explaining they needed someone who could not be identified as a working reporter. For his work Fenn would be offered five thousand pounds plus expenses— a sum large enough, it was estimated, to tempt Gemma into acquiescing.

Two months, Mallahide had said, and a simple assignment, nothing unpleasant. Just go back. Make contact with Banks. Remain as close as possible. Report.

Yet Fenn did not like it for many reasons. Not least, he did not believe it. It was a basic principle of intelligence work that the agent was never told everything. So, what next? How much deeper?

And even without that fear, there was the reluctance to be involved again at all.

Didn't they realize that he had changed? He was forty-five. It was over twenty-five years since they had recruited him . . . twenty-four years since the first major operation, the one meant to establish him in a useful position . . . over ten years since they had last made contact. Ten years!

"Something you must remember," Vladimir had said. "One day we may wish you to go to earth, to become a sleeper. Nothing may be said. We will simply cut off contact. But remember this—months may go by, years even. But when we make contact again the words will be the same: Josef's second cousin, Leonid, insisted I should seek you out to say hello."

But ten years!

Ten years in which a wife had died . . . in which Gemma had appeared . . . in which there had been children, a new country, a new life.

He was a different man.

Should he tell them to go to hell? Could he?

Mallahide had not threatened, but the hint had been there. If they *had* to do so, they could resurrect his past, destroy his present.

Yet that was not the only thing.

He owed. He hated to admit it, but he owed.

Fenn picked up the switchblade from the corner of the desk—Gemma kept reminding him to keep it out of reach of the girls. He pressed the button and the blade sprang out. He weighed it in his hand. It was beautifully balanced—the handle had been removed and then rebuilt, no doubt by the Foreign Legionnaire from whose body Fenn had taken it in an Algiers street. It was designed now for throwing as well as cutting. There was a darts board on the wall—Fenn often played at throwing at the board in periods when he wanted a break from writing.

He threw the knife, a quick, practiced flick. Over the years he had become good. The knife came to rest, blade quivering, just outside the center.

He owed his father, now long dead. Now *he* really had believed. *His* Communism had been forged in unemployment and poverty. It had been a real faith. Even Stalin's purges had only reinforced it. He had seen what was happening, condemned it, but at the same time the events had strengthened him. Only a faith that was so right could withstand such corruption.

Fenn's father had brought him up to believe too. He had done it, if anything, too well—although he had died not knowing this, convinced that he had failed. James had developed a faith so strong that everything else became secondary, family included. Like the early Christians, he had been taking on the whole world.

It had been necessary to rise above normal human weaknesses—even love for his father. When James had been noted, recruited, taken away for training, he had had to renounce his Communism publicly in order to serve the faith better. Not even his father had known the truth. Fenn had vowed to tell him before he died. He had arrived at the death bed too late.

He stood, pulled the knife from the board and returned to his desk. There was a sheath somewhere, a spring-operated wrist holder that, again, must have been made by the Legionnaire. A strange but highly effective device—a touch on the knife's handle and the weapon sprang into the hand.

He balanced the knife on his index finger, watching it.

And he owed *them* because of his first wife. When she was dying, slowly and painfully, they had helped. He had never asked for money, but they had seen he lacked for nothing. And one of the leading specialists in the Western world had "volunteered" his services. Now was the time to repay . . . but he did not want to—knowing he owed did not help.

Fenn put down his coffee cup and pulled down the ladder that led into the roof. The attic was large, lit by a window cut into the roof. They planned to convert it to a room one day. At present it was used for storage.

It took Fenn twenty minutes to find what he wanted—an old attaché case. It was locked and had been unopened for at least a dozen years.

He broke it open with his pocket knife.

Inside: the big lie. The newspaper cuttings were carefully stacked in cardboard folders. There were stories—by him, about him. Copies of the paperback book he had written. The written record of a daring young man, a freelance journalist who had quit his job on an evening newspaper to take a chance. A boy who had made for Hungary before the Revolution. Had become a minor hero.

He heard Gemma return. Friends who had brought her loudly refused a drink. Their car moved off. Fenn began to replace the cuttings.

A hero? A phony!

True, he had come close to being shot once or twice—the Soviet authorities could hardly have given their troops a picture of him—but that would simply have been an unfortunate accident.

In his haste, Fenn dropped a handful of cuttings. He began to scoop them up, but stopped at one: the one showing the baby being held by Lady Banks with her husband looking on.

Fenn filled the case, closed it. There was, he reflected wryly, a Maltese expression that was appropriate.

"X' Tista Taghmel?" It was said fatalistically. "What can you do?"

Twenty-four hours later, back in London, Mallahide began making the arrangements.

He figured he had at least three days before Fenn arrived— he had no doubt that the man would cooperate. Mallahide needed to rent a flat for Fenn, arrange a safe house, compile a list of Banks's known forthcoming appointments to help Fenn establish contact—and, of course, organize the forged letter.

He worked as fast as he could, partly because of excitement at being back in action, partly with knowledge that activity kept away the migraines that had plagued him since the shooting.

By the third day Mallahide had done everything that was necessary. That night he was due to be involved in a training exercise. He could have opted out—his new assignment took priority—but he knew nothing would happen yet, and he was still restless.

He did not tell Brighouse, who would not have understood. Besides, he would be back in the morning.

Mallahide took an early evening train to Birmingham. The "raid" on the factory was scheduled for eleven P.M. It was a routine training session—new MI5 men getting a taste of life in the field.

Tonight there would be five of them. Their task was to enter a rubber factory and steal a list of suppliers and prices.

No one at the factory knew of the exercise except the managing director. If anything went wrong, they had a telephone number to give the police. A call to this number would ensure their freedom. But they would have failed the test.

Mallahide was to be the observer.

The car he had rented by telephone was waiting. He ate a leisurely meal in a restaurant and drove to the factory. He had arranged a meeting point with the five. They were all sitting in a Ford car conspicuously parked in a side street. Mallahide knew they would have stolen it for the exercise.

Mallahide did not go near them. The first part of the test was to see what they did when he did not arrive.

He watched them through a night-scope—a device that used starlight radiated by the sky and made objects visible even in what seemed total darkness.

At last the five decided. They left the car and made for the fence around the factory. Mallahide watched them clear the wall, using sacking to protect themselves from the broken glass set into the concrete. Then he used the small two-way radio which he took from his raincoat pocket.

"Lunar Seven," he said, "they're in."

The reply came immediately.

"Roger, four."

Mallahide replaced the radio, strolled casually over to the men's car. They had left it unattended—a bad mistake. He tried to lift the hood and failed. It operated from a catch inside the car: a safety measure.

He checked the street around—a drunk in the distance, otherwise quiet. Then he leaned against the side of the car, drew back his elbow, and smashed it into the vent window. The glass broke clean. He reached inside, opened the door, pulled the hood catch.

Two minutes later he had removed the distributor cap, switched all the leads, closed the car and walked away. Whatever they did, the five trainees would not be able to start the car. His mission was accomplished.

He flicked on the two-way radio again.

"Lunar seven," he whispered. "All yours."

He slid into his car and drove off.

The factory break-in had been made purposely easy. The real test was a completely different one. While trying to start the car, wondering what had gone wrong, the recruits would be arrested. They would then be handed over to detectives who would refuse to believe their story, insisting the men must be enemy agents. The telephone number that the recruits had been given would prove to be a nonexistent line.

Then once the trainees were sufficiently confused and panic-stricken, they would be interrogated. That was the real purpose—to see how they coped.

Mallahide drove through the near-deserted outskirts of Birmingham and joined the motorway, heading straight home. He would return the car in London in the morning.

About halfway through the journey Mallahide's left eye began to throb. Before he reached London, the pain had spread to the back of his head. He staggered into his flat, lay on the bed in darkness.

The pain came in waves. In the blackness, he cursed them again. Another legacy from the Russians.

The letter arrived mid-morning. Fortunately it was not one of Gemma's teaching days—Fenn wanted her near when he read it so that she could witness his feigned surprise.

Because the envelope was unfamiliar and because few letters reached them from London, they played a guessing game as to who it could be from.

Finally, in mock exasperation, Gemma exclaimed, "Well, *open* it!"

She was younger than Fenn by eight years. Her black hair was swept high. Fenn looked at her affectionately as he opened the envelope. Her wide, full mouth was stretched in a smile. The laughter lines around her eyes added to her look of impishness.

The letterhead was different from the way he remembered it, but he had no doubt it was genuine. They must have changed the design.

It was a long letter, running to two pages.

"My dear James," it began "This letter will come as a surprise, I don't doubt, but . . ."

It ended, "I need hardly ask, I know, that whatever your decision you regard this letter as COMPLETELY SECRET AND PRIVATE. At the risk of sounding melodramatic, perhaps you would even go so far as burning it.

"If you are interested—at least enough to talk—all you have to do is use the enclosed air ticket and telephone me at this direct number when you arrive to make sure that I answer."

Fenn was conscious of Gemma's scrutiny as he read. He raised his eyebrows dramatically.

"Well?"

He slid the letter across the table. "You'd better read it."

She read it twice and then placed it in front of her.

"Will you go?"

"I don't know. It's *our* decision."

"But you're tempted?"

"Well, for Christ's sake. Five thousand pounds! We could finish the conversions, take a bit of a break."

"We *need* a break?"

She was angry. He was playing it wrong. He should have said that he was *not* going and let her talk him into considering it seriously.

He knew her fears, hidden though they were most of the time. She worried that he sometimes missed the old life, and that if he ever went back he would not return. That their life on Gozo would turn into an interlude.

"No," he said, getting up and walking around the table. "You're right." He put a hand on her shoulder. "We don't need the money. And sure as hell I don't need to get back to that rat race, even for a few weeks. I'll write back saying, thanks, but no."

And this *was* the right approach—because although Gemma had always feared him going, she had feared holding him against his will even more.

She stood, walked to the stove to brew more coffee.

She was wearing white cord trousers. Her body was starting to thicken—not to take on excess fat, but to go stocky, peasant fashion. It added to her fascination, made her look both sexy and motherly.

She poured more water into the pan, spooned coffee, and then turned back to face Fenn.

"Of course you must go," she said in her most practical voice, subconsciously stressing the Welshness. "It's only a short time. We'll be all right. It'll do you good."

She looked up. "And you're right. The money would be useful."

The immigration officer at Heathrow Airport took Fenn's passport, studied the bleak photograph, the pale face, and handed the document back without comment.

The Special Branch man sitting next to him stared down at the photographs of men and women whose arrival in Britain was judged to be of interest.

Fenn's picture was third from the left, but the officer waited until the man was out of sight before he moved off to the telephone to report.

The message was relayed to Brighouse less than thirty minutes later.

Brighouse gestured his visitor to remain seated and listened without interrupting. Putting down the receiver he said, "It looks as though our ferret is about to join the hunt. He arrived at Heathrow half an hour ago. It seems to be working."

"Good. I thought it would. I'd better get busy."

And Mallahide, who had never doubted the plan would work, left the room.

CHAPTER 10

Fenn checked into a small hotel in West London, went out for a coffee shop meal, watched a bad film, drank too much before he went to bed, and, waking early, almost decided to return home immediately.

The parting had been especially sad. Although Gemma had been quietly resigned, the girls had not. It had been a mistake to take them to the airport; they were not used to seeing him go away, and they could not understand. Their cries had followed him to the airplane's steps.

But by eleven-thirty A.M., the time scheduled for him to make his telephone call, the excitement of action and the unknown had begun to overcome the misgivings.

In a way, it *was* good to be in action.

Mallahide answered on the third ring.

"There's a block of small flats—Moon Court—in Charing Cross Road, about fifty yards from Foyles Book Shop. The entrance is at the side. The door will be open. Take the stairs to the third floor. Turn left. Number 14. I'll be there."

"Now?"

"An hour. Say twelve-thirty."

"It will take me that long."

As it was, Fenn was late. Although nothing had been said, he felt it incumbent on him to go through at least the basic precautions against being followed: changes of train, a walk through a busy store and out the emergency exit, hailing a cruising cab when it was the only one in sight. . . .

Throughout, he was conscious of how long it had been since he was schooled in the maneuvers, how long since he had had to put them into practice. The last time, he thought, had been on his way to pick up documents from a Chinese diplomat he had been ordered to cultivate. But it was so long ago—he might have been wrong. Certainly then the feeling had been different—he had felt like a soldier fighting for the cause.

The block in Charing Cross Road smelt of food, disinfectant and urine. The stairs were uncovered concrete.

Number 14 had a spy hole and two Banham locks on the door. Inside it consisted of a short corridor with a kitchen on one side, a bathroom on the other, and at the end a single, low-ceilinged room overlooking Charing Cross Road. That room held a bed, two armchairs, a coffee table, and, incongruously, a cheap but ornate cocktail wagon on which there stood one bottle of whiskey, one bottle of soda water and two glasses.

Mallahide poured without asking. "Soda?"

"Neat."

They drank.

"How was it?"

"Leaving?"

"Yes."

"Not good."

Mallahide showed immediate understanding. "They'll be all right," he said. "We'll keep a discreet eye on them, make sure there are no problems. Being apart—that's the worst part of the game, I know."

He was establishing rapport with his agent: kindness now . . . later, if need be, the heavy stick. A controller had to control. That was the first and last lesson of handling a man.

He opened his briefcase, taking out a package which he tore open, and handed Fenn the contents one by one.

"Keys. The address is apartment 9, 73 Kempston Court, Paddington. Not far from the station, smallish but okay—the right kind of place for your cover. It's taken for three months. Rent paid in advance. You use your own name."

Next came an envelope. "Money. Two hundred pounds. And a loan society pass book. You'll see there's a thousand on deposit there. It's easier to deal in cash, but if you find you need a bank account and check book, tell me."

Other items followed: a list of times at which he could reach Mallahide on the telephone, a Minox camera and accessories ("You remember how to use it?" He did), another sheet of paper with his cover story detailed. Finally, a dossier on Banks and his family.

Fenn drank and read while Mallahide sat, working his way through a copy of *Time*. Finished, Fenn handed back the papers. Mallahide burned them, then went to flush the ashes down the lavatory.

"Any questions?"

"Just the big one. How do I make contact with Banks? Or do you leave that to me?"

"You've been lucky, although someone else hasn't. There's been a death, early this morning. Kovacs. Remember the name?" Fenn didn't and said so. "He was one of your Hungarians. Jewish, so the funeral's tomorrow. There'll be a note in tonight's paper. Banks will be there. So will you."

It was raining when Fenn paid off the taxi at the cemetery and walked across the concrete approach to the chapel.

At the entrance he paused and put on his yarmulke, the Jewish skull cap that he had bought that morning. Although he was early, the hall was already crowded. He joined the men on one side of the square, simple building, facing the women on the other.

The coffin containing the body of Kovacs was already there

—a simple wooden box, according to Jewish law, and draped with a black cloth. Fenn tried to remember Kovacs, but the name meant nothing. After the escape from Hungary, Fenn had been told the names of his companions, but he had quickly forgotten.

As Mallahide had forecast, there had been a brief notice of the Hungarian's death in the evening newspapers—he was a well-enough known poet.

Fenn picked out Banks immediately. The tufts of white hair jutted out from the sides of his prayer cap. Banks was there in his position as President of "Remember '56"—an organization set up by Hungarian refugees to insure that the Revolution was not forgotten. Banks had been approached early because of Jennifer. It was not an onerous presidency. The organization met only once a year for an annual reunion. Occasionally the officers sent a letter to one of the newspapers.

The service began—the cantor's voice rose in prayer, first in Hebrew, then in English translation. The rabbi, his voice reverberating with sincerity—his own family had had to flee Hungary two generations before—paid a tribute. Then the body was being wheeled out into the drizzle. Fenn followed. The cantor's voice intoned the twenty-third psalm in Hebrew.

Four men lowered the coffin into the grave. A young man, no doubt Kovacs's son, shoveled the first earth on to the coffin. Then one by one, the other men, including Fenn, placed earth into the grave until it was full.

Fenn kept his eyes on Banks. The man could hardly have known Kovacs, surely, but his face contained as much grief as those who were obviously family.

On the return, outside the chapel, Fenn joined the line to wash his hands from the tap on the wall. He lingered outside, and from within, he could hear a prayer, the Kaddish, and the rabbi's intonement to Kovacs's widow and son: "May the Almighty comfort you among all who mourn for Zion and Jerusalem."

He entered and joined the other mourners walking slowly around the hall. Each, as they passed the widow and son, who sat together on a low bench, murmured, "We wish you long life."

And then Fenn was back outside in the drizzle and the faint sunlight.

Banks was holding a conversation. He broke away and headed toward a chauffeur-driven Rolls Royce. Fenn began to hurry after him, trying not to break into a trot.

"Sir Joseph."

The chauffeur was standing by the car and Fenn saw him tense.

Fenn put on what he thought was his most earnest face.

"I recognized you. I doubt you'll remember me. Fenn. James Fenn."

At first there was no reaction. Then Fenn realized that the other had registered the name, but was lost as to what to say.

The chauffeur interrupted. "Sir James, we should go."

At first Banks did not seem to hear. His eyes were staring into Fenn's.

"You've got a car?" he asked finally.

"No, I came by taxi. I'm heading back to town."

Banks stepped aside and gestured toward the passenger seats. "Please join me."

Fenn muttered thanks and, once inside, with Banks beside him, prepared himself for conversation. Banks, however, said nothing, and became businesslike in his actions; he changed his tie—replacing the black one with one that was dark lilac—inserted a pearl tiepin, and pulled up a hankerchief into his breast pocket. Fenn guessed that the man was going straight to a meeting.

An embarrassing silence lasted for most of the journey. Fenn had expected a series of questions. Instead, Banks worked through a mound of papers, making notes with a silver pencil. When he dropped Fenn at Trafalgar Square, few words had been exchanged. Suddenly he smiled the smile that had helped to make him, obese and ugly though he was, a man renowned for his warmth and charm.

"I must apologize, Mr. Fenn," he said. "I have been rude,

but I had to read these papers. That's the way of my life—and I have to confess that at my age funerals have the effect of silencing me. So has meeting someone I haven't thought of for over twenty years."

He took a card from his wallet, handed it to Fenn.

"But, please, you must join me for dinner. There is so much I have to ask you. Tomorrow? Eight o'clock?"

The chauffeur who was holding the door open for Fenn coughed. They were late.

Fenn got out, then watched the car disappear from view. He was on his way.

Banks's house was the last remaining private residence in St. James's Square, the oldest of the London squares. Two hundred and fifty years before, the square boasted six dukes and seven earls. Now most of it had succumbed to death duties, servant problems and high running costs. Houses had given way to commerce.

The Banks's London home would go the same way in another generation. In the meantime he kept it, having made one major compromise in his middle years—the top two floors had been separated from the rest of the house and sold to a banking corporation. The corporation, however, had its own entrance and could have been in a different building.

The butler, who was expecting Fenn, explained that Sir Joseph had telephoned to apologize that he had been delayed, but would be home soon.

Fenn followed him up the sweeping staircase into the main reception room on the first floor. It had once been a small ballroom, now it was a room that belonged in an embassy rather than a private house: long, high-ceilinged, polished wood floor, white leather sofas, and at one end a black display unit on which model soldiers stood between rare books on military history.

Sipping a drink, looking down on the square's private gardens, Fenn reflected that it was a potent combination:

wealth, intellect and power. Then he remembered the dossier he had read—Bank's incurably sick wife, their inability to have children, the never-to-be-realized longing for a son, the joy over Jennifer.

When Banks arrived he was effusively apologetic and at his most welcoming. They ate alone, Banks explaining that he "selfishly" wanted Fenn to himself.

Fenn, guarded and conscious of his role, found it almost too much. He felt the man was putting on an act. The only time Banks seemed genuine was when he talked of Jennifer. He expressed his sorrow that she was not here—abroad for a few weeks, he explained. He did not feel the need to say she had run off to the Bahamas with a man who wanted to open a club there, but that he knew she would return soon; her affairs never lasted. As he spoke, however, Fenn thought he caught a glimpse of Banks's true character.

As the evening progressed, Fenn found himself being quizzed gently. What was he doing now? Why was he in London?

His cover story was a different one from that provided for Gemma. His wife had been given the story of a newspaper investigation to provide an element of urgency. She needed to accept that he had to leave for London almost immediately. Such a story, however, would not do for Banks. He was told that Fenn was writing a book—one with a subject that Mallahide had calculated would fascinate him.

The provisional title was *1984: Where Are We?*, and it was to be a nonfiction work on what the world was soon to be like. Part of it would deal with modern weaponry developments and with psychological warfare.

Banks confined himself to a brief comment on the subject, but asked a series of prosaic questions. Did books pay these days? Was it commissioned? Who would publish? The questions had been anticipated, and Fenn answered each one directly. The book would pay a five-thousand-pound advance against royalties. He doubted whether it would ever earn more than that. But five thousand pounds was very worthwhile to him and to Gemma—living was cheap in Gozo.

He named the publishing house given to him by Mallahide at his briefing. Fenn took it that the firm, a small one, had Russian money behind it, just as one or two had been helped by CIA backing.

And yes, Fenn admitted, he hated being away. He would return home as quickly as possible.

Gradually Fenn became aware that Banks, though cautious, was genuinely interested, and quick to accept the younger man's replies. He began to relax his own guard. Banks, he realized, was probably like a number of other astute men he had met in the past—cynical and questioning in their work, almost naive away from it.

By the time the evening had come to an end Fenn was genuinely sorry to leave. A rapport of sorts had developed.

"You must come again," said Banks as Fenn prepared to go.

And outside in the street Fenn found he was congratulating himself on the way he had handled things and then, briefly, felt disgust: he had genuinely liked the man.

By noon the following day Banks had checked that Fenn was actually who he had said he was (it had been so long), that his background was as he had described it, and that he really did have a commission to write the book he had mentioned.

He had enjoyed talking to the man. Fenn was interesting. What he had done, what he was, formed a direct contrast to Banks's own life. He found this refreshing. It was not that he himself would have wanted the kind of life, but sometimes he thought he was becoming fossilized. His acquaintances were so predictable—politicians, academics, those who sought power—most of them, he suspected, greater or lesser reflections of himself.

Fenn was different, and Banks felt pleasantly intrigued. There were two further things. Jennifer, of course. The other was Fenn's first wife. They had spoken a little of her and how she had died. It had been gradual. The illness had been different but it reminded him of Pip. There were few people who could really understand. Perhaps no one who had not experienced it, or something similar. Like Fenn.

Over the next week he and Fenn met twice more for drinks in the evening. They discussed Fenn's book and the people he should see. Banks was noticeably less guarded, more forthcoming about his personal life. It was almost as though he needed someone to discuss such things with, and had no one.

Jennifer's name occurred often. It was obvious that Banks had no idea when she would return. He seemed to accept her lifestyle while regretting it. "She's a wild thing," he said at their third meeting. "And it would be ridiculous for me or anyone else to try to change her. All I can do is to see she doesn't get hurt."

At his meetings with Mallahide, Fenn repeated the conversations in detail, surprised he did not feel guilty. It was as though there were two completely separate parts of him: one that could do this and one that, while he was with Banks, could feel a warm friendliness.

It was helped, he realized after the third meeting, by his conviction that nothing he told Mallahide could be adding to the Russians' knowledge of Banks. So far he had not stumbled across the revelation that Banks was a homosexual, or went to bed with little girls, or was embezzling company funds or secretly owned arms shares. . . .

No doubt Mallahide's colleagues were doing some checking on Jennifer in the light of what he told them, but surely they would have been doing that anyway. And from Banks's attitude he doubted whether there was anything the girl could do that would make her father vulnerable to approaches.

He told them too about Banks's feelings for his wife, his hidden grief about her sickness, how, even ill, her presence helped sustain the man. But that too could hardly have hurt Banks.

In all, Fenn soon began to hope that life would continue like this for a few weeks, and that then he would be allowed home. Mission accomplished—as far as it went. His masters would have a nice thick file—useless for now, of course, but they could always persuade themselves that it might provide leads later. After all, intelligence was a business in which nothing could be discounted as useless forever.

It was with growing apprehension, therefore, that he faced a new line of questioning.

Mallahide produced a sketch that Fenn had supplied a few days before showing the layout of the house—or at least those parts he had seen.

He pointed one finger at a marked room on the first floor. "That you figure is Banks's study?"

"Yes. I can't be sure . . . but that's where he went when he wanted to fetch some papers for me."

"But there's another study as well?"

"On the ground floor. Not quite a study, more a cross between a library and a writing room. I'd suspect upstairs is where he gets down to the real work."

"So anything interesting could well be in there?"

"If there is anything, I imagine so."

"And the door is locked?"

"Yes. The night he went in to get those papers for me I heard him unlock it."

Mallahide thought deeply. He would have to refer it to Brighouse for a decision, but there was no harm in exploring the possibility.

"Could you," he asked at last, "help us get in?"

Under subtle but increasing pressure to produce "results," Brighouse authorized the break-in on condition that first he had to be convinced that it could be carried out safely.

Fenn was saved from having to participate directly by two lucky coincidences. The first was that he was invited to attend a cocktail party with Banks two nights hence. He was promised he would meet men who could be helpful to him on his project. Furthermore, Fenn knew Banks had a dinner engagement immediately afterward—Banks had, in fact, put it back fifteen minutes so he could manage both. The second coincidence was that Fenn overheard Banks's manservant, Parsons, arranging to be away overnight that same evening. The house would be empty—something that rarely happened.

Mallahide, as Fenn expected, leapt at the opportunity. Fenn spent two hours repeating everything he knew about the inside of the house, the locks on the doors, the burglar alarm system. Most useful of all was the supplier's name which Fenn had seen attached to an alarm box inside the building.

This enabled a policeman to call on the suppliers that same afternoon, ostensibly making inquiries because a well-known thief had been spotted in the area. The police officer was able to learn the name of the makers of the safe that Banks had had installed four years before.

It was a good safe, a modern one, a Clarke-Smith—closed with a combination lock, solidly built into the wall and held with metal bars. It was the kind of safe that would take an expert a long time to break open—and then there would be obvious signs of entry.

That was hardly a new problem for the Security Service, however. Sometimes there were safes in the offices and homes of diplomats, of foreign businessmen. . . .

The Service had long since found that the best way to cope was to recruit recently retired men who had *built* safes for the major companies.

In the case of Clarke-Smith their expert had retired four years before—lost with nowhere to go each day, resentful at the small pension and the watch, an eager recruit when he found he could help his country, be awarded some recognition and supplement his savings all at the same time.

The safe in Banks's house was of a kind he had put together himself. It wasn't a question of whether he could take it apart, just of how long he would need. He named it: three hours.

The alarm was even easier. Again, it was a good one—contact points on the doors, on the safe, and two microbeams across the room. The alarm, though, was of a silent type—meant to alert the police, not the thief. It sounded in the control room of a security company three miles away, transmitted over a Post Office telephone link.

And there was its weakness, because for Mallahide it was an easy task to get the number of that line. Shortly before the break-in, Mallahide would dial that number and leave his telephone off the hook. Until Mallahide replaced his receiver, Banks's secret link line to the security control room would be engaged, unable to transmit any calls of its own. The alarms would be triggered all right. They would simply not reach anyone.

When the time came, the break-in was as easy as Mallahide had hoped. Hollen regretted that they had not entered the house before—forgetting the crucial part their insider had played. However, the search yielded nothing in the way of spy paraphernalia—no microdot-making equipment, radio transmitters, code books.

In the safe, though, were two sets of papers, both with the highest security rating. One was on Soviet missile deployment. The other gave developments in antiballistic missile technology. It was copies of these that Hollen took to Chambers the following day.

Chambers was visibly shocked.

"My God," he said immediately. "*If* he has passed these on . . ."

He did not ask how Hollen had obtained them. Detail was better left to the experts. Carefully, he placed copies in his "destroy" tray. He would personally handle their destruction. It was a hard decision, but he knew it had to be made.

"If this is the type of material that he's taking home, I think we ought to consider more positive action. I take it there's still no real evidence?"

Hollen nodded.

"Then," said Chambers, "I think you should look again. And this time I am sure you *will* find something. And this time I am sure it *will* be convincing."

He looked into Hollen's eyes to see whether he needed to say more. He did not. Hollen understood, and he agreed. If there was not the evidence to prove the crime, then it would have to be created.

Banks *had* to be brought down.

CHAPTER 11

There was no dramatic event. No other man, no stand-up fight, no excessive demand for money, no feeling of guilt.

Boredom would have come nearest to the reason, but that alone was not it. It was more a feeling that the affair had run its course. That, just as a book had a beginning and an end or that a single day was not endless, this too had reached its conclusion.

Jennifer made the decision just after eleven in the morning. Stephen was still asleep. She wrote a note, kissed him on the cheek, murmured, "I'm going out," and left the bungalow they had been renting. The rent was paid for another two months with money raised from selling her watch. That could be Stephen's farewell gift.

She took the car, which was also rented, drove to the airport, used her credit cards to hire a small plane to fly her to Miami, and from there took the first London-bound flight. She left behind her clothes, the few bits of jewelry she had taken with her, even the suitcase in which they had been contained.

"When something's over, it really should be over," she had once said to an ex-lover who rather boringly had continued to follow her.

And the clothes and the jewelry and the suitcase were like Stephen. They belonged to something which was over. They were to be discarded too.

At London airport the customs officer questioned her for several minutes before letting her pass. His interest was professional—but he found her disturbing even though she was tired and had bothered little with makeup.

Afterward, driving home, he still remembered her, tried to pinpoint just what it was that had made her so memorable among the hundreds of people he had looked at during his shift.

Was it her height? She was taller than most women and it was accentuated by her slimness. Or her olive skin? Or her hair, long and jet black? Her features, though, were far from faultless: the bridge of her nose had a slight bend as though it had been broken and badly reset.

It was, he decided, none of them—or rather it was all of them, plus one other feature: her eyes. They pulled, they invited at some special chemistry shared just with you. She had presence, a charisma. She was, he thought, the kind of woman who once would have been a highly successful courtesan. Despite his brief moments of infatuation, however, the customs man was a professional. He had questioned her because a passenger on a flight from America with no luggage except a small handbag and a magazine had to be suspect.

Jennifer had expected it, and tired though she was, she bore it with resigned weariness. She had, after all, been through similar homecomings before.

"The problem," Hollen explained to Brighouse and Mallahide, "has changed somewhat."

Neither knew in any detail what the search of Banks's house had yielded. The report had been made direct to Hollen, and his first thought had been to talk to Chambers.

"It was," Hollen continued, "very, very interesting, but not conclusive."

Neither man spoke. After years of army discipline, Brighouse had developed patience. Mallahide had at least learned that to ask Hollen questions only further delayed him coming to the point.

"The documents we found there," said Hollen, "confirm the worst fears about the material Banks is seeing. There were papers that *officially* he hadn't access to."

No wonder he looked grave, thought Brighouse. Someone now had the agonizing decision of whether to tell the Americans. Whether Banks had passed on the information or not was not the most important immediate problem; the fact that he *might* have done so compromised the files. No one could any longer assume that the information they contained was secret.

Hollen detailed what had been found.

"But no *evidence?*"

"No. No evidence."

The two men waited.

Brighouse found himself reviewing all that had been done and was planned. The major ongoing activities were the watches on Banks and his mistress. Checks were also being made on everyone who lived in or regularly visited the apartment block. But so far neither surveillance nor checks had yielded anything.

He could offer no comfort to Hollen.

When the MI5 chief spoke, he did so slowly and carefully. "I think," he said, "that we should proceed on the assumption that if we haven't found evidence, we may never do so. I suggest that we should also assume that the *possibility* of guilt is great enough for us to take action anyway."

Neither man made any response.

"What I would like from you then is ideas—thoughts on how to deal with Banks if we assume that he is guilty, that we'll never prove it legitimately . . . and that despite that, we must do something."

He waved dismissal. "You'll want to think."

Mallahide, who had been getting bored with the assignment, felt new excitement.

"If we don't expect to get more information, shall we pull Fenn out?" asked Brighouse.

Hollen thought.

"No. We don't lose anything keeping him there. Let him stay. We may still have use for him. Who knows?"

Then to Mallahide. "But cut down the debriefings. Let him spend more time with Banks."

Three days had passed without a meeting in the Charing Cross Road flat. A terse message from Mallahide had instructed Fenn to go there only if he was alerted, not daily as before.

His immediate reaction was to welcome it. The pressures were easing. As he had suspected, his information was proving of limited value. Soon he would be allowed to return home.

And, God, he wanted that now.

The flat that Mallahide had found for him was small but comfortable—two rooms, a kitchen and a tiny bathroom above a row of shops, cheaply but recently decorated and furnished. His neighbors were mainly tourists. There was a pleasure in living alone and selfishly, able to do what he wanted, go where he wished.

This was living without problems. Money, suddenly, was no worry. He had all the things he had given up in some degree to enjoy the benefits and joys of Gozo. He would not want to live like this permanently. For a while, though, it was pleasant.

At the same time he missed Gemma with an intensity that grew daily, and he longed for the girls—for the crazy little things, like how they crawled into his bed on Sunday mornings and tickled him awake even though he had been waiting for them. And how Becky cooked exotic make-believe food in her make-believe kitchen and how Kate solemnly introduced him to strangers as, "This is my best friend, my daddy."

After the initial pleasure of fewer meetings, he grew nervous. Something must have happened to prompt the decision. That meant change. And change might also mean a greater degree of commitment for him later. He was nervous too that he had heard nothing from Banks. Had the man found signs of a break-in? And, if so, had he suspected that Fenn might be in-volved?

He tried to press on—researched the book as though it were real (perhaps, he thought, it might even be worth writing). He wrote daily to Gemma and the girls.

In the daily round, one small item brought home to him how much his beliefs had changed. In the rack of a newsstand below the flat he saw a copy of the *Morning Star*, the daily newspaper of the Communist Party. When his father had taken it, it had been called *The Daily Worker*. Fenn could not resist buying a copy. Just holding it brought back memories of his father reading stories aloud, marking passages, using news items to illustrate his convictions to his young son.

Fenn ran his eyes over the front page: "Certain government ministers who are little more than puppets of the bankers . . ." —"Car workers yesterday rejected a miserable pay offer. . . ."

Now it seemed so simplistic. Or had he grown cynical? Per-haps, he concluded as he tossed the paper aside, it would help if some remnants of faith still remained.

It was twenty-four hours later when Mallahide made contact again. The message was brief: a meeting, the following day at noon.

It came as a relief.

The strength of the Brighouse-Mallahide combination, Hollen had thought from the start, was that they perfectly com-plemented one another.

There was Brighouse—ultrasafe, cautious, a good man but a little lacking in daring. At most times, the ideal qualities for the department. And there was Mallahide—excellent instinct for the work, perfect background, good intellect . . . but a chancer: too impetuous, too willing to take risks. Carefully controlled, these characteristics were good too, now that there were areas of responsibility like Northern Ireland.

It was as a result of this combination of opposite talents that Mallahide and Brighouse finally came up with an idea after raising and rejecting dozens.

It was, at the end of it all, the simplest.

They would "lift" Banks's fingerprints and place them on documents. These would then be handed to one of the Russian spies operating from the Soviet Trade Mission whom MI5 had managed to blackmail into acting as a double agent.

They would have to arrest the agent. Sad, but double-agents took that risk. He would, of course, claim diplomatic immunity and be released and sent home. The Russians, knowing it must all be a charade, would doubtless send him to a labor camp or execute him. A loss, really; he might have fed the department interesting information over the coming years. Still, there were priorities.

Among the papers seized, though, would be ones containing Banks's fingerprints—surely enough to arrest and charge him.

Fenn was entrusted with the task of obtaining the prints, although he did not know for what purpose. He was given a new book with a shiny jacket. "Get Banks to handle it," he was told. "He'll probably be curious, ask to look at it. Otherwise, drop it, get him to pick it up." Then, Mallahide instructed him, handle it as little as necessary yourself.

Back in his office, Mallahide looked after the rest himself. He had done it before in Ulster when a little "evidence" looked as though it might prove useful. He placed a piece of transparent adhesive tape on Banks's fingerprint, pressed down, and carefully peeled the tape away. He then placed it on to the document to be handed to the Russian and rubbed it. Banks's prints were thus transferred from the book to the document—quickly, easily. And no one doubted the scheme would have been a success had not Hollen gone to the department's chief psychologist before the document was passed to the Russian. The psychologist deliberated and advised that Banks was a man who would fight such evidence, using all his skill and money to do so. In his opinion, it was not enough.

Brighouse and Mallahide thought he was wrong, were convinced that Hollen was being overcautious. They also resented the fact that, not for the first time, their chief was placing what they believed was too great a reliance on psychologists.

However, whatever the merits or otherwise of Hollen's decision, the result for Brighouse and Mallahide was the same: another search for a new plan.

CHAPTER 12

When Banks finally contacted Fenn, it was to explain he had been abroad, and also to make an unexpected offer. Among his books, said Banks, there were many Fenn would find useful in his research. Why didn't he work in the house for a week or so, studying them?

Fenn's feelings were mixed. He was struck by how alone Banks was in his personal life. As the man's wife became more sick and more distant and as Jennifer remained away, he needed someone near on whom to focus his emotions. Fenn was an obvious choice—the person who had given Banks a daughter and who also knew what it was like to lose someone loved slowly and painfully.

At the same time, Fenn was touched, though feeling more than ever a traitor, an impostor. In the end, he accepted. For an agent whose job it was to get as close as possible to Banks, it was an opportunity not to be lost.

At their next meeting Mallahide was visibly pleased—but he too had divided feelings. It was good that Fenn would have better access—although, no doubt, Parsons would keep a careful eye on this outsider—but it also meant that the two men were developing a degree of closeness that might prove dangerous. Fenn's loyalties could easily become divided.

The time was nearing, Mallahide decided, for the heavy stick. So far Fenn had had nothing but praise; soon he ought to be made to feel a little fear.

Fenn settled down to a new routine, a strangely businesslike and satisfying one. In the mornings he worked in libraries; the afternoons were spent in the house in St. James's, where he was conscious of how closely Parsons watched him.

Occasionally there were meetings with Mallahide. In the evenings he went to cinemas or theaters, but fought back from taking any women. It would be innocent—but who knew where it would lead? Frankly, he did not trust himself.

He vowed that the coming weekend he would fly home to see Gemma and the girls whatever Mallahide said and no matter how terrible the parting again would be afterward.

There was a meeting scheduled for the next day, Thursday. He would raise it then. He wouldn't ask, he would *tell* Mallahide—and, furthermore, he would pin the man down on how much longer he was expected to stay.

That morning he went straight to St. James's, planning to work through another pile of books he had taken from Banks's shelves the previous day. Parsons admitted him and announced almost immediately that he would be out for half an hour, calling at the London Library across the square. Apart from making his presence known, Parsons had shown no reactions to Fenn's presence in the house. Did he resent it? Suspect anything? Even welcome a new face? Fenn had no idea.

He sat at the desk in the room that Banks had provided, a small room at the back of the house, perfect for his purposes. It was quiet, light; there was nothing to distract him. He was taking the book seriously. It would probably never be written but the subject was absorbing him . . . and that was the only way to behave on such an assignment. Not to play-act, but genuinely to live the role you had been given.

He heard Parsons leave the house.

He worked for perhaps ten minutes. Then, in the cloistered silence of the house, he heard a crash . . . then another, followed by the distinct sound of breaking glass.

At first he thought it was outside. He soon realized, though, that it was coming from inside the house. He opened the door. Silence for a few seconds, followed by another crash, louder now.

Fenn gazed around the room, looking for something that would improvise as a weapon. He picked up a heavy glass ashtray. Going down the stairs, he put one edge into a folded handkerchief in his right palm. He would jab with the open side.

He followed the sound until he located its origin: somewhere beyond the doorway that led into Banks's daughter's apartment. He had never been inside.

He tried the door. It opened and the sound was louder. Vandals smashing an empty flat? They could have broken in through the entrance door to the flat that led directly to the street. There was time to call the police—the sensible thing to do.

Then he heard the sobbing between the crashing noises. He pushed a door with his foot and it slid open slowly and smoothly. She was standing, systematically smashing vases, small ornaments and bottle after bottle of perfume by throwing them at the wall. Broken glass covered the crumpled bed. The room smelled of stale sleep, liquor and perfume from the broken containers.

The girl was naked. She stood at the end of the bed, bleeding slightly on her left shoulder from a splinter of glass that had rebounded from the wall.

At Fenn's entrance, she turned. Her makeup had been washed by tears into a weird surrealistic pattern. She had nothing in her hands, but she advanced toward Fenn with her fingers outstretched, reaching to claw his eyes.

Fenn was puzzling whether to hit her with the ashtray or his hand when she stopped, began to vomit, and collapsed.

He waited a few minutes and then turned her over with his

foot. She rolled on to her back and began to snore. She was completely unconscious.

Fenn's first reaction was to turn the girl on to her side so that if she vomited again she would not choke, then he covered her with a sheet and began to check the room for the inevitable bottle of pills.

That was still intact when he found it. Nine tablets remained. According to the label, there had been thirty, but Fenn had no way of knowing how many had already been gone.

He gazed down at the woman. Was this really the young girl he had taken out of Hungary so long ago? The thought was replaced by a more urgent one: Should he call an ambulance?

He was still wondering when he heard footsteps in the passageway. It was Parsons returning. The manservant took immediate command. He felt the girl's pulse, checked the bottle, then made a telephone call. A doctor and private ambulance arrived within minutes. Parsons whispered to the doctor in the corner. It was obvious that it was not the first time the manservant had dealt with such an emergency.

As soon as they left by the private entrance to the street, Parsons began straightening the room. He opened the windows wide, but the smell of drink, perfume and vomit still hung in the air.

Fenn stood quietly, looking around. Even in chaos it was a beautiful room—a red carpet and soft pink art nouveau wallpaper, costume prints on the walls, heavy walnut furniture, chair seats covered in tapestry. The door was open into a large adjoining bathroom.

Parsons turned and saw him, looked surprised that he was still there.

"Was that Jennifer?"

"Miss Jennifer? Yes, sir."

"When did she get back?"

Parsons answered reluctantly.

"Yesterday morning. From the United States, I understand. Perhaps I should have warned you, but I thought she was sleeping."

"Does Sir Joseph know she's home?"

"No, sir, she asked me not to tell him. Said she would make it a surprise."

"This isn't the first time?"

Parsons didn't answer, but from his silence it was obvious that it was not.

"Do we call Sir Joseph?"

"If you really think he ought to know, sir."

"You don't?"

"I think it's more a cry for attention and affection, if you understand me, sir. I think you might find, sir, she's more drunk than drugged."

Parsons had dropped his guard, permitting himself, for one second, to be human.

Mallahide knew the girl was back. The customs officer had passed his suspicions to Immigration; Special Branch had checked her identity against the passenger list; and because she was Banks's daughter and because of his connection with the Prime Minister, the fact that she had arrived at Heathrow without luggage and had taken a flight at the last moment was fed into the intelligence machine.

And from there it passed to Brighouse and to Mallahide.

At the next meeting between Mallahide and Fenn, Mallahide waited for news of the girl's return to be given to him. The man *must* know. Further checks showed that she had taken a taxi home and Mallahide knew that Fenn had been working in the St. James's house.

Fenn said nothing.

Mallahide waited until the end of the debriefing. There is a rule any controller disregards at his peril: He has to show his agent unmistakably who is master. That moment had come, although neither his voice nor his expression showed it.

"So it's been quiet? Nothing unusual has happened?"

Fenn simply nodded agreement.

Mallahide walked to the window and looked down at the traffic. Without turning, he said, "Not even the girl's return?"

Fenn's mind raced. He should have realized they would know. Why hadn't he said anything? He knew why—a sense of guilt. She was, in a strange way, almost his own child. He had found her, carried her to safety, probably saved her from death. He was damned if he would destroy that part of his Hungarian escape, the only honest one.

"I didn't think it mattered."

"Didn't think it mattered?" Mallahide's voice rose in anger. His left eye began to throb again.

He walked toward the table and Fenn tensed his body for the attack he thought was coming, but Mallahide only wanted to reach his briefcase.

He took out a folder and threw it in Fenn's lap .

"Read it. It's just a selection. There are tapes too."

It was a dossier on Fenn's activities—dates, places, transcripts of conversations, photographs.

"What's the point?" Slightly bemused, not understanding.

"The point, my stupid friend," said Mallahide, "is that if we ever decide you are not useful any more, we can throw you into the sea and let you drown."

He gestured toward the file. "That sent anonymously to the right people would, I think, get you at least ten years, more if we embellished it nicely, which I think we could."

Fenn pushed his feet into the floor and launched himself forward. The file went flying, paper swirling, his head aimed for Mallahide's stomach.

Instead there was a knee in his face and a stiffened hand on the back of his neck. As he lay, semiconscious, bleeding onto the floor and gasping for breath, he heard Mallahide continuing as though he had not been interrupted.

"Just think of life without your beloved family for that long."

* * *

An Indian doctor packed his nose with gauze.

Mallahide had sent him there. Neither he nor Fenn wanted a curious hospital doctor asking questions, perhaps making a report to the police about a man who seemed to have been in a fight.

He prodded, and Fenn almost lost consciousness.

"You're lucky," said the doctor. "It doesn't seem to be broken."

Back at his flat, Fenn lay on the bed and, dosed with pain killers and a large drink, drifted into sleep.

The doorbell woke him. It took a long time to get off the bed. His head was still pounding and it was hard to focus.

He did not recognize the woman in the doorway. He stared at her.

"Oh," she said, "your poor face." She lifted her hand as though to touch him.

Fenn stepped back, still not fully awake.

"Who are you?"

"Jennifer, you silly," she replied. "Jennifer Banks. You saved my life and I've come to thank you."

And, outside, the men in the observation truck noted the time and jotted down details.

From them the information about Jennifer's visit would go to Brighouse. From him to Mallahide. And it would crystallize an idea that was already growing in his mind.

CHAPTER 13

In his fully conscious moments, Fenn suspected he must be suffering from slight concussion. He slipped in and out of a half-sleep and twice he stumbled to the bathroom to be ill.

Twice, too, almost unbelievably, the girl tried to seduce him in his waking moments. Once she began stroking his chest, once she felt gently between his thighs. But it was useless. He felt nothing, wanted nothing except rest and darkness.

And finally, resignedly, Jennifer wiped his forehead with a damp cloth, helped him hold the glass as he sipped water, and then settled down on a sofa to watch over him as he slept.

The man inside the surveillance van called Mallahide soon after seven A.M. as ordered.

He was brief. "Still there," he said.

Mallahide pulled himself out of bed. He would see Brighouse just as soon as he could. He would have preferred to go straight to Hollen, but suspected that would be self-defeating. Brighouse was so damned cautious. Surely, though, he would not dare to kill the suggestion without referring it upstairs.

On the way out of his room, Mallahide checked his face in the mirror tile stuck on the wall. Almost healed now. More than could be said for Fenn's face! He had been forced to hit Fenn hard and viciously to defend himself. He rehearsed his story, ready to report his actions to Brighouse.

Brighouse, of course, would worry about what Fenn would need to tell Banks to explain his injury. Mallahide would make sure he called Fenn before then to suggest a cover story. An attempted mugging might be the best; that could even gain Banks's sympathy.

Mallahide was still staring at his own reflection. Suddenly he began to smile. Necessary, yes. But it *had* been good.

"Hit them!" he hissed at the mirror. "Hit them all! That's the only way."

It was just after eleven-thirty when Fenn woke. He tried to breathe through his nose before remembering the packing in his nostrils.

He stood. Apart from the numbness in his nose and a slight dizziness, he felt reasonably well. No worse than a decent hangover.

In the bathroom he examined his face. There was a long, black bruise on and around his right cheekbone. He turned his head, winced. The back of his neck, above the right ear, was swollen and tender to the touch.

He washed carefully, ruefully remembering his dive at Mallahide. Crazy! The man was a pro. No doubting that. Fenn, foolishly, had underestimated him. Next time, if need be, he would take him from behind. Fast and with something heavy in his hand.

And then he remembered: if there *was* a next time. He began to sweat—the injury and nerves. He was trapped and it began to look like a whole new game.

Still naked, he went back into his room. Then he remembered: the girl!

He walked through into the living room. It was empty. For

a moment he thought he must have dreamed her presence in his hallucinations. Then he saw the crumpled, makeshift pillow on the sofa formed from cushions. He lifted one and held it near his face. It smelled of her perfume.

CHAPTER 14

It was a frustrating day for Mallahide. In his impatience to see
Brighouse, he had not once anticipated that the man might
not be available. When he arrived at Curzon Street, however,
Brighouse's office was locked, and all his personal assistant
would say was that he was away and unlikely to be back that
day.

For a short moment Mallahide wondered whether it could
have anything to do with his fight with Fenn, but he quickly
discounted that. He toyed, equally briefly, with the idea of
trying to see Hollen direct, but he concluded that his earlier
decision against this step had been right.

He spent the day restlessly bringing himself up to date on
papers. He left early, checked the newspapers, and found that
one of the suburban cinemas was showing an old Sam
Peckinpah film.

It exactly suited his mood. When he left the cinema, he felt
more relaxed. There was, he thought, something almost cleans-
ing about violence, even on the screen.

* * *

It was not until early afternoon that Fenn decided he would keep to his daily ritual of his visit to Banks's house.

It was not just that he felt well enough (which he did). Or that his face in the mirror did not look *too* bad, and that he had a good cover story. (Even though Mallahide had not called, he had independently decided to blame it on an attempted mugging.) The real reason, he had to admit to himself, was that he was drawn by the girl. She was a hazy image, a dream almost. He wanted to see what she looked like, experience how she behaved to him. It was not, he persuaded himself, a sexual thing, despite the way she had touched him during the night. It was more ephemeral than that. Perhaps, he thought as he left the flat, it was simply loneliness.

When he arrived at the house, there was no sign of the girl—only Parsons, as inscrutable as ever. There was not, Fenn noted, even a glimmer of interest of questioning at Fenn's face. Nor was there any reference to the previous day's finding of Jennifer; it might never have happened.

The book he was studying was a long, detailed work on mood-control drugs and gradually Fenn found himself becoming interested. He was so deeply involved in the text and his note-making that he took some seconds to register that the door had opened and someone had entered.

It was Banks. He looked tired. He stared at Fenn's face. "You've had an accident?"

Fenn lifted his head, touched his nose and smiled wryly. "A disagreement with someone who wanted my wallet," he said.

"You resisted?"

"Foolishly, yes. I must have thought I was younger and fitter than I am. Fortunately he thought he'd killed me and ran away." Fenn forced a laugh and waited for a reaction that did not come. He prompted. "Did you want to ask me something?"

Banks seemed to emerge from a daze. "Ask you something? Oh yes. My daughter, she's home. Wondered if you'd stay on this evening for a bit, have a drink, meet her."

He turned, without waiting for an answer.

* * *

Jennifer was wearing a long white dress as though it were a formal party, not just a meeting of three people.

Parsons had been told to leave the drinks; Banks poured.

Fenn found Jennifer staring at him. He purposely pretended to misunderstand. "Someone tried to mug me," he said.

"But you fought them off." Her voice was mocking.

Banks saved him from having to reply. "You know who Mr. Fenn is, darling?"

"I know." She held out her hand, formally. "I've had to wait a long time to thank you."

It was, Fenn realized looking back, a strange evening—three people trying to formalize their relationships with one another.

Whether it was Jennifer's presence and flirtatiousness or whether it was Banks's skepticism over the reason he had advanced for his injury, Fenn found Banks more cautious than normal. Whenever he glanced in the man's direction he was conscious of his wary gaze. Jennifer, on the other hand, seemed to revel in his presence—she used him as a foil to sparkle and to dominate the scene.

Fenn was simultaneously fascinated by her and repelled. At times she displayed those attributes that made her father likable—the steady gaze that told of total concentration on what you were saying; the fulsome smile that embraced the whole of the face and the eyes; the occasional self-deprecating remark.

At other times, though, she came across as just a rich bitch, a girl with too much, someone spoiled, for whom almost everything was a plaything.

When he left just after eight, heady with champagne, Fenn was still confused. The streets were quiet and he decided to walk for a while before taking a taxi. He realized that, whatever she was really like, Jennifer had gotten under his skin.

Waking, he thought it was a dream. Then he realized it was not.

Fenn lifted himself on one elbow, checked the time—12:55

A.M.—and waited to see if the doorbell rang again. It did. After the day's activity, he was feeling battered, and it was an effort to heave himself out of bed, but he opened the door, carefully, not sure what he would find.

She was giggly, drunk, a bottle of champagne unopened in her hand.

"I thought we'd continue the party," she said.

She went ahead of him, found the bedroom and lay down on top of the covers. Fenn watched from the doorway as she fumbled with the champagne cork. Suddenly it burst loose, shot across the room and bounced off the ceiling. Champagne gushed from the bottle and settled on Jennifer's face and dress.

Fenn's mouth went dry. He wanted her. He moved toward the bed and began to reach out. The bottle fell from her arms and rolled onto the floor.

At first he thought she was asleep, then he heard her mutter, "Last night it was you . . . now it's my turn."

Moments later all he could hear was her breathing. Fenn pushed her to one side of the bed and got in next to her. He ran his fingertips over her face, stroked her hair, then lay for a long time, looking. Finally the waves of exhaustion took over and he sank into an uneasy sleep. He woke twice to find she had not moved.

The third time the bed was empty and the room was filled with light.

He was still trying to focus when the door opened. She was carrying two mugs of coffee, handed him one, and slid into the bed beside him.

Jennifer's face was fixed in a half smile. Her expression said, I'm beautiful and I know it. He sensed this but had to agree. Her eyes drew him—dark, large.

Fenn put down his mug and was about to reach for her when she swung herself out of bed. Minutes later she was outside the doorway again, dressed.

"Rule one," she said, mock seriously, even though it had been she who had passed out on him. "Those who spurn me one night don't get me in the morning."

He heard her open the front door. Then she was back, briefly.

"Rule two," she said, "Don't be late picking me up this evening."

Mallahide finally saw Brighouse at eleven thirty the following day.

The younger man carried a sheaf of papers—a psychologist's report, notes on Jennifer Banks, and a résumé of the latest American pressures. Brighouse listened to him in silence, squiggling seemingly absentmindedly on a pad. Most of his doodles looked like fish.

At the end, he asked, "You really think it would work? You're serious?"

"I think it's worth trying. What else do we have?"

Brighouse squiggled some more. One of the fish was given what looked like a smile. Then he picked up the telephone, pressed a button and spoke briefly.

"He'll see us in fifteen minutes," he said as he replaced the receiver. "I can't say I altogether like it. But like you, I suspect we've little left."

Mallahide spoke almost nonstop for twenty-five minutes.

It was, he knew, a plan which would make the cautious men who ran the department nervous. More the kind of operation they would have thought suitable for the boys of SIS or their cousins, the CIA spooks. But then one of Mallahide's major assets to the department was that he did think the near-unthinkable—and this time he knew he held an ace: even ultracareful men like Brighouse were becoming desperate in the light of American pressure that showed signs of growing as the disarmament talks grew nearer.

Mallahide kept his voice flat, unemotional. The scheme he was outlining was bizarre, and he wanted it to be seen that he had thought it through calmly. He started from one basic premise: it was agreed that Banks must go.

Manufactured evidence did not seem a dependable enough method. Therefore, he suggested they contemplate blackmail. There were, he went on, two problems any blackmailer faced: finding the weakness, and anticipating how the subject would react to the demand. The problem with Banks was that he seemed invulnerable to both—none of them had been able to find an exploitable weakness; the psychologist argued that Banks was the kind of man to fight.

Hollen and Brighouse caught each other's eyes. It was sounding uncomfortably like a lecture. If Mallahide sensed their feelings, he gave no indication. He continued in the same even tone.

"The next point to consider then, it seemed to me, was whether he could be reached through those he holds dearest, those he really cares about, cold fish that he is."

"You mean his wife and daughter?" Hollen felt he had to show his presence.

"Exactly."

"All right. Go on."

"First I considered the wife. There's no doubt about the strength of his feelings for her. The psychologist suggests that it may even have been intensified since she went mad—guilt over whether he'd spent enough time with her, that sort of thing. But I came to the conclusion that there was no real scope there. I can detail the reasons why if you wish. . . ."

Hollen shook his head. Brighouse remained inscrutable.

"That left the daughter."

"But surely from what we've seen and from what we've said before, it's accepted there's virtually nothing she could do that would make her so vulnerable that Banks would feel he *had* to do anything to save her."

"I agree, sir—virtually nothing. But there's one thing he could not survive. If his daughter took the documents he takes home and if *she* passed them to the Soviets. And if we could prove it."

He looked for expressions, still saw none.

"Imagine," he continued, "what would happen if it came out. The girl would be destroyed, Banks would be pretty well finished. Moreover the scandal would bring down his friend's government. We could insure that it did by a few judicious leaks about earlier investigations pointing to the Bankses household."

"The publicity wouldn't do us or the country much good either. A big price to pay," Hollen noted.

"But there would be no need for publicity. No one but he and us need ever know. Not if he quietly resigned, that is. Overwork, a heart condition—something like that. I'm arguing —no, I'm *certain*—that faced with the choice I've just outlined he'd happily settle for retirement."

You young bastard, thought Hollen. You nasty young bastard.

He was about to speak when Mallahide delivered his trump card.

"Oh, and I forgot to say that the psychologists agree with my assessment, sir."

"Who are these Soviets she hands the secrets to?" asked Hollen.

"Why, Fenn, I thought. No problems there in proving that he's been a Soviet agent for twenty years. There's a file six inches thick on him."

"Supposing she'd do it, has she enough access?"

"No problem with the house. She's every right to be there. The study? We can arrange a key. The alarms? We know how to fix them. The safe? As the result of our visit we have the combination."

Brighouse spoke for the first time.

"And *why* would she do it?"

Mallahide permitted himself a smile. "Now she's a different animal from her father. I'd say she *is* blackmailable."

"It would have to be good."

"Well," said Mallahide, enjoying the drama, "I was thinking of her killing someone."

CHAPTER 15

"Tell me about it," she said.

"Hungary?"

"Yes. I've seen some newspaper reports that daddy kept, but I'd like to know more."

"I find it hard to remember, let alone think about it."

"You mean you'd rather not." She was being uncharacteristically understanding.

"Please."

They were in a corner of an almost empty restaurant they had stumbled upon. The tables were lit by dripping white candles in old Chianti bottles and it would have been romantic to say that the meal was perfect. It was, in fact, almost inedible. It did not seem to matter.

"Is the story that you told about your face true?"

A smiled grimace. "Do you mean, did I do it myself?"

"No, silly." Then she added, "But Daddy didn't believe it."

Fenn fought not to show an expression. Jennifer's words confirmed fears that Banks had become much less certain of him.

He wanted to ask more, but Jennifer changed the subject. "You miss your wife?"

"Very much."

"So why are you here?" Was Banks suspicious about this too?

"I need the money."

She started to say, "I'll give you money," but stopped. She had given men money before—Peter so he could open a restaurant, that boy who had wanted to run his own recording company. But large cash sums were no longer forthcoming from her father, and she had sold many of the easily disposable things to pay for the Bahamas episode. Even if she had the money, though, she realized she would not offer it to Fenn. It was not only his age, although she was conscious that he was older than any other man with whom she had become involved. She knew it would offend him . . . and she was glad he needed the money. It meant he had to stay. She realized she wanted that.

Her feelings were strange. She could not analyze them. Partly, of course, it was what he had done—he had saved her life. Without him, she would probably not exist . . . but that was not all. What was especially good was that she felt *comfortable* with him.

Of course, there would be a moment when it was all over. But she did not have to think about that yet.

"More coffee?"

She pushed her cup away.

"Come on. I'll make you some at home."

Outside, in the empty street, she reached out, took his arm. He tensed and then relaxed. It seemed right.

Inside the van parked fifty yards away, the camera began to turn.

It was a reasonably innocent set of film that was being taken. But it was the beginning of Mallahide's dossier. Soon, perhaps, he could improve on it.

It had been six months since Mallahide had been home.

First there had been the undercover assignment in Northern Ireland, then the surgery and recuperation after the shooting.

He should have visited them after that but he had wanted his face to heal.

His father would not have been unduly upset by the sight—after thirty-five years in the Metropolitan Police he had seen it all—but his mother would have reacted badly, and that always made him wish that he had never gone. Like his father, she knew what he did, but she liked to think it was safe and uneventful work, that she did not have to fear for him as she once had for her husband.

Brighton was full of tourists, foreign students, brash and noisy in the September sun. The terraced house his parents had bought on his father's retirement was Victorian, one hundred and fifty yards back from the seafront, beautiful on a day like today, windy and viciously cold in the winter. But they seemed to thrive on it.

His mother was in the kitchen, baking, because he had telephoned and said he was coming. Even though it was nearly healed, she was solicitous about his nose. "Just a bang," he said. "Something I got in training."

His father was in the small garden, dotting ant killer onto pieces of wood. "We've had an invasion."

Mallahide's mother brought out cold beer and the two men drank.

"You've been away?"

"Over the water."

His father nodded toward his face. "You got that?"

"It's nothing."

"Come on," said his father taking his arm, "we'll have another down at the pub."

Both men knew the burden of carrying secrets. Mallahide was glad to be with someone who could understand but did not ask.

It was after lunch, again out in the garden, that Mallahide asked his questions.

"Pop," he said, "road accidents where the car doesn't stop. Tell me about the evidence that the driver leaves behind. . . ."

*   *   *

They made love at his flat.

As soon as they were inside the front door, they began to undress each other. A trail of garments soon lined the route into the bedroom.

He lay on his back in the darkness while she went to the bathroom. He found himself nervous over whether he could satisfy her; she must have known so many men.

When she returned she went straight down on him with her mouth. He had to pull her away to take her. It did not last long. He was too excited, too nervous, they were too new together. But when she felt he was about to come, she dug her nails into his back and faked a climax. She had never had an orgasm, but normally she did not even pretend. This time—she was not sure why—she wanted to please him.

Afterward he held her and she liked that. They talked too and she liked that as well.

For a brief moment, in one of the silences, Fenn found himself comparing her with Gemma—Jennifer was rougher, less understanding . . . but exciting.

They talked some more before they drifted into sleep. And on the wall, the apparently innocuous plug picked up every word.

Mallahide's apartment was on the seventeenth floor of a modern building in West London.

It was oddly anonymous—within an hour it could have been cleared of every trace of its occupant. Less a flat, more a hotel room. Mallahide liked it like that.

After his day with his parents he had one of his headaches. He really should consult a doctor, not necessarily the service's resident man. He was afraid, though. A doctor might read too much into it.

They would go. He took aspirin, struggled to go on working.

His desk was at the window. Below, London was spread out before him as far as the Houses of Parliament.

He had a pad in front of him and he began to make notes.

Key words were written in capitals. "BLOOD." "HAIR." "SKIN PARTICLES." And in capitals and ringed, "GLASS FRAGMENTS."

Next to that were two notes: "Check if Porsche has special glass for headlights." And "Does *she* own Porsche?"

He began to find it hard to focus. The migraine was producing double vision. He wanted to lie down in a dark room . . . but there was one thing first. He dialed a number.

"George?"

The tapes had been back for an hour.

"He's there."

Mallahide put down the telephone, eased his tie as he walked into the bedroom. He lay on the bed, clothed, and stared up at the ceiling.

"The damned fool," he thought. "The fool. All for a piece of pussy."

He rolled over, took two sleeping pills from the bedside drawer.

He needed to sleep. Tomorrow it would begin to happen.

The telephone rang just after seven-thirty in the morning.

Jennifer was already up, making tea—she had soon learned of Fenn's addiction to the drink. She answered without thinking.

"Yes?" she said.

She realized her mistake immediately. The voice at the other end of the telephone was a woman's.

"James? Is James there?"

Jennifer replaced the receiver.

When it rang again five minutes later, Fenn answered.

"Gemma!" Then, alarmed because of the time, "What's happening? There's nothing wrong, is there? . . ." They had agreed they would talk on the telephone only on Sundays unless there was an emergency.

Her voice was puzzled. "But I received a message that you wanted me to call you."

In the silence that followed, Fenn heard the rattle of cups in the kitchen, a friendly domestic sound that he hoped was not being picked up by the receiver.

"And James—who was the woman who answered?"

He surprised himself at the readiness of the lie.

"Who? Oh, just a secretary. She's been working since dawn transcribing my notes. Things have reached a pretty urgent state."

He waited for a reaction. When it came, he was relieved—Gemma seemed to accept the story.

He wanted Jennifer, but he did not want to hurt his wife or put their marriage at risk.

Oral permission for the operation to go ahead was given by Hollen shortly after eleven. Nothing was being committed to paper.

Before making his decision Hollen had insisted on reviewing all the information collected so far. He had a vain hope that he personally would come up with something less dramatic, less risky. The file on Banks was now vast, but at the end of his reading Hollen was forced to concede he could see nothing.

A great deal of hope had been placed on investigating Stella Harding, the mistress. Hollen's men had probed her past, interviewed friends and old colleagues—although, as with Banks himself, they had been hampered by the need for discretion. They had found no link with the Soviet Union, nor with Communism, though that in itself did not mean much. The likelihood, an officer had concluded, was that *if* Banks was using her as a messenger he had begun to do so after genuinely setting her up as a mistress. Surveillance—physical and electronic—of her apartment had yielded nothing. But that again was not conclusive—it was a busy building with constant streams of callers, and the woman herself went out a great deal.

News of Hollen's decision did not, however, reach Mallahide

until early afternoon. He had been visiting an old colleague of his father's in anticipation of such permission.

He showed no sign of elation. His mind was already totally occupied with the mechanics. Because they were keeping the operation as tight as possible, he was handling as much as he could himself. That was why he hoped to keep away from the department's "experts."

"Will *you* see Fenn next time?" he asked Brighouse. "There's a meeting tomorrow. We'll need to add to the pressure. It'll be easier from a new face."

"I look too gentlemanly, too British," replied Brighouse. "Let's use Kirby."

Mallahide nodded assent. Kirby, because of his Slavic looks, would be ideal. He occasionally acted the Russian interrogator in training sessions.

After Mallahide left, Brighouse remained seated, unmoving, thinking again how cold an operator the younger man was. He did not know, would never have guessed, that Mallahide's feelings as he headed away from the office that morning were far from cool.

Mallahide's hands tingled, there was a tight feeling in his stomach. Banks, the daughter, Fenn. All of them were now simply the opposition. People like those who had been behind his shooting in Northern Ireland.

Despite the telephone call from Gemma, Fenn spent the day with Jennifer.

A calm day, a relaxed day. They had made love once more—in the middle of the morning before sleeping again. Jennifer had said one thing, half-asleep, which had touched him: "I know what I'm like," she had murmured, "and I can't help it. But I'll try to be good to you."

Late morning they took a bus, and then walked like lovers hand in hand in Hyde Park. They bought rolls and beer and picnicked on the grass. Jennifer talked a lot—as though it was a relief to have someone to communicate with.

Some of the talk was of her father. Fenn found her behavior toward him odd, but as she talked he saw a facet of her he had not realized: Jennifer shut people out of her mind when she was not actually with them. It was as though they did not exist at such times. That was why her attitude to her father seemed so ambivalent. It also explained, Fenn realized, why the lovers simply vanished, never again to be mentioned.

Jennifer was due to go to the theater with Banks that evening, one of their rare evenings out together. Fenn persuaded her not to cancel it. Partly he was afraid of alerting an already suspicious Banks to what was happening between him and Jennifer, partly he wanted the time the evening would give him, time to write to Gemma. He would repeat that the girl who had answered the telephone was just a secretary.

It was after eight when he finished the letter. He posted it, strolled, went for a drink and sandwich in a local pub.

He was beginning to like Paddington—a community of itinerants like him. They smiled at each other, respected each other's presence, but remained apart.

"But I thought you did. . . ." A snatch of conversation drifted toward him from between a couple further along the bar.

He remembered Gemma's voice: "But I received a message you wanted me to call you."

It had been received by telephone at the school. Both agreed it must have been a mistake—the teacher who took the call had gotten it wrong. Gemma was probably being asked to call a parent.

But?

Fenn stared into the swirls of cigarette smoke hanging above the fruit machine. Then he finished his drink quickly, left the sandwich unfinished and made for the flat.

He began searching immediately. A physical check yielded nothing, but Fenn remembered his tradecraft—those lessons near Moscow when he was supposedly somewhere else. He left again and bought an FM radio in a nearby shop—the salesman seemed amused that Fenn did not seem to care about the tone, only if the radio covered the FM bands and those used by aircraft and public services.

And if it had an earpiece for "silent" listening.

Back in the flat, Fenn extended the antenna, switched the radio on, and turned the volume control to full. Then slowly he tuned the radio through one band, then another, then a third. . . .

Nothing in the hallway.

He repeated the exercise in the center of the living room. He was on the second band when the sound came from the loudspeaker. Unmistakable. A high-pitched howling noise.

Carefully Fenn tuned the set until the howl was at its clearest, then he turned down the volume and plugged in the earpiece. With the ear socket in his ear and the radio held in his left hand, he began tapping furniture gently with a coin.

Nothing at first. Then he reached the radiator, tapped softly. The sound of the tapping, picked up by a bug and transmitted to the radio, came through loud on the earphone. Now that he had pinpointed the site, it took minutes to find the bug itself. He picked it out in the beam of a flashlight.

Small, but not too small. Hidden, but not so well hidden that he had not been able to find it. Even without the help of the FM radio, a careful physical search would have revealed it in time.

Which was exactly what Mallahide wanted.

CHAPTER 16

The dinner was being given in a room overlooking The Mall. The guest of honor was the station head of the CIA at the London Embassy who was returning home.

Three of his colleagues accompanied him. The other eight men around the table were from the SIS, including its head, Sir Edward Crimpton, and the Foreign Office.

The meal was being provided out of British Government Hospitality Funds. The setting—deep red silk-covered walls, glittering chandeliers—and the wine, which included a 1971 Château Lafitte-Rothschild with the lamb, was better than the food. That was overambitious, and was not helped by the fact that it had been cooked four floors below and brought up in a slow-moving dumbwaiter.

Nevertheless, it proved a good evening, much to Crimpton's relief. These things could easily go wrong, backfire, worsen relations rather than cement them.

He had been a little worried about the cartoon they had had drawn for the station chief—a caricature of the American disguised in a false beard and heavy rimmed glasses hiding under the table at a banquet at the Chinese Embassy—but the station chief, who had never done anything even vaguely like that in his life, was visibly amused.

Outside on the street as Crimpton accompanied him to his car, he was warm and effusive. It was only at the very last moment that he turned to professional topics. "The Banks affair. It's going through?"

Bad form, thought Crimpton, but he had to answer. "As far as I know, yes. It's right on schedule. We're not handling it, you know, but I keep a careful eye." It was at times like these that he wished he had stayed in the regular Foreign Office stream and had attained the ambassadorship with all the pomp and privilege his wife would have liked so much.

The station chief's car pulled up at the curb beside the two men, but the American beckoned the driver to remain in his seat.

"I'm only raising this now because I'm leaving first thing in the morning and it's my last chance. I'll try to persuade the people back home that you're doing everything and not to cut back on stuff. I've done my best so far, you know that."

Crimpton nodded. The station chief had got the flow of material partially restored to its normal level after being convinced that something was being done about Banks.

"But they're worried and impatient people," the American continued. "Oh, hell, I don't need to tell you that."

He let himself into the car, pressed the button to let down the window.

"What I'm trying to say, I guess, is that I'll give you as much time as it's in my power. But you must hit him soon, Edward. You really must."

By three o'clock, the scheduled time for the meeting in Charing Cross Road, Fenn had brought his fear and anger under control.

The purpose of the bug was obvious. First they had threatened him with disclosure if he did not cooperate, now they were adding a second threat—they were collecting material that could be passed to Gemma. There could be only one conceivable reason. His Russian masters were about to increase their demands upon him and wanted to be certain he would not refuse.

But where did Jennifer stand in all this? Was she one of them? Had she set him up? He discounted the thought. He and she had been a lucky accident for them. Without their coming together, his controllers would have found something else to compromise him.

Fenn found himself wondering what his father would have thought of it all. Where would it have fitted into his philosophy of man's equality and the need for Communism to satisfy it? Would he have dismissed it as necessary for the cause just as he had Stalin's excesses and the Nazi-Soviet pact?

Fenn arrived at the underground station early, and spent half an hour in Foyles Book Shop, finally buying two books to send to the girls. Guilt?

At the door to the flat he paused to gain his composure. This would be the first time he had seen Mallahide since their clash and since the discovery of the bug.

Mallahide was smiling when he opened the door. Fenn did not see the stranger until he was well inside. The man stood at the window, his back to the room. He turned slowly, arms folded, his face set and unsmiling. He was a heavy man and could have been a wrestler. His eyes were hooded, but his lips were incredibly thin for such a full face.

"This is Colonel Greshnikov," said Mallahide. "He wishes to meet you now that the playing is over."

Jennifer left the restaurant table four times to call Fenn's number before deciding she was making a fool of herself.

"Where's your cool, for Christ's sake," she said to the mirror in the ladies' room before leaving.

Her companion was a young stockbroker she had known for about a year. It was not a torrid affair, not even a real affair. He called her perhaps once every six weeks.

Outside, he hailed a taxi.

It was taken for granted they were going to his apartment. For a few moments she considered excusing herself, claiming she felt ill. God, she *was* taking Fenn seriously.

But when the taxi drew up she got in meekly.

Afterward he did not hold her and they did not talk. She lay and gazed at the ceiling and felt numb.

"I need some cigarettes," said the colonel.

His voice, which had the faintest of accents, was pleasant, but there was no mistaking the command.

"I'll fetch some. Which brand?"

"The strongest you can find. French, perhaps." He shrugged in Fenn's direction. "Your English cigarettes are too mild. I must arrange a good supply again."

The colonel returned to the window and gazed down into the street until he saw Mallahide begin to cross the road.

Fenn stared at his back. The colonel's hair was cropped short —a look Fenn well remembered from his secret visits to Moscow. Soviet officialdom's standard look. Because the colonel had not let his hair grow, had not had it styled in Western fashion, Fenn suspected that the man's cover was probably one of the official Soviet organizations in London.

When the colonel turned, Fenn noted the shoes too. Black, very shiny, a style from perhaps fifteen years before.

The colonel came close, produced his cigarette case, offered it and then lit one.

His thin lips smiled. "I thought we should be by ourselves. Besides, I always need more cigarettes." He gestured toward the door. "He is a good man, but sometimes, being young and impatient, he gets things wrong."

There was a fresh bottle of whiskey on the cocktail wagon. The colonel poured two large measures, one of which he handed to Fenn.

"To you," he said. "And to brave men like you."

He drained it at one gulp and refilled his glass.

"Our young friend has the wrong idea," he went on. "He

thinks that you need threatening—disclosure. Perhaps a word to your wife about a certain lady. . . ."

Fenn stiffened and the colonel raised his hand and made a patting motion.

"No. No. Don't worry. I know he is wrong. I have already reprimanded him."

He refilled Fenn's glass. "Now," he said, "we will talk no more of it. You will leave it to me."

He patted his pocket. "To business." The photograph he produced was of Jennifer out walking. Alone. But Fenn recognized the clothes, the background. He had been with her. Despite the colonel's assurances, it was a reminder they had been filming him.

"It is vital," said the colonel, "that we see the papers that Banks takes home with him. Regularly. Not just an occasional quick break-in like last time."

He poured himself more liquor, slumped into one of the chairs, gazing down at the glass. Fenn looked at the bottle. It was already half empty.

"It won't be easy," said Fenn.

The colonel swirled his drink, began to lift the glass to his mouth, stopped and looked solemn. "I know," he said. "But it's important. Vitally important."

He hauled himself up and began to pace the floor.

"*They* blame us for the arms race," he said. "They—the Pentagon hawks and the arms manufacturers. Do you know what the American defense budget is this year?" He spread his arms dramatically, spilling some of the drink.

"One hundred and fifty billion dollars!"

He finished the drink, put down his glass abruptly.

"What happens? We have to spend more on arms. We don't want to, but we have to match them—not just quantity but all the new developments. Money we'd rather spend on other things, peaceful things."

He came closer to Fenn, slowly spread his hands.

"That's *why* we need information like that. Why we are proud there are people like you."

Fenn felt lost, did not know what to say.

The colonel shook his head as though waking himself, picked up the picture of Jennifer, held it out again.

"Now," he said, "I understand she has access to the whole of the house all the time. I think we must *persuade* her to help us."

The door opened and Mallahide entered.

The colonel put his arm around Fenn's shoulders.

"Mr. Fenn and I have had a *most* useful talk," he said. "I have told him about your silly misgivings and how I *know* they are unfounded.

"I have told him what we want. All you have to do now is tell him how."

The map was spread out over the floor.

Mallahide knelt, jabbed at a spot. Fenn had to bend almost double to see where the finger pointed. The nearest town seemed to be Northampton.

"There's a party there on Saturday night. The Banks girl has been invited."

They must have been intercepting her mail, Fenn realized. "I know," he said. "Friends have a house they use for weekends. She asked me if I wanted to go, seemed relieved when I didn't."

"Probably realized you'd meet too many former bedmates," said Mallahide.

Fenn tensed, but did not look up.

"Well, you're going." Mallahide's words were an order, and Fenn was conscious that the colonel was watching him closely.

He remained silent.

"About eleven you'll quarrel with her and walk out. Just how is up to you. But it should be pretty easy. What do you think she'll do then?"

"How the hell should I know?" Almost immediately he regretted his tone. Better to remain cool.

Mallahide answered his own question. "She's a little tart,"

he said. "She'll drink like a bloody fish. Maybe take a couple of pills. That's what she'll do."

And Fenn thought with sickening understanding, "She'll also crawl into bed with someone."

"What you do then," said Mallahide, "is give her an hour or two—you'll have to judge how long yourself. Then you'll go back, make it up and say you want to go back to London."

"You think she'll have me back and that she'll come?"

"Oh yes," said Mallahide, and the voice was the one he reserved for lectures. "At the moment you are *the* one. It can't last—that's her pattern—but while it does you can get away with anything. The more you flatten her, the more you make her crawl, the more she'll like it and cling to you."

Fenn walked to the drinks wagon and for the first time at one of their meetings poured himself a drink. He was again conscious of the colonel's gaze and he fought to stop his hand trembling.

"Go on," he said.

"You make sure that she drives. Provided that she isn't totally incapable, that shouldn't be too hard. Drink and driving don't seem to worry her."

"It could worry me."

Mallahide disregarded him, leaned over the map again. "About there," he said, jabbing once more, "she'll hit someone."

"Someone?"

"Some*thing*, but she won't know that. We'll probably use an animal carcass, rig it up so that it looks human in the headlights. All you have to do is make her drive on. It should be nearing dawn by this time."

"And what then?"

The colonel walked over and again put his arm around Fenn.

"Now Mr. Fenn," he boomed, "don't let's be impatient. We will save that for another day."

*   *   *

The telephone rang three times that evening as Fenn lay on the bed staring into nowhere.

He did not want to eat, drink, read, walk, anything. He wanted Jennifer with him. And yet he knew that if she were there he would want to be alone.

He kept thinking of Mallahide's assessment of her and—for the first time—of the succession of men of whom he was only the latest. And yet, at the same time, he felt ashamed that he had not defended her. There was much about her that was good, much that he could admire. As for the rest, wasn't it Bank's fault—or rather that combined with the absence of a mother. Jennifer *needed* parents.

Gazing at the ceiling, Fenn wondered what she might have been like if she had never left Hungary, if there had been no revolution, no need to flee, no being orphaned. . . .

Suddenly, he found himself thinking of the girl with whom he had stayed for a number of days—the student with the tommy gun. Briefly he wondered where she was now. Could Jennifer have been like her?

He fetched himself a drink and returned to the bed. Christ, what a mess! What did a man do? Go along with them? That was the easiest. But where to? Stage by stage, he went deeper and deeper.

Though, once this was done, was his role ended? Mallahide had been right—the affair with Jennifer would be short-lived. He did not delude himself. Once it was over, surely his use was gone?

But the colonel had told him not to be impatient. Didn't that indicate further demands upon him?

Or instead of obeying them, did he say No! No more! This is where it stops! What then? Disclosure? Imprisonment? Or—and again he did not delude himself—even stronger pressures from British counter-espionage to become a double agent? And a dossier to Gemma?

Or should he vanish? It could, he was sure, be done—but only if he was prepared to give up everything. You could not disappear and retain any of your past. Worse even than going to prison.

It was Gemma who made the decision for him, without knowing.

It was almost one in the morning and this time he answered the telephone.

Her voice was breathless. "I know I shouldn't call, but I just had your lovely letter. I've just reread it. I just wanted to say I love you. And we all miss you."

And before he could say anything she hung up.

He fell asleep two hours later—sad in the certainty that, for now anyway, he would continue to do what he was told.

CHAPTER 17

"Will he do it?"

It was Sunday morning and Brighouse and Mallahide were sitting in Bedford Square. The trees were just beginning to shed their leaves.

Brighouse came into the square every Sunday morning if the weather was fine and spent precisely an hour reading his Sunday newspaper before going home to tend to his fish.

"I think so. We may need more pressure."

"No." Brighouse was firm. "Not yet. If we *need* to apply more now, it's no good. He's under enough. Later, perhaps. Not now."

Mallahide was surprised and impressed by the other's firmness. He'd often thought the older man a bit of a dodderer. "All right," he said, and then, graciously, "You're the best judge."

A woman pushing a baby carriage paused nearby and looked as though she would sit on their bench. She saw Mallahide's look and moved on.

"You want me to go through it again?" said Mallahide.

"Yes, I know the outline, but I'd like the detail. Please." Brighouse was under orders to keep strict watch over Mallahide's activities. There was to be no improvising once a plan had been agreed.

Mallahide ran through the arrangements—places, timings, people to be involved, equipment needed and being arranged.

Brighouse asked questions until he was satisfied.

"Just one last thing," he added. "Fenn's being briefed on *precisely* what to do afterward?"

"To make sure one of the girl's first thoughts is the effect it will have on her father at a crucial time?"

"Yes."

"All arranged. Fenn'll make sure that on the way there the conversation includes the wife's illness worsening and the forthcoming arms talks—and how heavy the strain is on Banks."

"Good. *That's* what will insure she doesn't go near the police."

A flurry of wind blew a pile of leaves. Some settled by the bench. Mallahide bent, picked one from the ground and began to tear it into small pieces.

"Funny, isn't it," he said, "that their weakness turns out to be each other?"

"You've been seeing a lot of Jennifer?"

Banks's words were more a statement than a question.

It was the first time Fenn had seen Banks for almost a week. The older man had been attending a series of meetings and, Fenn had been told, had also had to make two sudden visits to the Cotswold house to confer with doctors about his wife.

For the first time since they met, Fenn realized the man's age. He looked even more tired than he had at their last meeting—transparently a man giving out more energy than he was replenishing.

Fenn's reply was guarded. "We've been out once or twice. She's very good company."

Banks studied him over his claret glass. They were dining in one of his clubs. Fenn had been surprised by the invitation to meet. Banks had been noticeably less friendly recently.

Banks found the next question difficult to ask. "She knows that . . . ?" The question tailed away.

"That I'm married and have children? Oh yes. And that I'll be going home once this is over. It's not like that. It's just nice to have someone to do the occasional things with."

Banks fixed him with his eyes.

"I'm glad," he said. "I'm not sure it would be a good thing for you two to get too involved."

His voice was cold.

Fenn was not surprised when minutes later Banks asked him if he had finished going through the books in the house.

Banks obviously wanted him out.

His ease of access was over.

By Friday Mallahide had everything arranged.

There had been no difficulties. The road signs had been obtained from the police via Special Branch, ostensibly for an exercise. A medical expert in the SAS had been consulted. Blood, skin and hair had been obtained in the most direct way—from a pathologist who worked for the department as a part-time adviser. (It would, Mallahide thought, have been a nice touch to have a real body—but obtaining a corpse in total secrecy was not an easy task.)

The blood, stored in a plastic, sealed balloon, had to be prevented from clotting—easily achieved by adding a few five-milliliter tubes of sequestrine to "fix" the calcium content and keep it liquid.

Mallahide's Indian doctor made up a flask of alcohol and barbiturate for Fenn to carry in case the girl sobered up. With it he delivered a warning about its potency—one small whiskey, he said, could increase the effect of a drug tenfold.

He would collect the pig carcass from a deep-freeze center on Saturday morning. That left only the van to be arranged today.

He did not want to take one from the pool. He toyed with the idea of stealing one. It would be pleasing to see if he still had the touch . . . but it wasn't necessary. He was making a simple job too complex.

He reached for the evening newspaper and began to read through the "Vans to Rent" column. He wanted a small firm, the kind unlikely to blazon their name on the side of their vehicles.

"Do you *really* want to go? *Really?*"

She was clinging to his arm and playfully being seductive.

They had lunched in a pub overlooking the Thames near the London Docks. The streets as they made their way back to the car were deserted. This was a working area, away from the immediate vicinity of the tourist pubs and, on Saturdays, empty.

"What else could we do?" he said, entering into the game.

"Well, maybe I could think of something if I tried *very* hard."

They reached the Porsche and she slid into the driver's seat, opening his door from the inside.

"We've time for both," he said.

"You pig," very girlishly.

She turned the ignition key. The motor whirred, stopped. She tried again.

"It's only just been serviced. Oh no!" Anger at a fault in twenty thousand pounds' worth of nearly new car.

Fenn found himself thinking that if the car did not start, that night's events would have to be canceled. He willed the engine not to catch—even though he knew that would only postpone things.

Jennifer turned the key again. The car purred into life.

CHAPTER 18

The M1 Motorway, leading north out of London, was crowded
—Saturday visitors heading home from the capital.

Behind the wheel of the Porsche, Jennifer was impatient.
Several times Fenn had to restrain her from taking crazy risks
at overtaking, and once, when she did have a clear run in the
outside lane, he had to talk her down to a near-legal eighty
mph from one hundred and ten mph.

"You're chicken," she yelled, "I've done one hundred and
forty on the *Autoroute*." She had been in a bad temper ever
since they had gotten out of bed. "Let's just stay here all
night," she had urged. And when Fenn had said her friends
would be disappointed, "Who cares about them? They're only
shits." And then, with what he feared was frightening percep-
tion, "Why the hell do you want to go anyway?"

Near Luton, though, the traffic eased and so did her temper.
Driving had always been good therapy for her. She drove with
concentration and instinctive skill, though sometimes recklessly,
relying on the car's superior power to get her out of trouble.

As they turned off the motorway, she stopped the car briefly,
turned and kissed his cheek.

"Sorry," she said, restarting the car again immediately. "I'm a bitch sometimes. You'll have to forgive me."

Fenn could not bear to speak. He felt like a traitor.

The van was dark green and had no distinguishing marks.

Mallahide had drawn false number plates—a fairly routine procedure. *If* anyone spotted anything unusual and reported the van, the trail would end nowhere. The plates would show on the vehicle licensing computer as having no owner: in other words, Security—so leave alone.

They kept off the motorway, using the A road, the one Fenn would persuade the girl to drive along on her return to London.

After an hour Mallahide pulled off the main road on to a track. While Kirby stood outside, eating sandwiches and drinking beer from a can, Mallahide busied himself in the back of the van.

The pig's carcass, wrapped in an old blanket, lay on several thicknesses of industrial-weight polythene. It was still frozen but beginning to thaw, and the smell of animal was already strong.

It was difficult to maneuver. He consoled himself that it would be easier once it had thawed more: less slippery to handle, lighter in weight.

The "head" was ready—taken from a store window dummy, stuffed with the balloon of blood. He fixed it to the carcass by driving four long meat skewers through it and into the collar of the animal. Then, painfully, he pulled the coat around it and secured it with staples.

The sight when he had finished was bizarre in the extreme. No one would ever have thought it other than what it was—a sickening looking dead animal with a mock human head. Certainly no one would have mistaken it for a person. But that did not worry him. He only had to fool a semidrunk woman driving too fast in the darkness. All she would see was a shape and that for seconds only.

Satisfied at last, he tapped the door.

Outside, Kirby looked around. No one in sight. He let Malla-hide out.

"How's our poor victim?" he asked.

"Getting smellier by the minute."

Kirby held out a sandwich. "They're cheese," he said. "I thought I'd show some tact."

Jennifer parked the car in the grounds but well away from the house.

Mallahide was being lucky. That would help the team who would "fix" the car later that night.

"I don't want some fool trying to see if he can get it started and take it for a joyride," she explained.

"Nice friends you've got."

It was a stupid remark. She stared at him in the dim light of late evening, puzzled, about to say, "It's *you* who wanted to come—*why?*"

He saved the moment. "Sorry," he said. "I'm nervous. You realize these are the first friends of yours I'll have met . . . and I'm afraid they won't like me."

It was the perfect remark. As they walked away from the car, toward the house and the noise, she clung possessively to his right arm with both hands.

For a brief moment, Fenn realized one of the reasons he was so attracted to her. He was flattered! She could have almost any man she chose—and, for now at least, she chose him.

She squeezed his arm tightly.

"They'll love you." And then quietly—but not so quietly that he could not hear—"Like me."

Mallahide and Kirby left the van in an attended parking lot in Northampton, twenty miles from where they intended to intercept the girl, and ate a leisurely meal in a steak pub.

At eleven-fifteen they left, with between three and five hours still remaining before action time, depending on when Fenn got the Banks girl to leave the party.

Mallahide drove carefully. It was the time of night when police patrols, looking for drunks, stopped drivers. He shuddered to think what a patrolman would make of the sight in the back of the van.

They arrived at the site just over an hour later. Kirby had found it and Mallahide had seen detailed maps and Polaroid photographs, but this was the first time he had been here. Right now there were still other cars on the road, as people returned home after a Saturday night out, but even so it seemed ideal. The road narrowed, there was a sharpish bend, and, best of all, there were woods on either side with tracks cut wide enough to take the foresters' vehicles.

Following instructions, Mallahide pulled off the road, drove about seventy-five yards into the trees, stopped and doused the lights. The other van was already waiting, also in darkness, but Mallahide had checked its license plates before killing his headlights.

He made no move to get out yet. First he needed more reassurance.

"The nearest house is about two miles?"

"Yes." They had been through it in London, but Kirby answered patiently.

"Police patrols?"

"Arranged. From about the time the car leaves the house, any patrols around will find themselves pretty busy."

A number of false emergency calls.

Mallahide jumped out of the van into the blackness and walked over to the other vehicle.

They did not bother with names.

"How long does it take you?" asked Mallahide.

"Say an hour. I *can* do it in less if I have to."

Mallahide checked his watch. 12:28.

"You've got at least that much time," he said.

"I'll start now."

Back in the Bedford van, Mallahide confirmed that the radio line was open, put his hands behind his neck, closed his eyes and was asleep within seconds.

He would awake in exactly an hour.

Kirby shook his head in admiration. He had always heard that Mallahide was a cool operator.

Jennifer was in the best of moods. She waltzed through the party, clutching Fenn's hand, drinking little and pretending not even to understand the invitation to the upstairs room where the cocaine and silver spoon were being passed around.

All the blackness of earlier that day had gone. She clung to Fenn, danced only with him, laughed at his jokes. There was, in fact, no excuse for Fenn to stage a scene. By midnight he was panicked.

But Mallahide, advised by the psychologist, had anticipated even this.

"If *nothing* happens," he had said, "walk away, leave her alone. She'll destroy herself."

On the excuse of going to the lavatory, Fenn drifted away and walked in the grounds. The cool and the darkness and the innocence of the open air soothed him. In the distance he picked out the houses of the small village. No lights—they were all in bed. He wondered what the villagers thought.

He waited thirty minutes before returning to the house. He entered a side door. It took a few minutes to find her. She was surrounded by a group. It was obvious that they were all old acquaintances.

Occasionally her eyes darted around the room. She was not holding a glass. He could not hear but he watched bodies contort in drink-aided laughter. One man handed Jennifer a drink. She stared at it for a moment, then smiled and drank it quickly. Accepted another.

Fenn looked at his watch. 1:40. He would give it an hour. That should do it.

There were three checkpoints, twelve, eight and four miles away where the accident was to be staged.

Watchers were equipped with two-way radios and infrared glasses.

They were so positioned that each had unrestricted views of upward of a mile north.

None knew why they were there. Only that they were to report the car coming into sight.

At two o'clock all were alert. Traffic was almost nonexistent.

It took fifteen minutes to "prepare" the Porsche. One man handled it while another kept watch in the shadows. The girl who had arrived with them had been told to remain behind in the parked car a quarter of a mile away. If the Porsche had been parked near other cars, she and one of the men would have necked beside it while the second man carried on with his work behind them.

The headlights were criss-crossed with a glass cutter to ensure that the glass would shatter apart on impact. Traces of blood, hair and skin were smeared onto the front, pieces of clothing material were attached to the metalwork under the bumper.

Finally satisfied, the man and his colleague melted into the darkness. Two hours later they and the girl were all back home. None had the slightest idea what the point of the work was they had carried out. But that was the way it went.

Just before 2:30 A.M. it began to rain. Fenn had been crouched drowsily under a tree on the edge of the grounds, staring into the sky and thinking, wryly, that this was where his father's almost religious beliefs in Communism had brought him.

With the rain, he pulled himself up, decided he had waited long enough.

Jennifer was dancing when he got back to the house. He stood just inside a doorway, oblivious to the couples who rushed past him as they fled from the downpour.

He felt cold. Nervous. He wanted a drink but dared not fetch one in case he lost sight of her.

She looked at him twice, averted her head.

The music ended. Her partner held on to her hand, tried to lead her away.

It was all ridiculously easy and Fenn realized that Mallahide had read things right.

She broke away from her partner and came toward Fenn, unsteadily and, he thought, angrily.

"Why did you go?" Her voice was pitched like that of a child.

"I just needed some air." He hardly recognized his own voice.

She made it very easy. "I told you that we shouldn't have come."

He reached out his hand. "Please, can I take you home?"

And without looking back she took his hand and went with him.

CHAPTER 19

The moment the car started Fenn knew she was drunk, but not too drunk.

"You're sure you're all right?"

She shifted gears for a bend, took it racing-style close to the center of the road for maximum visibility. She had kicked off her shoes and was driving barefoot.

The trees on either side of the road were just blurs. Then she began to slow.

"I forgot you were chicken," she said. She giggled. "For you, I'll take it gently." And then, more seriously, "I'm all right. I wouldn't drive if I wasn't."

"Let's keep to the A5—it's a nicer road than the motorway."

"Fewer police, you mean."

"There's that too."

She did not argue.

Once more, Fenn checked his watch. It was 3:11. She had slowed the car down to seventy mph on the straights—a speed the car could almost achieve in first gear.

He made rapid calculations, figured they would arrive at the spot in about twenty minutes. He instinctively checked that his safety belt was tightly fastened.

She misunderstood. "Relax," she said. "I'm not going to crash us." Her voice was drowsily slurred. She began to sing softly.

The first checkpoint picked up the car at 3:24 and the observer was already radioing ahead as it swept past.

It was a bright moonlit night after the rain and the roads were almost totally empty. There was no need for the infrared.

Mallahide and Kirby hauled the roadwork signs out of the van and manhandled them into position. The signs closed half the road and directed cars to slow. That done, the two men took up positions on opposite sides of the road.

Mallahide pulled the carcass erect, checked the wires attached to see that they were not snagged, then tugged and verified that Kirby was holding the other end. He would throw the carcass as the car approached. And as he felt the tension in the wires relax, Kirby would pull.

They had practiced it with a large, stuffed bolster a dozen times. Timing was the most important thing, but they had found there was a wide latitude for error.

"Bingo two," said Mallahide's radio. The car had passed the second checkpoint. Only one more now. He estimated another four minutes. He screwed his eyes into the distance and waited.

She had turned on the radio, and he had to say it twice.

"Hey. Watch the signs. Slow down."

The headlights had picked out a "Roadwork Ahead" warning.

She began to slow immediately, but jerkily, and Fenn realized she must have been dozing.

The speedometer came down to fifty-five mph and then Fenn saw the single lane traffic signs. For the first time he feared her going out of control after the impact.

"Slower!"

Fear and the tone in his voice pulled her fully awake.

"Who the hell's driving this car?"

Nonetheless she slowed.

The car swept into the narrow funnel produced by the road signs.

For a few seconds, Fenn thought he must have gotten the place wrong or everything had been canceled. Then the shape loomed. One moment there was nothing, then there was a man immediately in front of the car, rising up to meet them.

The face shone sickly white in the moonlight.

"Brake!" Fenn screamed.

Jennifer spun the wheel, sending the car screeching into a skid through the road signs.

The car caught the body close to the left headlight, pitching it high into the air. It filled the windshield and looked as though it would come through the glass. Fenn crouched forward, his hands in front of his face. There was a thud as the body bounced off the roof of the car. Then the car stopped. It had turned around completely.

Fenn looked down at himself, almost expecting to see blood. He turned toward Jennifer. Her hands were at her face and she was mouthing words that he could not at first make out.

A few moments later he realized that she was repeating "My God" over and over again.

"Stay here."

He eased himself out of the car, tripping over the remains of a road sign. There was no need for him to act. He genuinely felt numb, sick, frightened.

Then he realized that Jennifer had not obeyed his command. She had gotten out of the car too and was standing, swaying from side to side, on the road. He moved to head her off and escort her back into the car, but he was too late. There was a small pool of light and he realized she was carrying a flashlight.

She was shrieking.

He joined her, and looked down, expecting to see the obscene carcass. Instead, he saw a body. Twisted out of shape, a great gash in the head, blood oozing out of the mouth.

He dragged Jennifer back to the car, took the light and examined the bodywork.

Part of one fender was smashed in and a headlight was shattered. There was a deep dent in the roof. Blood was spattered over the hood. He leaned inside and turned on the windshield washer, using the water to try to remove some of the blood. He realized he was acting crazily, that he ought to get away from here.

Jennifer was still looking down at the corpse, shivering, whimpering.

Fenn took her elbow and led her to the passenger seat. Her body was a dead weight and he had to heave her inside.

Once in the driver's seat, he adjusted the steering wheel, forcing himself to be calm. He turned the key, praying the car would start. It did, first time.

He pulled away, nervously wrestling to master the controls. London was forty miles away. The road ahead was empty, lit by just one headlight.

Beside him Jennifer leaned forward, and moaned.

Mallahide and Kirby watched the car until it was out of sight. To them Fenn seemed to have taken an eternity.

Every second Mallahide had scanned the road in both directions, even though other traffic was unlikely.

The moment the Porsche finally disappeared from view the two men rushed forward. The "corpse" rose from the roadside. He was a professional victim—a man used in military exercises to teach emergency first aid in battle situations. His wounds were said to be so realistic that even tough recruits had been known to retch at the sight of him.

As he stood, he threw away the wooden splints that he had used to distort his limbs, and spat out the remains of the capsule that had filled his mouth with "blood." Before he reached his van he began peeling off his jacket—again soaked with imitation blood.

Mallahide meanwhile backed the van out on to the road,

leaped out, opened the doors and helped Kirby load the road signs.

Handling what was left of the carcass was messy, and Mallahide cursed that he had not had the foresight to bring overalls. However, at last it was finished.

Mallahide checked the time. 3:41. The whole operation from beginning to end had taken only eleven minutes.

"Okay, let's go," he called.

A look of triumph flickered across his face.

It was almost half an hour before Jennifer said anything.

"Was he dead?"

"We'll talk when we get home."

Her voice rose to a shriek. "Was he *dead?*"

Fenn was remembering the blood slowly trickling out of the corner of the man's mouth. "Yes," he said.

"Oh my God."

She began to sob, and then went quiet except for occasional choking noises as she fought back tears.

They neared London and Fenn reviewed the best routes to keep him away from other traffic. Mallahide would have removed the "evidence" so there would not be an alert, but the car had obviously been in a crash. Any police patrol car would stop it.

On the outskirts Fenn doused the single headlight and drove on the unbroken sidelights.

His eyes constantly searched the streets ahead, then shifted to his rearview mirror. Once he thought he saw a police car. Immediately he turned off into a side street and killed the lights until it was clear.

He kept remembering the body.

Beside him, Jennifer began to shake and mumble hysterically.

"What are you doing? Where are we going?"

"Shut up!"

He wondered whether to slap her. He remembered the

drugged flask. It was in the dashboard where he had placed it. He leaned forward, found it, handed it to her.

"Oh, no! Not more drink."

But nevertheless she drank.

"Not too much!" He took it from her.

At last they reached the Euston Road, busy as always despite the hour. He turned right, his hands tightening on the wheel. Only minutes now. The Porsche attracted no attention among the rumbling trucks crossing from east to west London.

He turned off and headed toward Oxford Circus. Near it, he pulled into the automatic parking lot and found a dark corner. Easing himself out of the car, he checked that the crumpled fender was hidden by the corner wall, helped Jennifer out and supported her as she struggled upward through the echoing coldness of the empty streets.

It was 5:25 A.M. and the light was gray when they reached the flat.

Neither said anything. He helped her on to the bed.

"What will we do? What will we do?" Her voice was soft, pleading.

"Easy. Just sleep now. Just sleep."

He waited beside her in the darkness until her breathing became deep and regular.

Then he went into the living room, sat in an armchair, hunched forward and began to sob.

CHAPTER 20

After the events and excitement of the previous night Mallahide felt spent. It was almost as though he had had a tre-
mendous orgasm that had drained him physically and emo-
tionally.

It was seven before he reached home after making a detour
to dump the carcass in the River Thames and to leave Kirby
near his house. At first he had felt restless and edgy, then had
come the feeling of exhaustion. Nevertheless, he forced himself
to shower and change. He had to report to Brighouse at ten.

This time he resented it. They should have allowed him
some sleep. That was not really the reason, though. He was
being peevish. Their lack of trust, the closeness of their control,
was being made too obvious. Fuck it, he was the man who actually *did* things while they sat behind their desks.

Brighouse anticipated Mallahide's mood, and when they
met, again in the square, he went out of his way to be attentive
and full of praise for the way Mallahide had handled things.
He was, in fact, hearing the story for the second time that
morning. Kirby, after being dropped by Mallahide, and before
going home, had picked up his own car and reported direct.

Brighouse noted without surprise that Mallahide's version of what had happened made no mention of the fact that he had already begun to drive away when he had remembered that he had not collected glass particles from the road. Such an omission would not have been crucial. They could, after all, show the girl any pile of broken glass and assure her it was special to her car. But it showed that despite all the cool Kirby said Mallahide had displayed before the simulated death, he had felt a degree of panic afterward.

Something to be noted.

Brighouse contented himself with listening. "A non-too-pleasant operation," he commented when the account was finished. "But excellently handled. Pity in a way there are no papers on this, but I'm sure the powers that be will make sure it isn't forgotten."

It was faint praise and he knew it. Brighouse struggled for some way to be more glowing without being patronizing.

"How's he taking it?" he asked after a few moments' indecision.

"Fenn?"

"Yes."

"It's too early to tell. We picked up some crying on the bug. His, we think."

Two other microphone-transmitters had been placed in Fenn's flat, better-hidden than the first. At the time Fenn had conducted his search they had been switched off by radio beam so they would not emit a signal the FM radio could pick up. Later they had been reactivated.

"Is the girl with him?"

"Yes, but out cold judging from the snoring. There's been some gibberish in her sleep but nothing that's worth reporting."

"It's all being recorded?"

"Yes."

"I'd like to hear it later."

He noticed Mallahide's quick glance—the man was touchy, resentful that he wasn't being trusted enough. Brighouse could not help that. This was too sensitive an operation for him to take chances.

"He'll need handling *very* carefully," Brighouse continued, adding as a concession, "I need hardly tell *you* that." He moved his newspaper from his lap, placed it beside him.

"Why not send him home for a couple of days?" he said. "It would be a break for him. And it would give him a reminder of what he's risking if he tries to opt out now."

Not for the first time, Mallahide was surprised by the older man's callousness. He accepted it within himself, but he expected Brighouse to be less calculatingly hard. Nevertheless, he liked the idea. "It would have another advantage," he said. "It would give *her* time to sweat a little by herself."

They had that at least: the contact of mutual professionalism.

And, suddenly, it dawned on Brighouse how he could make his gesture to Mallahide. Brighouse knew that his colleagues regarded him as a lone man, an aging bachelor who when the day was over walked home alone to his apartment and—it was rightly rumored—his tropical fish.

None of them had ever been invited home. An invitation would be an accolade.

"Come and have coffee with me," he said. "At the flat—if you have time, that is."

Fenn awoke just before eleven. He had fallen forward, so that the top half of his body lay supported over the arm of the chair.

It took a long time to focus and to remember, and when he did, the previous night seemed mad and unreal.

A genuine corpse!

The doors of both the living room and the bedroom were open and he walked across and peered through, not quite certain he would find her there. She lay curled, like a fetus, her face composed and angelic. It could have been peace. More likely it was the drug. At least she slept. He realized that he dreaded facing her when she woke.

He tried Mallahide's contact number although he was not supposed to do so. No reply.

Fenn stared down at the receiver for a long time before realizing he had to go on. Mallahide had given him the name and telephone number of a small repair shop which, he assured Fenn, specialized in getting work done and not asking questions. Although Fenn did not know it, Mallahide had gotten the information from his father's old police friend.

The telephone rang for a long time before it was answered. The voice was blurred. Fenn had no doubt he had gotten the man out of bed.

Fenn introduced himself as he had been instructed—"A friend of a friend of George gave me your number"—and explained what was needed. There was a long pause and Fenn feared the man was about to refuse. Then greed won.

"A Porsche, you say. Difficult, precise work that. Even harder if you want it done quickish."

It was Fenn's turn to remain silent. The man was hooked.

"What I mean," said the voice at the other end of the telephone, "is that it all gets a bit expensive."

"I'll bring it round around ten tonight. Okay?" Fenn wanted to drive in the dark. He would risk the broken light.

"Make it quarter to eleven. Now you know where to come. . . ."

Mallahide had two tasks left that Sunday before he could sleep.

The first was to check over the van and get rid of the polythene and old blanket. The van did not need cleaning—the little blood that had run had been caught by the coverings. He disposed of these by driving northward out of London until he chanced upon one of the inevitable illegal gypsy sites. On either side of the camp rubbish littered the hedges and roadside. He tossed out the polythene and blanket without even leaving the driver's seat.

On the way back to London he stopped to make two calls from a pay phone.

The first—brief—was to Fenn. He did not give the other a chance to talk. "The body," he said. "It wasn't for real. A fake. I'll tell you more tomorrow."

The second was longer and more diplomatic.

"I believe Andrew Brighouse told you to expect my call."

The voice that replied was deep and slow and had a faint country burr. "You wanted to come today?"

"Tomorrow. Late afternoon if that's all right."

"There's a train at 4:10, gets in at 5:20. Does that sound all right?"

It did.

"I'll meet you. Don't worry. You'll recognize me."

The telephone finally woke her. She had slept for eleven hours.

Fenn had checked her often, concerned whether he should call a doctor. There might have been drugs he did not know about at the party. Her breathing had been steady, however, and her pulse strong, though fast, and he had decided to let her sleep it off.

She entered the room seconds after the call from Mallahide. Fenn was still glaring. The shit hadn't even asked if they were unhurt. But the news about the body was a huge relief; it did not occur to him to doubt Mallahide's word.

"Who was it?"

"Just a wrong number."

She sat on the carpet near his feet. "It really happened, didn't it? I haven't just had an awful dream."

He began to stroke her hair.

"Don't!" She pushed his hand away and looked up, her eyes wide. "Just tell me. Don't treat me like a child. Have I killed someone? I have, haven't I?"

"You've killed someone." It did not seem like lying. It had been so real and the memory was still vivid.

"Who was it?"

"I don't know. A man. A tramp, I'd think."

"But he was dead?"

Fenn didn't answer and then she remembered the sound as the body bounced on the roof and she shuddered.

"We should have called an ambulance."

Fenn's voice was flat, resigned. "It wouldn't have helped him."

"We should have called the police."

Fenn remained silent.

"*Please*," she said. "*Please* what shall I do?"

"We can still call the police. Do you want to?"

She remembered the conversation early yesterday—was it *only* yesterday—about her father, how tired he was looking, how the strains on him were mounting. Could she add this to his burden?

"If we don't, will they find us?"

"I shouldn't think so."

"I don't want to call the police. Please."

"Then we won't call them."

She reached out for his hand, attempted to smile. For a moment he sensed that part of her was enjoying the drama.

"What about the car?"

"I'll try and do something about that. I know someone who might know someone. . . ."

She squeezed his fingers. "It will be in the papers, won't it? I mean we'll find out who it was. If there's a family we can send something anonymously. . . ."

He squeezed back. She mistook it for reassurance. It was anger. The rich bitch! "We can *send* something. . . ."

Unwittingly, she gave him the excuse to go on.

During the late afternoon Fenn pretended that he had to meet a man to talk about the car.

He told Jennifer he would try to deliver it to a repair shop that evening. In the meantime the Porsche was best left where it was.

Acting on instructions, he made sure she knew exactly where it was parked.

Jennifer waited for fifteen minutes and then, as Mallahide had anticipated she would, she took a cab to the parking lot. No one followed her inside, but when she reemerged the man following her noted these words for his subsequent report: "Numbed-looking, white, drawn face, might have seen a ghost. . . ."

He noted too that she kept looking down at the index finger of her right hand.

Brighouse interpreted what that meant when he read the report. She had run her finger over the front of the car in the darkness. It would have come away flecked with dried blood and perhaps a trace of hair.

The repair shop was exactly as Fenn had envisaged it—straight from a television thriller.

It was in a quiet side street, backed by a disused warehouse. The yard was protected by a high brick wall, barbed wire at the top. A small man in a sweater and cap was already waiting to swing back the heavy wooden gates when Fenn arrived.

In the yard there were two covered garages and Fenn was signaled to drive into one of them. The man walked around the car examining the damage.

"It'll take me a good three, four days," he said. "That's if I start first thing tomorrow. Not going to be easy matching that paint."

"How much?"

"Hard to say yet."

"I'll need a price. It's not mine."

"I know, you're handling it for a friend." The voice was cynical.

They settled on seven hundred pounds. "Half now and the rest when you collect."

Fenn knew no one would expect him to have that money without notice. "I've got two hundred now," he said. "The rest later. After all, you've got the car."

The man ran his hand over the gashed fender. "But I don't know how hot it is, do I?" he said. "Two hundred now, another one and a half tomorrow at this time—just drop by. The balance when it's ready."

This time Fenn agreed.

He walked for a long time before hailing a taxi. All the pubs were long closed. He regretted that—he wanted the noise and bustle of strangers. He needed assurance that the world went on, that for others life was normal. He thought of looking for a nightclub, but finally weariness won.

Tomorrow he had to face Mallahide again. Perhaps then he would discover how much deeper he had to descend.

Outside the door of his flat he paused, key in hand, and steeled himself to face Jennifer. The rooms were in darkness. The apartment was empty.

Her note was in the center of the table. "I just *had* to be by myself for a while."

Dramatic. Had he read her right earlier? Was she enjoying the excitement? Finding it a kick?

Whatever she was feeling, he was glad to be alone.

One conscience—his own—was enough.

CHAPTER 21

Neither Mallahide nor Brighouse knew how close their scheme came to failure on the morning of September 15.

Banks, feeling guilt at having seen so little of his daughter recently, left a message inviting her to have lunch at one of her favorite restaurants. At midday, given courage by the amphetamine she had taken to keep her going after a bad night, Jennifer had decided to tell her father. *He* would save her, he would get her out of trouble. He had done it before. Nothing was beyond him.

Half an hour later, sitting in the restaurant's bar, having arrived early, she was no longer so sure. There was the effect it would have on him. And what was the point? The man was dead. It was sad, but she couldn't bring him back to life now. She could only ruin her father's.

She also thought about herself. What would they do to her? Her father would see she got the best lawyers, impeccable character witnesses, everything, but would that be enough? Might she still have to go to prison? Rich girl kills old man. The mood of the country for law and order was strong, that of the courts tough. Being at one with that mood was one of the many reasons Godwin was now Prime Minister.

Prison!

She took a smoked salmon ring and shivered.

Nevertheless, with her father facing her, and relaxed by a drink, she might have said something.

News that she was wanted on the telephone interrupted her thoughts. She took the call in the lobby.

"I tried to reach you at home. You'd left."

She knew what her father was about to say. She anticipated his words: "Something's cropped up? You can't make it?"

"I *am* sorry. If it wasn't vital. . . ."

It always is, she thought. It had happened before.

Later that afternoon when she bought yet more editions of the evening newspapers to see if they contained anything about the accident, she saw a photograph of her father leaving Downing Street with the Prime Minister. And she *knew* it was too late.

She could not tell him now. She would do what Fenn had suggested: nothing.

The meeting with Mallahide, which Fenn had anticipated with dread the previous evening, became the one fixed, real point of his day.

Jennifer did not make contact and he did not know whether to telephone her. He realized that he needed advice—not just on this but on everything he did now. He had, it became suddenly obvious to him, become dependent on Mallahide to direct him. The man really was his controller. And that, strangely, was reassuring. It would be much easier to do the things he had to do if he accepted that he was not a free agent, but a puppet.

He found himself waiting for the meeting with impatience. Mallahide and the colonel were the only men to whom he could really talk and unburden himself, the only ones with whom he could be honest. Relations with everyone else were a lie.

Fenn's mood had been anticipated, and Mallahide greeted him warmly.

He handed Fenn an article, torn from a magazine, about modern training methods to prepare rescuers sent to emergency accidents. The photographs were grisly, but as the captions made clear they only depicted people skillfully made up.

"I'm sorry we had to spring that on you. We worried at the last moment she might insist on getting out of the car."

Fenn was not angry.

Mallahide poured drinks, the meeting's moment of regular ritual.

"You've done *very* well," he said. "Everything we could have asked and more."

He handed over the drink, then produced an envelope. "A copy of a cash transfer," he said. "Two thousand pounds have been credited to your account. There's also another thousand pounds in cash. You must be running low now."

Mallahide sipped, smiled over the top of his glass. "And there's a return air ticket," he added. "We thought it time you saw that family of yours."

He noticed Fenn's expression and hurried on. "Not for good yet. We still need your help for a little while longer—not too long, perhaps another three, four weeks."

Fenn slid the unopened envelope into his jacket pocket. "When do I go?"

Mallahide noted that the man needed direction and was pleased.

"No more meetings this week for us," he said. "Unless you have problems. Then you call and I'll be here. I'd like you to concentrate on the girl. Just stay with her, take her out, console her—whatever seems natural."

"What about the car?"

"What are the arrangements?"

Fenn told him.

"Fine. Keep them."

"So when do I go?"

"Say Thursday. You'll have collected the car by then. Tell

the Banks girl you've had an urgent message to go home—
daughter not well, something like that."

"What do I tell Gemma?"

He *was* dependent.

"Tell her you needed to see her, managed to get a break.
Tell her that it's almost over. Tell her the truth. That you'll be
back in less than a month."

"Is that a real assessment?"

Mallahide did not hesitate. "At the outside," he smiled.

Fenn was almost home before he realized that he still did not
know what that month still held for him—what the orders
would be next.

On the train to Cambridge, Mallahide tried to read a paperback book but found it hard to concentrate. He was too full
of self-congratulation. He found Fenn's dependence on him
heady. There was something godlike about it all.

What he liked about this operation was that it was so self-
contained—a rarity. So often in the past he had been a part of
something, not knowing what the other parts were, let alone
the whole.

Since Ulster, he had began to doubt whether he had done
the right thing in joining the department. His options when he
had left the university had been numerous. His degree in Sla-
vonic languages had been a good one. A number of people had
shown interest. He could have gone into banking, joined a
multinational corporation, would almost certainly have gotten
into the Foreign Service. Or, closer to his present job, he would
have been welcomed by SIS, the Security Service's more glam-
orous cousin.

He had finally chosen the Service when their invitation came
because he had thought he was just a bit too good for them. He
would start as a high flyer, remain ahead of the class.

That had been the theory. It had not quite worked out in
practice. He knew, without self-delusion, that he had been
regarded as a good catch—but in real terms that had not meant

much. In Northern Ireland, for example, he had done no more than an army undercover man or a Special Branch officer could have done. He had been there no more and no less than the department's presence in the undercover war.

Thank God then for this assignment.

It made the other things worth paying—the biting angers he had to fight down, the migraines that he dared not report.

Henry Noakes was the kind of man whose features and bearing exuded official authority. Nodding at the ticket collector, he swept through on to the platform.

It was a hot afternoon, but despite the heat Noakes was wearing a heavy tweed suit. He had moved to Cambridge on retiring from the Special Branch where he had been an inspector three years before. His main asset then, as throughout most of his career, was that he looked like an archetypal policeman—solid, reassuring, incorruptible, strong, a bit slow but honest and sure to reach the right solution at the end.

He was a good man to send to make an arrest or to have standing in the witness box to impress judges and juries. He was all that, and he was also a man who knew his assets and how to capitalize on them.

During his years in the Special Branch he had always gone out of his way to keep officers in MI5 more fully informed than his colleagues would have considered necessary. On his retirement, it had paid off—assistance in getting a security post at an electronics company in his beloved Cambridge.

And now he was about to help again. Nothing nasty like money would change hands. But Noakes's chief was about to retire, and influence might mean something.

"Don't talk about it," he said.

Jennifer had been waiting for him when he returned. She lay now with her head on his shoulder, naked, the bed clothes flung to the floor.

Neither felt like making love. Their minds were too abuzz with what had happened.

"But it'll be all right?"

"I told you it would, didn't I?"

He reached out in the half darkness for his glass of whiskey which was on the floor near the bed.

He was wondering when to break the news to her about having to go home.

The house was suburban and highly conservative. The only thing missing was plastic ducks on the wall.

Noakes had bought it six months before retirement and had lived there alone since the death of his wife. It had five rooms and was too large for him, but he saw no point in moving again.

The two men drank instant coffee and Spanish brandy which Noakes had brought back from a security conference in Barcelona. Brighouse had asked him if he would be available to impersonate a policeman and had hinted that it was a "rather messy one." Noakes had not had to think: "Whatever you want—after all, I don't think I'll find it too difficult."

Now Mallahide explained the details.

"She thinks she knocked down and killed some old tramp. She also thinks she's safe."

"That's where I come in?"

"Yes. Give it two, three days. Say till Thursday. Then call on her. We'd like you to put on the bite."

CHAPTER 22

The airplane was crowded with tourists and Fenn, who only had hand luggage, was first in the line for Immigration.

"You are on holiday?"

"Yes." He knew that to say he lived there would only bring more questions. He had also learned to change the job description on his passport; the Maltese government did not like foreign journalists. He now called himself "salesman." Today, as he pushed the passport back into his pocket, he thought wryly that the description was not so wrong—he had sold himself.

He quickly forced back the thought. He was here for three days and that was what mattered now. London and the crash and the aftermath, like collecting the repaired car, seemed far away. The heat hit him as he stepped outside; it was only eighty degrees, but he had quickly grown used to more temperate climates. He slipped off his jacket as he climbed into the first taxi.

There was an hour's wait for the ferry and it was late in the afternoon when he arrived at the house. He was silent—tired, but also moved by the crossing. He had come close to forgetting the things that had drawn him in the first place.

He had sat outside on the ferry. Halfway across, as the sheer cliffs of Ta 'Cenc had come into view, a mist had sprung up suddenly, making the sea look like a Scottish loch. And then minutes later the rain had come, chasing the mist away.

On the drive from the harbor he had delighted again in the yellow and white of the oxalis and narcissus at the edges of the road.

The house, though, was empty. It was one of Gemma's working days, but she should have been home by now. He cursed himself for not having warned her that he was coming. Had she and the girls gone to stay with someone?

There were new paintings by the children on the cork notice board. He was standing looking at them when the door opened. The girls saw him first and were running to him before Gemma even realized he was there.

She put down her shopping bag slowly and carefully and then walked toward him, not rushing, her arms outstretched, her mouth twisting into a smile.

"Thank God you're back," she said.

He had never felt more at home.

Noakes waited until Friday morning. The local newspaper for the area in which the "accident" had happened was published that day. He wanted to carry a forged clipping, ostensibly taken from it.

He had found that there was something about Fridays. Subconsciously, people began to wind down ready for the weekend. That being so, sudden shocks seemed to have great impact.

Noakes was dressed in a navy-blue suit, slightly shiny in the seat and at the elbows, and he carried a bulging briefcase that had obviously been his companion for years. He wore a hat which he normally kept for funerals; he had found that the ritual of removing it gave a suitably bureaucratic feel to the opening of any interview.

"Miss Banks?"

It was nearly midday but she was still wearing a robe. She had slept badly after receiving Fenn's call late the previous evening telling her he had to return home.

She stood on the doorstep of the street entrance to her flat, blinking in the light.

"What do you want?"

"I wonder if I could come inside. It's a little hard to talk out here."

"Who are you?"

He produced his identification with a sweep. "A police officer, Miss Banks. Now if I can come in, I won't keep you long."

Almost without realizing what was happening, she found herself retreating inside as he followed. They were in the living room before her mind began to function. "Perhaps I should call a lawyer. . . ."

Noakes was turned away from her, admiring a set of English country prints. "Now *that*," he said, "is what I call painting." He stood back to admire them better and it seemed he had not heard her. Then he added, "Of course you can call a lawyer if you like, miss, but I don't quite see why. I haven't told you what it's about. I might be looking for a missing cat for all you know."

He began to laugh at his own joke—his main aim at the moment was to make himself look a fool. He wanted her relaxed and feeling superior. He looked around for somewhere to put his briefcase, finally decided to place it on the floor, and then let it tip over.

He was conscious of her eyes. She would be pulling herself together, convincing herself that there was nothing to fear from this man, no matter what he wanted.

"Detective Inspector Noakes," he said as he straightened. "You didn't answer my question, but I take it you are Jennifer Isabelle Banks."

He did not give her a chance to reply. He moved off in the direction of a second alcove. In it, incongruous in such a luxurious room, was a shelf of small glass animals—objects of the kind that could be bought in seaside towns or won at fun fairs. He could not know that they were among the few touches to the apartment provided by Jennifer herself—the rest had been designed by professionals on the instructions of her father.

"Now that takes me back," he said, lifting one to examine it more closely. "My wife, my late wife that is, used to collect them."

Let her relax a bit—that was the secret.

"Would you like some coffee?" She was not calm, but she had to pretend.

"Ah. Now, that *would* be nice."

Alone in the kitchen, she spooned Nescafé into two cups and wondered what to do. Her father was away. So was Fenn, damn him. She could call a lawyer . . . but the policeman was right. What for? He hadn't told her what he wanted.

She poured water into the cups and decided she was being a fool. What was he? A stupid policeman. And who was she? The daughter of one of the richest and most influential men in Britain. She was handling it badly. But that, she knew, was one of her major problems—she was not equipped to handle things. From her earliest childhood, everything had been taken care of for her. All that was left for her was to rebel—and then only within limits that would not harm her or her lifestyle irretrievably. Still, this time she must take the initiative, ask what he wanted, listen and then show him out.

Back in the living room, she handed him a cup and tried to compose herself, ready to take the offensive.

Noakes took the coffee and as she was about to speak held out the newspaper cutting that was already in his hand.

"This might interest you, miss, if you haven't seen it."

The story was headlined, "Police Seek Hit and Run Driver." The article below began, "The grisly early morning discovery of a man's body on the A5 near Eardingly last Sunday started a widespread police search for a hit and run driver. Detective Inspector Herbert Noakes, who is leading the investigations, said this week, 'There is no way that the driver of the vehicle could not have known what happened. Driving on must have been a deliberate action.'

"The dead man was still unidentified yesterday, but police said he was believed to be aged between fifty and sixty and was five feet five inches tall with black hair and brown eyes. He was dressed in gray trousers and a blue jacket." The story continued for another half column.

Jennifer felt terrified and sick, but struggled to keep her face impassive.

She handed back the cutting. "What a horrible story," she said. "But why show it to me?"

Noakes folded the paper carefully and placed it in his wallet. He sipped his coffee. "Ah, nice," he said. "Just what I needed." His mind told him, slow, slow, slow, don't rush it now.

"Well," he said, "you'll appreciate, miss, that on something like this we try to follow up every lead. One of them is trying to trace anyone who was on the road that night. Not an easy task I can tell you."

If Jennifer had had time to think, the story would have been seen to be blatantly untrue: Who in a dozen years could make such a trace? But his voice and expression, confiding, were convincing.

"And it so happens that you've a distinctive-looking car that someone remembered seeing, so I thought I'd have a word. A long chance, of course. But it might be that you saw something."

Jennifer pretended to think . . . then she took in Noakes's face. He was smiling, and it was a sly smile. Suddenly she knew. Her palms began to sweat.

"How did you trace me?" she asked, still trying to appear calm. "You say I drive a distinctive-looking car and that's true. But how did you know it was mine?"

Noakes remained silent, took a long time finishing his coffee. He placed the cup on a table, retrieved his case and opened it.

He removed a small plastic container which he held out. She was forced to stand and walk over to him.

"Open the lid."

It contained broken glass.

"Glass is a funny thing, miss," said Noakes in a conversational tone. "Most people think there's just glass—well, they know there's stained glass and plate glass and window glass. But they don't realize it can be as distinctive as a fingerprint."

He began to pack a pipe. "You don't mind?"

She shook her head.

"This glass was found at the scene of the accident. So, good little detective that I am, I swept it up and off it went to the forensic laboratory." He took his time lighting his pipe.

"Now I don't know it you're interested in technical things, miss. Me, I'm fascinated. They heat the glass in a thing called a hot-stage microscope until it reaches a temperature where they can read its refractive index. Sounds complicated, doesn't it? Well then, they just check that against the records at Aldermaston where they keep such things.

"While they're doing this, they're also taking a close look at the paint. Oh, the paint—I didn't mention that, did I? There were a few fragments embedded in the corpse's skull—if you'll forgive me.

"Now here they are *very* clever. They look at the top coat and the layers of undercoat and they check these with the colors and *processes* of every make of car."

He stared into her face. White. "Maybe you'd like to sit, miss."

He continued. "Now there's not much hope at that stage. Likelihood is that it's glass from a Ford Escort or a Mini—something that could have come off thousands, hundreds of thousands of cars. Same with the paint."

He blew smoke and it hung around him. His face had a gentle smile and he looked like a benevolent uncle.

"But you know what—this time, jackpot! Paint, very distinctive. Not from one of your mass-produced pieces of rubbish. Same with the glass. Both from a Porsche. Even more specifically, a yellow 1979 Porsche. Realize how few of those there are, how easy to get a few names?"

He sipped coffee and then said, "You wouldn't have a cracker, would you, miss? My late wife always believed that you'd never get a bad stomach if you had something to nibble every time you had a drink. Sounds silly really, but you know, I've kept to it, and I'm one of the only men in the force who never gets indigestion. Occupational disease, that is."

She found a package of crackers and spread a few on a plate. The meeting had a mad quality. But she appreciated the few minutes by herself. She had to think. If only her father was here. Or Fenn. Someone she trusted, someone she could depend on.

"The other thing was that the car that hit our old man was traveling south. So all I had to do was look for people with 1979 yellow Porsches who lived south of Luton, probably in London. Shows you how easy detection is, doesn't it? Just plodding work for plodders like me."

Jennifer was mesmerized. Should she call a lawyer now? She would hear him out. What she must not do was say anything.

"But you know something, I didn't even need that. A young thug who does a bit of work in a dicey garage in south London is in a spot of trouble with his local police. He decides, sensible lad, that the best way to buy himself out of trouble is to keep his eyes open and pass on a few things. What people have a lot of spending money, who's talking to who about getting a gang together."

His pipe went out and he relit it carefully. He had gathered a small group of objects in front of him—matches, crackers, coffee cup.

"One little bit was about a smashed-up yellow Porsche that his boss was patching up in secrecy. Didn't mean anything to the local police, but they put it on the wire for any forces that might be looking for such a car."

He rolled his eyes. "You see how easy it all is, miss. Crime really doesn't pay."

Her car was now in her father's garage. She wondered whether Noakes had seen it. He would have had to break in, but she supposed such things were easy for a policeman. Suddenly she remembered the hair that had come away on her finger when she had examined it after the crash, and she shivered.

Noakes's voice interrupted her thoughts. "You don't want to ask me anything, miss?"

She was forced to react. "What's all this to do with me?"

"Ah, I was wondering when you'd ask that. Well, let's suppose something, shall we? Let's suppose I look at that car of yours, and let's imagine what we'll find, shall we? I'd say a new fender, new lights, perhaps a dent or two hammered out—the corpse looked as though it had been bounced a bit."

He reached in the briefcase, handed over a folder.

She opened it and was staring at the top picture before she realized what it was: a mutilated body. Someone *she* had killed!

"Oh, you bastard."

She dropped the folder at her feet.

"Not nice, is it, miss?" The voice had grown harsher. It went on, "Let's suppose what else we'd find. A few traces of blood—*very* hard to get rid of them totally. Group B negative, I'd say. Perhaps a bit of skin and the odd grayish hair. . . ."

Jennifer stood and rushed for the lavatory. Noakes heard retching and then the lavatory flush. He waited for her to return and then suddenly, he became suspicious.

He opened the door into the passageway and saw her heading for the street door.

"Stop!"

She stood still until he took her arm to lead her back into the living room. He placed her in a chair, found brandy, poured her a measure.

"I want to telephone a lawyer. I want my father."

The words came between sobs. She's like a child, thought Noakes. It had been almost too easy. His instincts told him she was a girl who had never been allowed to develop the normal self-reliance. Without someone to protect her when things got bad, she was lost.

He made his voice gentle. "Of course, miss. That's your right."

She struggled to her feet and made for the telephone.

"Of course, do that, and I'll *have* to charge you. I think we might manage manslaughter on this one. Shouldn't be hard to track down where you'd been from analyzing the gravel and soil dislodged from under the car when you hit the late lamented Mr. No-name. Find out what shape you were in when you set off. Even death by reckless driving's not too bad —five years inside."

It took time for his words to register. "What else could you do?"

"Well, miss," and the voice was confiding. "I'm a fifty-four-year-old man, retiring next year, not knowing what to do except I can't afford it. I'd say you could go a long way to making restitution by making a donation to charity. Say to the Herbert Noakes retirement fund for deserving coppers."

Fenn, Gemma and the girls spent Friday and Saturday like tourists—swimming, boating, eating long, lazy meals, watching a film.

All normal household rules were relaxed or totally abandoned —bedtime was when the girls wanted it to be, lunch was at five o'clock if no one wanted to eat before. And if Becky and Kate wanted three courses of different flavors of ice cream, that was all right too.

Gemma had never before seen Fenn like this. He was acting almost like a man with a known and short time to live. But even though she knew it would only add to the problems with the girls when he returned to London, she indulged him. And, in truth, she enjoyed it. She was a practical woman— almost too much so. It was good, just once, to enjoy some madness, particularly as money which had always been so tight was now so plentiful.

At one o'clock on Sunday morning, the girls only just in bed, she watched him as he stood outside, staring down at the sea.

She moved beside him. "It's beautiful, isn't it?"

"Yes." He was absorbing it, his mind a camera taking a photograph. He wanted to carry this picture.

"It *will* only be a month," slipping her hand into his.

"Perhaps less."

They did not talk again until almost an hour later when they lay still and satiated in bed, their bodies rich with the smell of sex.

"You're not tempted to go back, to stay there?" She had to ask, had wanted to ever since he had returned. Now there was only the night.

There was no hesitation in his voice. "No," he said. "I want to be back."

They lay a long time, silent, though conscious that neither of them was asleep.

When Fenn finally spoke, his voice was soft and hesitant. "Gemma," he said, "I have to tell you something."

She waited.

Looking back, he supposed it was the pressures that made him confess.

"Part of the job," he said, "has been cultivating a man called Banks—you remember the name, the man who adopted the girl?"

She did, but said nothing.

"The girl is grown up now," he went on. Again, no reaction.

He turned toward her and put his arms around her, feeling her naked breasts against his chest. Both of them were still wet with sweat.

"I got involved with her," he said. "God knows why. And God knows why I have to tell you. But I do."

There was nothing for a while and then she slid her arms around him and tightened them.

"You still love me? You still want to be with me?" she said.

"Oh yes. Oh God, yes."

"Then it's all right then," she said. "It's all right."

They held each other close.

It was not a good night for either of them. He slept a restless sleep, one in which bodies were hurled through the air and glass exploded and screams echoed. Gemma did not sleep at all.

In the morning a taxi arrived to take him to the ferry. They had agreed that it was best for Becky and Kate that this time they part at the house.

They kissed at the doorway. The words that she called after him as he made for the waiting taxi were sudden and unexpected despite his confession.

"A month," she called. "A month—no more. Or . . ." and her voice was so quiet that he could not be certain of the words . . . "not at all."

She turned and went inside. Fenn started to go after her. The taxi driver's voice halted him.

"We're late. You'll miss the ferry."

She was just being emotional. It meant nothing.

Fenn got into the taxi.

CHAPTER 23

There were three letters and a postcard inside the hallway.

Fenn carried them into the bedroom and tossed his case on to the bed. The letters were all circulars. The postcard showed the Trooping of the Color and the message was brief:

"Sorry to have missed you while I was in London. But hope to see you soonest." It was signed "Maureen."

"Soonest" meant that Mallahide wanted to see him the following day.

Purposely, on the flight and on the limousine ride from the airport, Fenn had tried not to think of what awaited him. Now the worry and the curiosity flooded back.

He checked his watch. Just after four. Should he telephone Jennifer? He decided not. He would have a drink from the duty-free bottle he had brought with him, perhaps watch television for half an hour and around seven go out for an early meal. A pleasant way of postponing the realities of what he faced.

He took the bottle of Crown Royal from its box and walked into the living room. Curled up on the sofa, legs crossed under her, staring silently at the door, was Jennifer.

She was wearing denims and a simply cut check shirt. For

the first time since Fenn had known her, her face was devoid of makeup.

It was less than seven hours since he had left Gemma, but Jennifer's silent presence pulled him. And as he reached out to touch her cheek she began to cry.

She took almost an hour to tell the story, insisting on including all the details—how she had felt and reacted, what Noakes had done as he talked, even the man's request for a cracker.

Fenn found himself forced to put on an act, the way she would expect him to behave if it were a straightforward blackmail. He had to suppress his anger at his controllers. Why, *why* hadn't they warned him?

But he knew the answer. It had not been necessary. It had been obvious what they planned to do if only he had thought. He had closed his eyes. Only the method had been in doubt. Now he found himself numbed. So much so that he hardly heard her next words, had to wait for her to repeat them.

"After I phoned you twice and was told you weren't there, I came here to wait. I didn't know how I'd get in, but I saw that nice caretaker and he remembered me and I told him this story about how you'd asked me. . . ."

"You phoned me twice?"

"Yes. It's all right. I made convincing excuses for wanting to get hold of you."

Suddenly it was clear. Gemma's farewell message was explained. She had known about Jennifer even before Fenn had told her. She had just wanted the story to come from him.

He started to say, "You silly bitch," but then he saw her face —hurt, contrite, white with worry.

He choked back the words. He felt torn in two.

"Why didn't you tell me?"

"We planned to. We didn't know she'd be waiting for you when you got back to the flat."

Mallahide was lying, but it was useless for Fenn to argue.

The long hot summer seemed to have broken. Rain rattled on the windows of the Charing Cross Road flat, and even though it was only early afternoon all the lights were on.

The colonel was present again, but this time he did not offer drinks, was much more direct, formal. He gave Fenn his orders while Mallahide stood silent.

"Noakes has told her he wants money. He hasn't told her how much. You persuade her to pay. Oddly enough, you'll find that she hasn't much cash."

"What then?"

"She'll have to raise it. Her first instinct will be to try to borrow from an acquaintance. You stop her—tell her it's not safe to involve outsiders."

"So how does she pay?"

"She borrows it from you." Mallahide was the speaker. He and the colonel now conducted the briefing together.

"He'll ask for a thousand pounds," said the colonel. "A respectable sum but not greedy, although she'll suspect he will ask for more later. You offer to lend it to her."

"And when he asks for more later? I take it he will."

"Then you'll lend her more still."

"I don't follow," said Fenn.

"You will." The colonel glared out at the rain. Without turning, he said, "Just do what you are told. It will all be over well within the month."

He turned. "Disobey and you will make life difficult for all of us. Just do and trust. That's not too much to ask, is it?"

Despite her anxiety about herself, Jennifer was genuinely concerned.

"How will you raise it?" she asked Fenn. "You told me you had money worries."

They were in her flat. She held a postcard. "A thousand thank yous for being so nice to me," it said.

There was no signature. Noakes was due to call the following day. To her, the point of the message was obvious. One thousand pounds. Money she hadn't got, but could just about raise by selling oddments. Fenn was offering to help her until then.

"I've had a good advance on the book. Take it for a while at least. When you've got it, give it back to me."

She squeezed his hand, looked directly into his eyes.

"All right," she said. "But not for long. Honestly. I don't know how I would have survived without you."

Fenn listened to the conversation from a cupboard, the door slightly open.

Jennifer was composed and practical today. "How can I be sure no one else will put the pieces together and trace me?"

"You can't. But while I'm in charge, it's doubtful, to say the least."

There was a long silence while Noakes lit his pipe. Then he added, "We still don't know his name, let alone whether he left any close relatives. There's no pressure to do anything. Apart from me, that's your biggest protection."

In the darkness of the cupboard, Fenn strained to pick out the sounds. He thought he heard the click as Jennifer opened her handbag. Seconds later it was confirmed.

"Do you want to count them?"

A brief rustle of notes.

"I'll take your word." A pause. "After all, you and I have to trust each other."

The sound of Noakes's briefcase opening and closing.

"I'll thank you and leave you, miss." The "miss" was heavily stressed, mockingly.

Then, "How do I know you won't ask for more?"

Noakes gave the only answer that made any sense.

"You don't."

Fenn held her until she went to sleep. It was then after ten. But still he remained awake.

Jennifer tightened and began to mumble in her sleep.
"Don't let them. Please don't let them."
Fenn lifted a hand and very gently began to stroke her brow.

CHAPTER 24

Godwin read the last piece of paper he intended to study that day and noted that he had finished with less than three minutes to spare before his appointment with the Secretary to the Cabinet.

He was a man who hated to keep anyone waiting, even now that he enjoyed his exalted position as Prime Minister. Every action had its allotted span. The greatest sin was to be late—or to make others late by keeping them waiting.

He was sitting in his study overlooking St. James's Park. For the first weeks he had worked at the table in the huge Cabinet Room, an isolated figure in its vastness. Now, whenever he could, he moved upstairs and worked in an armchair near the window, the red boxes of papers waiting to be studied ranged around his feet.

The internal telephone rang. "Sir Peter's here, sir."

Godwin looked at the clock. Dead on time. "Ask him to come up, please."

Chambers had a sheaf of papers, but put Godwin's mind at ease. "Not much to worry you with, Prime Minister. Twenty minutes perhaps."

Nineteen minutes later, all the points had been covered. Chambers, chameleonlike, adjusted well to his political masters. That was one reason—though only one of many—why he had survived, prospered and now enjoyed influence and power greater even than that carried by the office he held.

"Sherry?"

"Please, Prime Minister."

Chambers walked around the room admiring the early English watercolors on the walls as Godwin filled glasses. He paused to enjoy a landscape by Paul Sandby, father of the art form. The pictures were so far the only changes Godwin had made in the room. Otherwise it remained exactly as it was after former Prime Minister Edward Heath had enlarged it and his successor Harold Wilson had furnished it in pale colors. Godwin's immediate predecessors had hardly used the room.

Both men sipped.

"Always the best," said Godwin. "First one of the day."

He knew politicians who had given up drinking on reaching high office. They realized how easy it was to keep hitting the bottle a little bit harder to soften the strains. Godwin had compromised. He no longer drank during the daytime and he no longer took spirits.

He sipped again. "Banks tells me that he's heard that some of his friends and colleagues have been asked questions about him. People asking said they were Ministry. Know anything about it? I hope that silly business hasn't come up again." He paused. "Particularly without reference to me."

His voice was reasonable enough, but his stare was cold.

Chambers replied immediately. It was a question he had anticipated might be asked one day. "I did hear about it. A check for renewal of positive vetting—normal course of things in view of Sir Joseph's renewed access to sensitive materials. I didn't tell you because it was so routine. As you know, I try not to bother you with superficialities, Prime Minister."

Godwin's eyes were still steady on him. "And that's all it is?"

"To the best of my knowledge. I will make doubly sure if you wish, though I've no reason to doubt."

The Prime Minister thought. He wondered whether the time had come to confide in Chambers about the special assignment he had first entrusted to Banks when he was Defence Minister. He decided not.

"No," he said, "if that's all it is, leave it." Not worth giving Security ideas or let them think he was worrying. "Just one more thing, though," he added. "Are the Americans still making noises?"

Chambers finished his sherry. "Oh, the Americans," he said, bringing a laugh into his voice, "they're *always* worrying. You know what they're like, Prime Minister."

Godwin took Chambers's glass. "Yes, I do," he said. "So let's make sure we don't take them too seriously. More sherry?"

It was almost midnight before Chambers returned to the small apartment which was his home during the week. He made himself a brandy and soda, and settled down in a leather chair, his feet raised on a stool.

Since leaving the Prime Minister earlier in the evening he had been busy and had had little time to think. Now he deliberated on their conversation. Had Godwin been satisfied with his explanation about the routine nature of the investigation of Banks? He thought so. But it was, he also decided, going on far too long. The sooner it was over, the better.

He called Hollen first thing the following morning, and launched into the subject without preamble.

"The matter we talked about," he said. "The P.M.'s been asking questions. Nothing to concern us—yet. But it does seem to be taking *rather* a long time."

"Two to three weeks now. That's all. These things can't be rushed." There was resentment in Hollen's voice at having to defend his department.

"No more than three weeks? I can depend on that?"

Hollen had plucked the time scale from the air, but he could not back down.

"Unless there's anything really unsuspected."

"But there won't be, will there?" Chambers's voice was cold.
Before Hollen left that afternoon, he talked to Brighouse
and he, in turn, talked to Mallahide.

"Two weeks?" Mallahide's voice was incredulous.

"Well, three at the outside."

"We're already cutting it fine with plans for a month."

"I know." Brighouse's voice was weary with resignation. He
wanted to explain, to assure the younger man that the decision
was a political, not a professional one, but his training held him
back. He did not want to appear disloyal to those above.

Mallahide banged a fist into his palm in exasperation. "It's
hurrying it just that bit too much. It'll be like pulling a fish in
with a great yank, praying the line will hold, instead of playing
it gently. We risk blowing the whole thing."

He waited for Brighouse's response, for the man to argue
Mallahide was wrong. But Brighouse said nothing. He could not
disagree. He had already argued the same points. To no avail.

CHAPTER 2 5

Noakes shook his head in disbelief.

"It's only been four days since I collected," he said. "Another bite already is *too* greedy. She'd be mad to pay. Any idiot can see that if I'm going to come back this quickly, she'd be better off saying no now and taking the consequences. Any fool knows that the secret of a successful blackmail is to demand a bit *less* than the victim would be prepared to pay."

Mallahide wanted to explain, to justify himself, but like Brighouse the previous day felt unable to do so. He confined himself to a general remark that he hoped would be reassuring. "Things have hotted up, I'm told. I know it's not the best way to handle it, but you realize better than almost anyone that the game's often like that."

Noakes, who was putting up some shelves, began screwing in a batten. "It's no way to handle it at all," he said. But he was at least partly mollified. He would, of course, carry out his orders: he was a professional. At the same time, a botched and hasty job was alien to his orderly mind. Although he would cooperate, the whole business added to his growing distaste for Mallahide. The man, he had decided, was genuinely nasty. Noakes himself did unpleasant things, but only because it was his work. Mallahide, he suspected, actually liked doing them.

"Our concern," Mallahide went on quickly, "is to try to see it continues to work despite the new problems."

Noakes put down his screwdriver. "What we'd need to do," he said almost to himself, "is to convince her somehow that I'm not going to be returning every few days asking for another payment or else. . . ."

"That's the way I see it too."

Noakes started to fill a pipe.

"We could put on a big bite. Say something has come along that makes me need a big sum now. Tell her that this *is* the one and final payment, that I won't be back. But it would still be hard to convince her."

Noakes's knowledge of the operation was strictly limited. He knew the girl had to be blackmailed and that in borrowing the money to pay she would make herself even more vulnerable. But he knew no more.

Mallahide decided that more information now might help.

"We have something going for us that I haven't mentioned. It would just have clouded things before. The man that she's borrowing the money from—he's a friend of ours."

"Has she told him what the money is for?"

"Yes."

"So he can help convince her."

"Yes, but more than that . . . now this is just a thought, but do you think this might work . . . ?

Noakes made the call from a telephone box. On the first three attempts there was no reply. When she did answer she was breathless, as if she had just come in from the street.

"Are you alone?"

"Who is that?" Then she recognized his voice. "What do you want?"

"I said, are you alone?"

"There's a friend. He's gone into the kitchen."

"Close the door. Keep him there."

There was a pause while she walked over to the door.

"I've done it, but be quick. *Please.*"

He judged from the tone of her voice that she expected news, not another demand.

"I'd like some more thanks," `he said. "Ten thousand of them. Say by the day after tomorrow."

It took several seconds for her to absorb the demand—and the amount.

"Ten thousand. I couldn't. It's impossible. You said. . . ."

"Day after tomorrow. Ten o'clock. You'll manage it. You'd better."

He replaced the receiver. He just hoped the friend with her was the man Mallahide had mentioned . . . and that he was persuasive.

He picked up the receiver again and called Mallahide.

Jennifer was still holding the telephone when Fenn walked in from the kitchen, carrying the coffee cups. Her face was pale, and she was staring at the receiver as though paralyzed.

Fenn put down the cups, took the telephone from her hand and replaced it on its cradle. He knew what the call had been. But even if he had not, it would have been obvious. "Was it him?"

She nodded. He led her to a chair. "Is he having trouble keeping it from others? Is that it?"

She shook her head. "No. I don't think so. He wants more money."

"More money! Already? It's been less than a week."

"Five days."

"What does he want this time?"

She looked up, eyes wide open and watering with tears. "You won't believe it. Ten thousand."

"How much?"

"Ten thousand pounds. I know, it's hard to believe."

"You can't pay it. You mustn't. The man's mad. He'll bleed you dry and keep asking for more."

"I know. But what happens to me if I don't . . .?"

Fenn paced the floor in simulated anger.

"When does he want it?"

"The day after tomorrow."

"That soon?"

"Oh God," she said, "I can't go to the police now. Just having left it so long makes me look more guilty. . . ."

"Look," said Fenn. "I think I can handle him. I think I see a way it will be all right."

The money was in ten bundles, each composed of two hundred five-pound notes, well-used, secured with rubber bands.

"Whatever you do," said Mallahide, "be careful with them. Don't let them out of your sight until you hand it over. They'd have my head for it."

Fenn had never seen Mallahide so obviously nervous. Destroy someone, knee a man in the face, blackmail a girl—yes. But hand over ten thousand pounds of KGB money. . . .

He took the bundles and stuffed them into the shoulder bag he had bought that morning.

"Perhaps I should count it?" Mallahide's fear made him feel strong.

"It's all there." The colonel's voice was harsh. Its tone said: Don't argue, just do as you are told.

Fenn placed the last bundle in the bag. On top of the money he put a rolled-up sweater.

"Okay," he said.

Mallahide still looked worried. "You know exactly what to do?" he asked.

The colonel spoke again. "Stop worrying him," he said. "He knows. It will be all right."

Noakes arrived at precisely ten o'clock.

Had he been a genuine blackmailer, he could have been early—to make sure nothing was being plotted. Or he could have been late—to make Jennifer sweat some more. But he was on time to impress her that what he was going to say was genuine—that he was not lying or hiding anything. That if he said he would be there at ten, then he would be. And that if he promised that this would be his final demand for money, then that was true too.

He seized the initiative the moment he was inside. "You've got it?"

Jennifer had been dreading the meeting, remembering Noakes's first call, but with Fenn back, it was easier to cope. She had someone to tell her what to do. Now she followed his instructions, and she was calmer. "If I give it to you how do I know you won't return in a few days and ask for more? How do I know you won't hand over the evidence that you've got about my accident?"

His voice was mocking. "Won't my word do?"

She was more in command than he had anticipated. "No. No, it won't. I want more than that."

It was easy for him to fake anger. "Well you won't get more. Pay or be damned. You hit and killed some hopeless old man, and then drove on. I can prove it—if I have to. If you want to save your skin, you pay. That's all. The rest you damned well take on trust."

Although he spat out the words, the expression did not change once—still smiling, still benign.

The reminder about the body, the threat about her own future numbed her, but she forced herself to continue with the words Fenn had made her rehearse earlier. "And if I pay you, you'll destroy the evidence and you'll leave me alone. You won't bother me again."

"That's what I said."

Jennifer went over to a bureau, opened it and extracted a fat envelope. She handed it to Noakes. She so desperately wanted what he said to be the truth. She couldn't cope with more.

"Well?" she said finally.

Noakes took out the bundles, one by one, and dropped them into his case.

"Don't you want to count them?"

"I said last time we met that we'd have to trust each other."

"There's ten thousand," she said. "As you asked—for keeping quiet and suppressing the evidence."

Noakes closed his case. "I'll leave you now, miss. I'm glad we didn't have any problems."

He was halfway to the door when it opened. Fenn stood there. Jennifer's face showed her relief.

"Every word is down on tape," Fenn said.

Then, directly to Noakes, he added, "I think you and I ought to talk. I think you might find it's stalemate."

Noakes sat as Fenn stood over him.

"You can keep the money," he said. "But it's the last pay-off. You ask for a penny more and the tape gets sent to your chief constable with a copy of *The Times* just to make sure he doesn't mislay it."

"She'll sink too if you do that."

"Sure," said Fenn. "That's why I hope it's not necessary. But believe me, we'd rather you both went down than just her alone."

"I believe you."

At the street door, Noakes turned as though about to say something. He remained silent.

Fenn closed the door behind him. "I think everything will be all right now," he said.

It was not until 4:15 the following morning that Jennifer woke and looked down at Fenn's body beside her. He was naked and had pushed back the coverings. His body was taut, no wasted fat. He had kept himself in trim, looked fitter than many of the younger men she had known.

She reached out to touch him and drew back as a thought entered her head. She suddenly realized that, whether everything was all right or not, what had happened had cost her eleven thousand pounds—money she did not possess.

CHAPTER 26

With the increased activities generated by the forthcoming Vienna conference, Banks was rarely home now.

Fenn was relieved by this. He found it hard to face the man. He was certain that Banks did not suspect him of spying on him, but he was equally sure the other resented his relationship with his daughter.

They met briefly on the street near the house.

"You're going to see Jennifer?"

"Yes."

"I'm getting jealous of you, my boy. Wish I could see as much of her." Banks laughed as he spoke but it sounded forced.

Fenn was finding the mental pressures exhausting. It was impossible not to think about what he was doing. All he could do was persuade himself that he was repaying all his debts to the Russians and that, in any event, he had no choice in the matter. But it would have been easier to "kill" from a distance, to be pushing the button that launched a missile, not to be firing a pistol at close range at someone whose face you could see.

Not once had Mallahide or the colonel talked about ideology after the first embarrassing speech from the colonel. Did they take it for granted that he still believed? He doubted that. There was nothing in his lifestyle or his reactions to point to anything but political cynicism—although they could, he supposed, think *that* was his cover.

No. They could have no delusions about him. That was why he also was a blackmail victim.

The summons came two days after the confrontation with Noakes—after a shorter period than either Mallahide or Brighouse would have liked, but forced by Hollen's orders. Again both Mallahide and the colonel were waiting.

"You'll be glad to hear we achieved the return of the money," said the colonel. He was being affable again. "Our heads are safe."

Mallahide, thought Fenn, looked even more tense than usual—a contrast with the colonel's mood.

"We're nearly there now, Mr. Fenn," the colonel continued. "Two more stages and then you can bow out, go home, relax, forget things. What you have to do now is to persuade Jennifer Banks that you are in trouble over the money you raised to help her. Surprisingly, perhaps you'll find she has closed her mind to practical thoughts like how you could have got it. She's a girl who has never had to worry about where money is coming from."

He lit a cigarette. Fenn noted that he had managed to get a supply of card-filtered Russian ones.

The colonel exhaled the strong smoke. "A good story, I would suggest, is that you borrowed it from not very nice people who will do you a lot of harm unless it is repaid quickly. You will find that short of going to her father—which she won't do —she has no way of raising the kind of money we are talking about."

"Eleven thousand?"

"Precisely. You will suggest she sell her car—it's worth at least that. Make it clear that all along you've thought that's what she intended to do."

The colonel sucked in more smoke. Fenn watched fascinated. He had never before seen anyone smoke with such ferocity.

"You'll find that she will be embarrassed by the suggestion. You see, Mr. Fenn, she doesn't own the Porsche. It's her car, all right, but it is registered in her father's name. There is no way that she could sell it."

"So how does she pay?"

"In kind. Papers from her father's safe. Not for us, of course. We have a nice little story that we think should convince her."

He outlined it. "Do you think that's a good one?"

Fenn was noncommittal. "I'll have to be very convincing. It's asking a lot."

"Yes, but not too much. I agree, though. She must be convinced that unless she does this, something terrible really will happen to you. And we must remember what you mean to her—the man who gave her life, who is protecting her now, who is. . . ."

Fenn noticed that Mallahide was putting on a pair of gloves.

It took him several seconds to work out what was happening and by that time it was too late. The colonel gripped him with surprising strength and Mallahide's first blow hit him in the stomach, winding him.

"This is necessary, I'm afraid," the colonel said. "We'll hurt you as little as possible. A few marks and bruises are the main thing. This, you understand, is your warning to pay up. Miss Banks needs to see how nasty your friends really are."

Mallahide telephoned from a nearby pay phone to check that Jennifer was at home. He hung up as soon as she answered, and she was left wondering whether it had been a wrong number or whether it could have been Noakes again.

Although it was almost one o'clock, she was not in bed. She dreaded sleeping because of nightmares about the accident. If Fenn were here, it would be better, but he had been spending a lot of time engrossed in work—an escape from his own anxieties, she imagined. It might also have something to do with the money.

She poured herself another drink and wondered whether

sleeping tablets would help tonight. Then the doorbell rang. It was less than ten minutes since the telephone call. Her nerves were screaming. She would not answer. She looked into the passageway to check that the door was bolted and on a chain. It was.

She went back into the living room and drained the whiskey. Neat. Her hand was shaking. She waited for another ring. Nothing.

Given courage by the drink, she walked to the front door and peered through the spy hole. At first she could see no one. Then she made out what seemed to be a bundle near the foot of the door.

She stared for a long time, uncertain what to do. Finally, in a burst of courage, she slipped the chain and unbolted the door. For a moment, despite the light from the passageway, she could not make out anything about the bundle except its size and that it looked like an old blanket.

It moaned. She drew back, terrified. Her hand reached for the door to pull it shut.

The bundle moved and a face, bloodstained, battered but familiar, emerged.

And, ridiculously, it tried to smile.

"No doctor, no doctor," Fenn kept repeating as she helped him on to the sofa. It was hard to talk with his lip split open.

Jennifer pushed a cushion under his head and lifted his feet. Pain shot through his stomach, yet he was sure he was not badly hurt. The blows had been carefully placed.

"Do you have a first aid kit?"

"Not here. In the car."

"Fetch it. Please."

When she returned he was in front of the mirror in the bathroom, examining himself. He had removed his jacket and shirt and she could see blackening bruises across his stomach and shoulders.

Fenn bathed the cuts with water and disinfectant and

patched them with plaster. His only real worry was the pain
in his left side. Had Mallahide struck too hard, broken a rib?
He sometimes suspected that Mallahide was slightly mad. He
bent sideways. The pain shot through him, but he convinced
himself it was all right—only bad bruising.

"Can I stay tonight?"

"Oh God, you must be crazy. Of course you can."

He hobbled to the bedroom and lay under a sheet while she
fetched him a drink and found aspirin. She had not asked
questions and he was glad. That could wait until morning. He
would volunteer nothing now.

He fell asleep before she returned. He awoke in the night,
his body wet with sweat and full of pain. She was lying beside
him. The drink and the aspirin she had fetched were on the
table beside the bed and he swallowed them both.

He fell back into an uneasy sleep, experiencing the strangest
of feelings. He should be hating Mallahide and the colonel for
the beating, and when it had been happening he had tried to
scream obscenities and threats at them.

But now, he felt oddly purged.

The beating, in some way, seemed an atonement for his sins,
for the lie he was living, for the hurt he was bringing to others.

The idea was Brighouse's, and once more Mallahide found
himself surprised by the man's cold-bloodedness.

"It may not be necessary," Brighouse said. "But I've been
thinking about that little extra bit of pressure you mentioned
a while back. I wonder if this might not be a good moment to
apply it."

Mallahide listened. "All right," he said when Brighouse
finished. "You want me to arrange it?"

"Please."

"James, please. Please tell me. Who was it. Who did it?"
Jennifer's voice was pitched high.

She and Fenn faced each other over coffee cups and the kitchen table. He was dressed, feeling stiff, but experiencing less pain than he had feared. Drinking, though, was difficult. Because of the cut, he had to sip through one side of his mouth.

"I don't know."

"You're not telling the truth. James, *tell* me."

He reached out to take her hand. "Please," he said. "For now, let it lie. I need to go out. I have to see someone. Perhaps we can talk later."

Obeying orders, Fenn spent the day away from Jennifer.

"You must let her worries build up before you tell her anything," the colonel had instructed.

It was impossible to work or even to pretend to do so. Fenn walked around the National Portrait Gallery and painfully ate lunch in a steak bar. He read a newspaper as he ate. The lead story was about a spectacular breakout from East Berlin by a family of four. Fenn read it because of the story itself and because of the man who had written it—Frederick Donovan, the newspaper's Defence Correspondent and a man well known for his exposés of security scandals over the years.

Fenn wondered what Donovan was like these days. How long since he had last seen him? A year after leaving England? Yes . . . five years then. Many, many years before that, before Fenn's first marriage, they had shared a small flat. It would be good to see him again . . . but obviously not now. Not while Fenn was involved in this operation.

The car picked him up on his way home to change. The colonel was seated in the back. The car moved off as soon as Fenn was beside him.

The colonel studied Fenn's face with concern. "I cannot tell you how much I regret it was necessary to do what we did last night."

"You picked me up to tell me *that?*" Fenn's voice was half-mocking, but he was concerned—something must have gone wrong.

The car headed south. The colonel nodded in the direction of the driver. "Don't worry. He will hear nothing." Then he continued. "It was partly that. I worried that our friend had been too vicious. He is a good man but impetuous. Sometimes he goes too far. I was afraid he might have hit you too hard."

"I'm all right. Sore, but all right."

"Good. I am reassured."

"There's something else?"

"I wanted to tell you. This meeting we are having, it is unprofessional. I would like you to forget it ever happened . . . but I wanted to tell you."

"Tell me what?"

"Our impetuous friend, he went above me . . . persuaded them that you are still a risk, that you might not do what we asked. Despite all I had said." His voice was weary and full of hurt.

"And?" Fenn prompted him.

"I believe they have sent some warning to your family. They make them hostage to your behavior."

Fenn clenched his fists.

"Believe me, I knew nothing of this until after."

"Drop me here."

"Here?"

"Yes. I want to walk."

Nearly an hour later, he tried to telephone Gemma. No reply. He paced the floor, wondering what to do. Should he telephone someone else on the island, get them to call round? Where was she now?

Then he remembered. There were new visitors due about now to occupy one of the apartments they rented out. She might be there. He would keep trying.

The consoling thought was that it was only a *warning* they would be sending; nothing would actually happen. Provided he obeyed.

The message was very clear, though. Gemma and the girls

were hostages. And he did not delude himself—there was no
way he could protect them except by obeying orders.

The colonel's dramatic gesture, of course, had just been a
way of making sure he understood the situation.

He began to change. Suddenly he was in a rush to get back
to Gemma. The sooner it was over now, the better.

CHAPTER 27

For the first time in her life Jennifer found herself genuinely concerned about a man.

She had had occasional worries about her father, of course —mainly that he drove himself too hard—but he was someone who seemed indestructible. Fenn was suddenly so vulnerable, however. And it was because of her.

Long after he had gone to bed in her apartment, she sat thinking back on the evening. They had eaten at home in the kitchen, the stereo playing from the living room—an attempt to create a false gaiety. Gradually under pressure from her, he had told her the reason for the beating.

"And they did—*that?*" she had said.

"The collector did," he had replied. "Just to warn me that I was already overdue."

It wasn't just eleven thousand pounds—as if that wasn't enough—but twelve thousand pounds to include interest, he had said. Then he had begun to laugh hysterically. "I *must* be mad. Twelve thousand. I'd have a job raising twelve hundred."

Jennifer fetched a drink and looked through the open doorway into the bedroom. It was too dark to see Fenn's face, but she shuddered at the recollection of his cuts. She had always been insulated from violence.

She swallowed the drink in one gulp and walked over to pour another. God, she really didn't want him hurt any more. But what could she do?

She downed the second drink as quickly as the first.

Not knowing the answer to her own question, she sought escape in the way she knew best.

The parcel had a Valetta postmark. It was addressed to her and the two girls by name.

Gemma opened it, puzzled at what it could contain. A present for the children from one of their friends?

There was a great deal of wrapping paper and in the middle of that an envelope. The envelope contained a single sheet of paper. On it, one word.

"BANG!"

She shuddered. What kind of madman would do such a thing? Gemma pushed the wrapping paper aside and concluded she would be silly to call the police—there would be too many questions. Besides, she had to look over the apartments —though, now, she would take the girls. She would, however, tell James. She lifted the telephone and asked the operator for his number. There was no reply.

She replaced the receiver, and then remembered Banks's name; James had told her he had been working in his home. Twenty minutes later she had the number and was being connected. Persons brought Banks to the telephone.

"Sir Joseph Banks? You don't know me, but I think you've been helping my husband."

"Yes, Mrs. Fenn." The voice was noncommittal.

It seemed silly now, but she had to go on even though she couldn't tell him about the note. "I need to contact him urgently and I wondered if he was with you."

Banks wondered what she wanted. He would have liked to tell her about Fenn and his daughter, tempt the woman into some action that would destroy their friendship. But he dared not—it might not work. It might get back to Jennifer.

"I'm sorry, Mrs. Fenn. I see him rarely now. But if I do . . . you've tried his flat, of course."

Gemma mumbled thanks. It had been useless to call. At the other end of the line, Banks heard a click. He stared into space for a long time before hanging up. He wished he knew what to do.

The relief when Fenn finally reached Gemma was intense.

"Thank God," he said. "I've been trying to call you."

"The flats," she said. "You know. There were things to do."

The conversation was strained, things both of them were thinking but not saying.

"Is everything all right?"

She told him about the parcel. "Don't you think it's sick?" She did not tell him of her call to Banks.

"It's all right. I was warned that something like that might happen. But it's over now. You don't have to worry."

"It's something to do with the thing you're involved in?"

"Yes, but it's nearly over now."

"I hope so. I can't take very much more."

"Honestly, it's all right." Then he had to spoil it. "If there are any more parcels, don't open them."

He got out of bed just after three o'clock and deliberately made enough noise to waken her.

Jennifer came through into the living room. He was drinking tea. "You want some?"

"Please."

He made her a cup and they sat facing each other, she in a robe, he in a pair of pajama bottoms.

"Have they been in touch again?"

The genuine concern in her voice made it harder. Hesitantly, "Yes. They've given me forty-eight hours."

Her voice rose. "For all that money?"

"For half."

The fear and the concern for him welled inside her. She moved next to him and clutched his hand. "You must have been mad. It's me who really owes the money. How could you have thought you could pay them back?"

"Remember what the alternative was," he reminded her.

"I know." She stared at the carpet, faced for the first time in her life with a problem no one could solve for her.

Fenn pressed on. "They're threatening my family, too." He told her about the parcel.

Jennifer put down her untouched tea, stood and fetched a tumbler of whiskey. "Oh God, my God," she said. She had forced herself never to ask Fenn about his wife or his children, but in a strange way their existence had comforted her. She had not been concerned that one day they would draw him home—she expected it to end anyway—but she liked the fact that their being gave him a solidity. He was a father, a man who coped.

Jennifer drank the whiskey, poured more. God, she thought, she really was a shit! She'd killed a man; now her actions threatened someone she genuinely cared for—and his family.

She realized he was staring at her. "I've tried to think of what I can do," she said. "I've gone through everything I own. I think I could raise about two thousand. It's not much, but would that help—keep them away a little while?"

This, Fenn knew, was the moment. He hated it, but he had to go through with it.

"Jen," he said, "could you sell the car? I know you love it, but it would bring in all we need and more—even sold quickly to a dealer."

Jennifer raised the glass to her lips, began to sip, and then began to rock with hysterical laughter. The glass tilted and whiskey poured on to the carpet, but she was oblivious to it.

"Oh Christ, Christ, Christ," she said. She put her free hand to her face. "You don't know, do you? You couldn't know."

"Know what?"

"That I don't own the car. It's always been in daddy's

name. It's mine but I could never sell it."

Fenn slumped in the chair, head in his hands. Now he either succeeded or failed. He wanted to fail for her sake. He wanted to succeed even more so—for himself, Gemma, the girls, their future.

"There's one other way," he said haltingly. "But I don't know if I dare ask you. I'm not even certain it would work now—it goes back a long time to when I was working as a journalist—but I think it would. . . ."

Jennifer looked at him attentively. Fenn averted his eyes so that he would not have to look at the tears on her cheek as he lied.

"You sometimes get strange approaches when you're working for a newspaper, especially when you're doing the kind of globetrotting work I was."

He had her complete attention.

"There was one man from an electronics company that was doing a lot of defense contract work. He sounded me out once, offered to pay for anything that I could pass on that would give his firm knowledge of what the government and other governments were thinking arms-wise. A lot of money."

He looked at her. She nodded her head to show that she was following him though she didn't understand.

"I checked today. He's still there. I think he'd still be interested."

"But how could you tell him anything interesting now?" She wanted him to come up with a solution, but she was genuinely puzzled.

Fenn moved over to her, took the glass from her hand. There was still half an inch of whiskey in it. He drank it.

"Jennifer, love," he said, "your father brings home loads of stuff—this kind of stuff. I know. I've seen it. Just a few bits of it—the least secret, the most innocuous. Believe me, these people have so much money they'd pay for it—and they'd get me off the hook before we even knew what was happening."

*　*　*

She got very drunk very quickly and fell asleep saying, "You shouldn't have asked me. Anything but that."

She woke just before five. She was alone in the bed. She lay for a long while, her mind a jumble of thoughts. Mostly she tried not to think. There were things too painful—her mother's absence, her occasional self-disgust at actions she seemed unable to control . . . even her father. She loved him; of that there was no doubt . . . but if only he had reached out more, been demonstrative, more open in his love for her. Instead, he had cared by proxy—taken infinite trouble in finding the right school, encouraging the right friends, providing her with the most beautiful home.

The room began to lighten with dawn. She heard Fenn moving in the living room, but still made no move. For the first time since waking she focused her thoughts on the immediate problem: his suggestion.

Fenn *had* been demonstrative—she kept remembering how they had talked after the first time they had made love. And he had proved his caring—after the accident, that terrible accident, he had done everything he could to protect her without thinking of himself.

She got up and walked through to the living room. Fenn was awake, seated, bent forward, hands over his eyes.

He looked up. "I'm sorry," he said. "You're right. I shouldn't have asked you."

There was only one point on which she had to satisfy herself. "If I got you papers, you would be careful what you copied and passed on? You wouldn't give them any real secrets?"

"Jen, you were right. It was a bad idea. Let's forget it."

She took his hand. "Come with me." She began to lead him into the bedroom. "But you would be careful. You wouldn't do anything that could harm him?"

They lay in the bed, his arm around her.

He lay for a long time waiting for her to speak again, but there was only silence and then the sound of breathing as she drifted into sleep.

She would, he knew, do what he had asked. But there was no elation.

The first handover took place thirty-six hours later.

Jennifer had accepted Fenn's story that he knew the safe's combination because he had watched her father open it one evening. The key, it emerged, was no problem. Jennifer knew where her father had hidden a spare.

Fenn had asked her to take the papers to his flat. "I need to copy them," he had explained.

He rushed to meet her as soon as she arrived, held her for a long time in the doorway. Then he led her over to the small table near the window where the Minox camera was already set up on its stand.

"You know you're probably saving my life," he told her.

She handed him the papers. There were three sets. Fenn looked at them for a long time, holding them in such a way that they were easily visible from the curtained window of an apartment opposite.

There, in a room borrowed from the occupants, two men filmed every movement—the actual handing over, close-ups of the faces of Fenn and Jennifer, and zoom shots of the papers that Fenn held. Enlarged, the pictures would show some of the text, identify them.

Fenn handed back one set of papers. "That one looks too sensitive," he said. "We won't copy that."

He switched on the single light uner the copying stand and placed the first sheet of paper under a sheet of glass below the camera. A piece of cardboard covered with foil was propped up opposite the bulb to reflect light and take the place of a second lamp.

Fenn began to take the photographs. He worked quickly, but to Jennifer, nervously pacing the floor, it seemed an age.

Finished, Fenn handed back all the papers with the exception of one sheet.

"I need this until I've seen him," he explained. "To prove

that I'm copying from master copies. It's not an important document—it won't be missed."

She was nervous, reluctant.

"Please," he said. He looked at his watch dramatically. "I have less than twelve hours."

She stared at his face. At the cuts that had not yet healed.

"All right," she said. "But for God's sake, take care of it."

As she left, she asked, "What time are you seeing him?"

"The electronics man? In just over two hours."

"You think it will be all right?"

He shrugged, resigned. "I hope so. If not, you'll have done everything you can."

"You'll phone me as soon as you know?"

"Of course."

Fenn gave her a half hour's start before leaving for the Charing Cross Road flat.

Mallahide was waiting impatiently when Fenn arrived. There were no preliminaries. He held his hand out for the film the moment Fenn entered the room.

"And you have an original?" he said.

Fenn produced it. "You'll have it back by the morning," said Mallahide. "There are tests we have to conduct."

Fenn had accepted the story that Mallahide and the colonel needed to show their superiors that Fenn had gained access to the originals. Suspicion all along the line. The truth was a lot more complex. The paper would be checked for fingerprints. Mallahide would not be surprised if in addition to Fenn's, the girl's and Banks's, they did not include those of the Prime Minister.

That would be a useful additional piece of evidence to have around.

Fenn delayed telephoning until well after the promised time. A cruel touch but again, he consoled himself, one that had been ordered.

Jennifer answered immediately.

"Was it all right?"

"Can you meet me?"

"Was it all right?"

"Say outside Embankment Station. I'll tell you everything then."

She arrived before him and as he struggled through the home-going crowd, he saw she kept trying to read the front page of a newspaper and then, almost immediately, putting it down. He hoped they would leave her alone soon. And then he realized. What did he mean *they*? It was him as much as anyone else. He, of course, was only obeying orders. But weren't they too? And perhaps they even believed in the rightness of what they were doing.

As soon as she saw him she ran, arms outstretched.

"You're all right?" The concern in her voice, the tightness with which she held him, moved him more than anything she had done before.

He hugged her, glorying in the warmth of her. They began walking, his arm around her.

"I'm fine," he said. "It worked. I'm only late because my man got nervous at the last moment—he thought someone was watching us. So we parted and met again two hours later. I'm sorry. I didn't want to tell you on the phone. I'm so nervous. It only needs a crossed line or something."

"Did you get the money?"

"Yes. Six thousand."

"And you've handed it over?"

"Yes. And I've got a week to supply the balance."

He stopped and turned toward her. "Just one, perhaps two, more consignments. That will do it. Then we can stop."

He took her hand and began to run. "Come on," he said. "Let's go and celebrate."

They had slowed and they were breathing heavily and giggling when the words hit her.

Two more consignments.

*　　*　　*

There were fewer papers the second time, but Fenn expressed himself satisfied.

"They'll pay up," he said. "The stuff is probably useless to them, but they can't afford to take chances. For what's no more than petty cash they're buying something their rivals probably haven't seen. Even if it's only a chance in a million that it will pay off, it's a fair gamble for them."

The handovers were filmed again, and in his office Brighouse put together a folder of photographic enlargements that were enough evidence in themselves. Jennifer Banks had been taking documents from her father's safe and handing them to a known Soviet agent.

But there was more than that: carefully edited and re-recorded voice tapes of the handovers, the evidence of the fingerprints. These showed the passage of the documents. The prints included those of the Prime Minister, Banks, the girl and Fenn.

All that remained now was to pounce and to pray that they had gauged Banks accurately.

It had been a risk speeding up the operation but, as he prepared to go home that evening, Brighouse was forced to concede it had worked.

It was Hollen who decided there should be one more raid on Banks's safe.

"I don't understand," said Brighouse. "Surely it's not necessary. We'll only get more of the same sort of evidence."

It was the nearest he had ever come to questioning an order.

"By now," said Hollen, "the P.M. will have the latest NATO position paper for the Vienna talks. If *that* found its way into Banks's hands and got handed over. . . ."

Brighouse nodded, suddenly in agreement. "I see. That could be the clincher." It was, after all, worth taking the further risk.

"Will you arrange it?"

"Yes. We'll plan it for Saturday. That'll give it time to seep through to him. And that's the day Banks visits his mistress."

A watch was still being kept on Stella Harding and her apartment.

"Good," said Hollen. "We can have it out and back before he returns."

CHAPTER 28

Banks rose later than usual on Saturday morning. He switched on the radio, caught the end of the eight o'clock news bulletin, and decided to breakfast before showering.

Parsons was away again and he was alone in the house. He considered asking Jennifer to join him, but he remembered she had said she would be away visiting friends.

Banks suspected she was with Fenn. Although part of him still liked the man, he regretted and resented it. This time, he thought, Jennifer really could be hurt. He had had to end Fenn's casual access to the house when the man had been working here; it came close to encouraging the liaison. But in truth it would be easier now if Fenn were still about. He would have a better idea of what was happening.

Banks stirred a tablespoonful of wheat germ into a carton of yogurt—breakfast was his only abstemious meal of the day. He ate in the kitchen, perched on a stool, a morning newspaper propped in front of him. As always, he had every newspaper. He would read two carefully—which ones varied according to his mood and the day—and skim the headlines in the rest.

This morning it was hard to concentrate. It had been a late

night, but usually he was able to shrug off fatigue with the minimum of rest. He must, he told himself, be getting old. Only he did not believe that for a moment. It was, he knew, an exhaustion produced by his fears and emotions. The previous night he had been told by telephone that his wife was refusing to eat or take any liquids—her voices had told her that all food and drink was poisoned.

Today was the day he saw Stella. He wondered whether he should cancel that, go home instead—but he knew he would not. There was nothing he could do . . . and Pip had not even recognized him for three weeks.

He finished the yogurt, poured coffee and carried it into the main living room. He stared for a long time at the portrait of Pip, the one showing her looking remarkably the way Stella did now.

This was not the reason he had sought a mistress but it explained why he had chosen the one he had. A silly pretense? A betrayal? No, not that. Stella had proven a good choice, understanding as well as satisfying his sexual needs. And later, of course, the apartment and her loyalty and discretion had proved a useful combination.

He was still staring and thinking when the telephone began to ring. He disregarded it for a long time before remembering he was alone in the house.

"Sir Joseph? This is Dr. Madden."

"Yes. What is it? What's wrong?" The doctor was struck by the worry in Banks's voice.

"Now don't get overanxious. Your wife is all right, but she's suddenly lucid again . . . keeps insisting that you have left her. I'm giving her something to make her sleep for a while, but I think it could be useful to her if you came over. It might help, seeing you."

Banks peered at the clock. Despite the traffic, it was probably quicker to drive than take a train.

"I'll be there in two hours," he said.

* * *

"Okay," said Fenn. "You decide."

At 8:30 A.M. they were both still in bed, but were sitting up, eating toast, drinking tea and studying a large map of Britain that was spread over the bed.

"I can't."

"Well, close your eyes and touch somewhere with your finger."

She did. He looked. "No good unless you really want a week in the middle of the North Sea."

At Fenn's suggestion—unexpectedly made late the previous evening—they were planning to go away together for a short while.

Mallahide had told Fenn he wanted him to remain away from Gozo for a week. Then he could go home. Fenn knew the week with Jennifer would make his life more complicated, would make the parting harder when it came, but he wanted it.

"You know where I'd really like to go?" Her voice was suddenly serious.

"Tell me. It's your choice."

"Ireland," she said. "And drink Guinness and eat fattening food and make illicit love all day."

"I thought you wanted Britain. Ireland's not Britain."

"They can speak English, can't they?"

"Yes."

"Well!"

Fenn thought. He could not see how Mallahide would object. His orders were not to go home yet, but to leave a contact telephone number if he went away.

"All right," he said, pushing the map to the floor. "But let's start the illicit sex right now."

It was not good. Both were thinking of the afternoon: the last raid on Banks's study.

She killed herself twenty minutes before he arrived.

One of the nurses, believing that Lady Banks was heavily drugged and unable to move, left the door open when she went into the main house to try to find a magazine to read. Lady Banks was not drugged. She only feigned sleep. She held the tablets in her mouth, wedged against the inside of her cheek. As soon as she was alone, she spat them out.

She had a task to perform. Her voices had told her that she had to prove to everyone that she was immortal. Nothing could harm her.

She found the rope in the stables, entered the main house without being seen. She hanged herself from the bannister, tying one end of the rope around the handrail, the other around her neck. Then she jumped.

A professional hangman would have approved of the distance she fell before the noose bit into her neck. By coincidence the rope was nine feet from the bannister to her head—the ideal distance for a clean kill of her weight. Longer and she would have been mutilated. Shorter and she would have slowly asphyxiated.

Banks was not allowed to see her until the police had cut her down, taken photographs and measurements, and laid her body out in what used to be her bedroom.

The undertaker had done what he could on the spot—pushed her tongue back into her mouth, closed her bulging eyes, dressed her in a high-necked frock that hid the burns made by the rope.

Banks sat beside her for half an hour, angrily gesturing people away on the two occasions they tried to interrupt him. She had been gone from him for many years now, but the finality of it hit him harder than he had ever imagined.

He sat, hunched forward, eyes lifted staring at her face, remembering it—in repose, in laughter, in anger at him, for her moods had often been violent.

He wanted to cry, but he could not. The grief was too deep for that. He wished he could pray, but that would have been a lie—for her as well. She too was an unbeliever—he remembered her saying after a friend died painfully from cancer, "I'm glad there is no God, because I would not have enough curses for him."

Finally he tried to telephone Jennifer, first at her flat, then at the house, finally at Fenn's. There was no reply from any of them.

A number of people had gathered now, including a police superintendent anxious to know how they should announce the news if they had calls from the press.

Banks dealt curtly with them all.

Madden tried to console him. "At least she died immediately," he said. "The fall dislocated her neck."

"No one knows the death's instantaneous," snapped Banks. "Doctors have been arguing over it for years." He knew too much of the mechanics of death to be deceived.

Declining all help, all sympathy, he made for his car, announcing that he was returning to London. In truth he wanted to be with Jennifer. Not only must he tell her before she heard from someone else, but he needed her presence. She was all he had now.

"You callous shit," muttered Madden under his breath. The police superintendent overheard him, agreed. "You can see how a man gets to the top and stays there," he said.

There was only one document when Jennifer entered the study soon after 2:30 and opened the safe.

It was about a hundred pages thick, though, and heavily stamped with security classifications. It was also numbered— a sure sign, even she knew, of a highly restricted circulation.

For several minutes she paced the floor wondering whether to leave it and tell Fenn there had been nothing. If there had been other papers she would have taken them and left this one. Her memory of the morning, however, her anticipation of going away, and the fact that she had taken papers twice before overcame her reluctance.

Nearly 2:45. She had already wasted fifteen minutes. She slipped the document into her briefcase. She should have it back in the safe by five o'clock.

*   *   *

Banks arrived back in London soon after four.

He wondered briefly whether he should visit Stella. She would be someone to talk to, someone with whom he could share his grief. She would be wondering where he was, knowing nothing of what had happened. He would not, though. He could not. It was not that it would have been a betrayal of Pip. It was that he could not bear to see that face, so like hers. Best not.

He walked unseeing for about half an hour before realizing he must return home. He had to find Jennifer, check funeral arrangements.

The house felt strange. It was just as he had left it that morning. The empty yogurt carton was still on the kitchen table, his coffee cup stood beside the telephone. Yet the world —his world—had changed totally. Had changed more than he could ever have imagined.

Jennifer was still not at home. He tried Fenn's number once more. It was engaged. He would try again soon.

The quietness of the house, one of the things he had always loved, depressed him, but he did not want to go out. He did not know what to do. Drink? pills? call a doctor to come round? Telephone people and talk? Who?

None of the possibilities appealed to him. Then he thought of the one thing that had always helped him through crises— his work.

In his study, he opened the safe. He would read the NATO paper. He really ought to get it back to the Prime Minister anyway.

At first he thought it must have got caught up with other papers he kept in the safe. Then, when it became obvious that it was not there, he wondered whether he had forgotten to put it back after glancing through it the previous day. Strange, he was normally so careful. But he searched.

Only then, when he still could not find it, did he begin to feel panic. Someone must have broken in and stolen it. He stared at the safe. No sign of a forcible entry. But then did a good safebreaker leave signs?

He was so engrossed in his new worry that he did not hear the door open.

He heard the gasp and turned.

"Jennifer, darling," he said, grateful that she was back.

Her face was white. She must have heard already.

And only then did he focus on her outstretched hand, in it the missing document ready to be replaced in the safe before her father returned.

CHAPTER 29

They did not talk about the classified document for a long time.

"Your mother is dead," were his first words.

Then she cried and called Fenn to explain why she would not be back that day, and she and her father sat together for several hours, talking in short bursts of conversation, mainly, though, just being silent.

As the evening progressed, she became solicitous.

"You must eat. Something. It won't help if you're ill."

"We'll both eat."

It was a comfort to do something. She made sandwiches, he uncorked a bottle of wine. The fear of being discovered with the document had been submerged by genuine and awful grief —and guilt. She should have visited her mother more often. How could she explain that she could not bear to see illness and suffering, even in someone she deeply loved?

Her father was grieved more than she would have thought possible. She'd known he had loved Pip, but she had thought he must have become at least partly reconciled to her not being with him, not sharing his life.

The telephone rang. It was the lawyer Banks retained in Oxford. She heard a brief conversation about the inquest and the funeral. The inquest would open the following morning. The body would then be released for cremation and the simple service Banks wanted. The problem was that Banks wanted the funeral virtually immediately.

"Tomorrow," he repeated flatly three times. He was not prepared to argue.

Jennifer placed the sandwiches on a small table, poured wine.

"Then get them to stay open longer. Pay overtime—anything —but tomorrow."

He replaced the receiver without saying goodbye. "Sorry," he said to her. "I want it over. You'll come?"

She was surprised he felt he had to ask. "Of course."

The telephone rang again. Banks's voice this time was calmer, grateful. "Thank you. I *knew* you could do it. Four o'clock."

He took one of the sandwiches. "You heard that? Four o'clock."

She nodded.

He walked to the window, eating as he went, and gazed out at the moonless sky.

"Why did you have that paper?" he asked.

He had to know, no matter what his grief, no matter how great Jennifer's sorrow.

"Can't it wait until afterward?"

"Until after the funeral?"

"Yes."

He turned, walked over and reached out to take both her hands.

"No," he said, "you must tell me now. You know you must."

When, a long time later, she had finished, all he could say was, "And you couldn't tell me."

Long after she had gone to bed, heavily drugged with sleeping tablets, he sat in his favorite leather chair, retelling himself the story she had detailed.

He made two telephone calls that night and a third early the following morning.

The first was to the Thames Valley Police to ask whether Inspector Noakes was on duty. He was not surprised to find there was no one of that name. The policeman had obviously used an assumed name.

The second was to the small firm of private investigators his lawyers had used for years to keep watch on Jennifer's lovers on his instructions. They had one great virtue: They were totally discreet.

Scott, the senior partner, was in bed and was surly until he realized the caller's identity.

Banks gave the date and place of the hit-and-run accident. He wanted details as soon as possible, he said. The private detective was pleasingly matter of fact.

The third call, in the morning, was to make an appointment with the Security Service man he had met when first being investigated for access to classified material. He was pleased to find that the man was still with the department.

That done, he showered and changed. He had had no sleep. He did not need any.

Even as funerals go, it was a particularly depressing one. By insisting on simplicity so as not to be false either to Pip or himself, Banks had succeeded only in looking unfeeling.

A resentful crematorium employee stood by the coffin and mouthed the minimum number of words. The funeral director stared stonily into the distance, as though he was in the presence of someone who was spitting on the dead. The staff from the Cotswold house obviously resented the lack of any display of grief or affection.

Banks had even insisted that there should be no flowers. He neither noticed, nor cared. He had withdrawn into himself. He was thinking of another funeral—the one at which he had met Fenn. A fearsome thought was growing. He hoped he was wrong.

Back in London, he dropped Jennifer at his house and drove on to his appointment with the Security Service. Parsons, who was chauffeuring him, noted that Banks suddenly did look like an old man. True to the cliché, he had aged twenty years in two days.

The man from the Security Service was polite and just subservient enough to convey that he knew exactly who Banks was.

Banks found it difficult. "There's a young man," he said finally. "He appeared almost from nowhere some weeks ago. He has been cultivating my daughter, calling at my house. I'm a little worried that he might have motives that concern your field."

"You mean you think he's after something?"

"I don't know. It would be nice to be reassured."

The man pulled over a pad. "All right," he said briskly. "Let's check, shall we? His name?"

And Banks began to give details.

The telephone rang at regular intervals, but Jennifer did not answer. She suspected it was Fenn and she did not know what to say to him. Like her father, she had retreated into herself.

At the other end of the telephone, Fenn worried and wondered whether to call Mallahide. He finally decided against it. Jennifer was mourning the loss of her mother. There was nothing anyone could do about that. To call Mallahide would simply tempt the man to reinvolve him in something. Better let it all lie.

She would contact him soon. In the meantime he contented himself with drinking too much and writing long, warm, guilty letters to Gemma.

The replies all seemed to come together.

There was no Noakes. Not even anyone who answered that description who could have been masquerading under that name.

There had been no hit-and-run death in that area on the night mentioned.

And Fenn was indeed a suspect figure.

It had taken long discussions within MI5 before it had been decided to admit this fact. Then Hollen had concluded there were advantages in doing so. When they came to blackmail Banks into resigning by revealing Jennifer's treachery, this would reinforce the story.

It was the truth about Fenn that hit Banks hardest, even though he had been half-prepared for it from the previous day. Sitting in his leather chair, trying consciously to get drunk for the first time in his adult life, he wondered how much the other had learned. Fenn had had everything working for him—first Banks's friendship and the invitation to work in the house, then Jennifer's devotion.

Banks knew they had raided the safe. But what else? Did Fenn and his masters know about the Saturday meetings, the handovers? He thought not. But *if* Fenn had stumbled on something. . . . How long then before his contacts ended up in front of firing squads or in concentration camps or died in torture chambers?

Finally the drink worked, but only for three hours, and then he awoke, knowing that he would not sleep again that night. He lay and waited for dawn, and thought.

Pip's death.

Jennifer's betrayal.

Fenn's treachery.

At three in the morning, that time when the body is at its lowest point, Banks finally got up, made his way to the study, and searched in the corner of the safe for the small pill box.

He took it out, opened it, and extracted the white tablet from the cotton wrapping.

His wartime L-pill—cyanide, something he had kept for over thirty-five years, always determined to use it if he was ever stricken by an incurable disease.

CHAPTER 30

It was time, Godwin concluded reluctantly as he shaved, to enlist the support of the Security Service. It was the most useful thing he could do to prepare for Banks's reinvolvement.

Godwin had spoken to Banks on the day of Pip's death. He had respected the other's wish that no one attend the funeral, but he had written later making it clear he was only a telephone call away when Banks wanted to talk, virtually no matter what his commitments.

Apart from that note, however, Godwin had left him alone, as the other obviously desired. He would have to approach him soon—the forthcoming conference and the preliminary work made that imperative—but it could wait two or three more days . . . better to give Banks a chance to withdraw from his lone mourning at his own pace.

On one thing Godwin had no doubt—that Banks would want to continue. The work meant too much to him. He would probably welcome it more than ever—therapy in his grief. There was much to do, not least on the special assignment which Banks had handled so delicately and so well. More time would have to be devoted to that.

And that was where he needed outside help. A chance, he thought as he walked to the telephone, for Hollen and his department to earn their keep.

Three, perhaps four days more, before Mallahide had said he could return home.

Fenn was finding the waiting almost unbearable. He wanted the time to come so that he could return to Gemma. At the same time, he feared it might arrive before he saw Jennifer again. He felt totally and frighteningly alone. He was now without Banks, Jennifer, Mallahide or the colonel. He could ring Mallahide, but to say what? That the waiting was tearing his nerves to shreds?

He pulled on his coat and left the flat. Walking, surrounded by people, he felt better. The loneliness of the apartment made it worse. On impulse, he stopped at a telephone box and dialed Jennifer's number. There was no answer. Should he call Banks, ask if she was there?

He decided against it. He would try later.

Banks was still staring down at the pill when Parsons entered the room to ask if he was ready to take breakfast.

The butler saw the tablet and was immediately solicitous. "You have a headache, sir?"

He was surprised when Banks began to laugh. "Something like that," said Banks. He placed the cyanide pill carefully back into its box.

He realized Parsons was still waiting.

"Breakfast," he said. "Ah yes, breakfast." He should eat. There was a lot to do, all of it necessary, all of it unpleasant.

"I think we'll put the yogurt back in the refrigerator this morning," he said. "I'll have eggs, lots of them. Scrambled."

Before Parsons had reached the door, Banks had begun to list mentally everything he had to do.

*　　*　　*

Knowing the Prime Minister's phobia about time, Hollen erred so much on the side of caution that he had to ask his driver to make another circuit of Whitehall so that he should not be too early.

He was nervous. Godwin rarely made direct contact with his intelligence chiefs, preferring to work through Chambers or one of his ministers. This time not only did Godwin want to see him personally, but he had insisted upon doing so at very short notice. Hollen could not know that this was due more to a canceled appointment of Godwin's than to the urgency of the matter.

Hollen checked his watch: 11:15, fifteen minutes before the scheduled time. Just right. He tapped on the glass partition, ordered the driver to head back toward Downing Street.

The worry went beyond that. There was no indication as to the point of the summons. Perhaps—and he hoped this was so—Godwin simply wanted to discuss his retirement, perhaps sound him out on possible successors.

The car stopped outside Number-10. He was such a rare visitor that the policeman on duty had to look carefully and dig deep into his memory before saluting.

Even though Hollen was still a few minutes early, Godwin was ready for him. Hollen was swept upstairs and ushered into the study. It was some months since he had last seen the Prime Minister and he was impressed. Godwin still looked as he had on that previous occasion. It was noteworthy and surprising because the stresses of leadership normally aged a man so quickly —the reason why so many of the world's statesmen could hardly have survived without their doctors and the drugs they dispensed.

"You'll take coffee?" Godwin was behind his desk, the coffee pot on a tray in front of him. He already had his own cup.

"Please, Prime Minister."

Godwin poured. "Milk? Sugar?"

Hollen signified agreement to both, and wondered whether Godwin's solicitousness might not be the prelude to bad news— the clasp of affection before the knife thrust.

He sipped the coffee. Godwin picked up his own cup and saucer and carried them to the window.

"It's worth being Prime Minister just for the view," he said.

Hollen obliged with the nervous laugh that was expected of him. Godwin was notoriously short of small talk. *That* had been it.

Godwin became brisk. "I need your help," he said. "To you it will be a routine matter. To me, to the government, it will be of vast importance."

Hollen knew he should have reacted, but he sat riveted by the relief. It wasn't anything to be feared. The Prime Minister wanted his help!

Godwin poured himself more coffee and drank, still standing, the cup held in his hand like a glass at a cocktail party.

"What I'm going to tell you," he continued, "is highly secret—no need to ask you to keep it confidential, of course." He attempted a laugh, and Hollen smiled dutifully. Godwin had his full attention again.

"Some time ago when I was Minister of Defence in our previous administration, I had the opportunity—with, I should add, the blessing of the then Prime Minister—to establish some highly delicate but potentially worthwhile talks with some people in the Kremlin who shared our fears about the madness of the arms race.

"Just how contact began isn't important. What matters is that it *had* to be us—the Americans, even then, and God knows it's worse now, were so besotted by the Chinese that even the most reasonable Russians wouldn't trust them."

Godwin put down his cup. Hollen realized that the man had not prefaced any of his remarks with any sort of apology for dealing with Soviet politicians—the reason was obvious: He did not need to. His loathing for the system was too great, too well-known. He took it for granted that his listener would realize that his actions were pragmatic.

"That contact," Godwin continued, "has progressed over the years—less, obviously, while we were out of office. Nothing sensitive in the way of information, no secrets, have been passed on, although the meetings and the contact themselves have been both those. But certain accommodations have been made, certain points agreed.

"Will they mean anything?" He spread his hands. "We can only wait. Time will tell. We understand each other much better. They—those who have talked with us—have to sell to their masters, of course. We, if anything useful is to emerge, need to sell to *our* paymasters—the Americans."

Godwin lifted the coffee pot. A trickle emerged. Not enough to make it worthwhile raising the cup.

"Forgive the lecture," he said. "It's by way of background. The discussions, such as they have been, have proved difficult to arrange—I suspect I hardly need tell you that. Much of the time we have had to confine ourselves to messages through third parties. Fortunately my armaments adviser, Sir Joseph Banks, has proved himself very adaptable—a real cloak-and-dagger operator whom I'm certain your department would appreciate."

Hollen fidgeted with his empty cup. He was becoming nervous again.

"Yes," Godwin went on, "he's taken a leaf out of your book—meetings on the way back to London from conferences, messages passed through a friend . . . all that kind of thing."

He obviously found it amusing and he watched carefully for Hollen's reaction. Seeing none, he continued. "But that's no longer enough. Before the new Vienna talks we need some more detailed discussions, and that means opportunity and time. In safety."

He walked around the desk and took Hollen's cup from his hands.

"What I would like from you," he said, "is somewhere that Sir Joseph and our contacts can meet. Somewhere safe, somewhere free from prying eyes. And, of course, some way of spiriting Sir Joseph there—and perhaps even me—without the risk of being followed."

Hollen was glad he no longer had the cup in his hands. He would have dropped it. His fingers were trembling with shock.

It was late morning and Fenn had finally succumbed to his desire to talk to Jennifer even if it meant calling Banks's number.

If Banks answered, he would hang up. By luck, it was Jennifer who came to the telephone. The conversation, though, was brief. She was obviously still in a state of shock.

She walked back to the drawing room. Her father looked up at her questioningly.

"It was James," she volunteered. "He wanted to know how we were coping, whether there was anything he could do."

"You're meeting him?" He hoped that Fenn was not coming to the house.

"No. I don't want to see anyone. Not yet."

Banks had held back from what he knew had to be done. Now, he realized, he could delay no longer.

He fetched brandy and poured two glasses. Jennifer watched, bemused, but even though she did not feel like a drink, she took one.

"Jennifer," he said at last. "There's something I have to tell you, and I don't know how."

Her face remained impassive as he recounted the story—of how Fenn had ingratiated himself, of how the road death was a fake, of how the blackmail had been planned.

When he finished, he expected her to break down, to cry, but she continued staring ahead, saying nothing. He moved to touch her, but she stood for a moment and then started in the direction of her own apartment. Banks began to follow but stopped. It was a time for her to be alone with her thoughts.

Minutes later he decided he must proceed to the second part of what had to be done. He began dialing Godwin's private number.

The screams interrupted him. He ran toward the door into

Jennifer's flat as quickly as he could. Nevertheless Parsons was there first.

Blood was running down Jennifer's face where she had torn her flesh with her own nails. She was staring ahead, eyes unblinking, and her mouth was open with one continuous high-pitched scream.

Parsons led her to a chair and she became silent. It was Parsons who suggested the clinic. Banks nodded his agreement. It was a relief when the ambulance arrived and the doctor led her away.

"No more action," said Hollen. "Nothing more unless I say so."

Brighouse stared at him, stunned. Had the man gone mad?

Hollen lifted his head and looked into the other's eyes. He would not go into detail now. He needed to think. But some explanation was necessary.

"We made a mistake," he said. "I'll tell you more later." And then, more weary than angry, "Just call off the dogs."

Godwin was shocked by Banks's appearance. It was not just that he had clearly failed to take his customary care in dressing —the tie was somber, the silk handkerchief missing—but everything about him looked crumpled. It was as if his massive body no longer filled his suit. Even his features seemed somehow shrunken.

Godwin had realized from Banks's voice when he'd telephoned that the matter was personal and urgent, but until now he had not realized how painful it must also be.

He listened without interruption.

Outside, the light began to fade, but the Prime Minister did not even rise to switch on a lamp.

Banks took his time telling his story. It lasted well over half an hour. He did not want to risk leaving out anything. He also insisted on spelling out the main points and implications—the Russians, by raiding his safe, had gotten key documents; through following him, they might have learned about his secret negotiations on behalf of Godwin—though he doubted that.

His major preoccupations now were protecting Jennifer ("Can *you* see what else she could have done?") and, for Godwin, avoiding scandal—publicity would not only destroy Banks, who was doomed politically anyway, but also Godwin and his government.

At the end, he said, "So obviously, I resign. But what else? What more can I do for you?"

Godwin lay back in his chair, closed his eyes and rubbed his face. It was hard to realize how much everything had changed; how the last hour had taken his world and turned much of it upside down.

He picked up a paper knife and began tapping the desk. It was a hard sentence to speak. "The talks—the unofficial ones—can't go ahead," he said. "It's too dangerous." Then, almost to himself he added, "And they could have achieved so much."

He snapped his eyes back on to Banks's face.

"I'll have to accept your resignation, Joseph," he said. "I'd like to blame it on ill health."

Banks nodded.

"And your daughter?"

Banks waited.

"Can we keep her in her clinic for a while, for her own good? I see no point in letting this become any less secret than it is now."

Again, Banks agreed.

Godwin threw down the knife. It bounced on the desk and fell to the floor: a rare outburst of anger. Almost immediately, Godwin pulled himself together. He walked around the desk and stood in front of Banks. "Don't torment yourself, Joseph," he said. "It wasn't your fault."

His sadness was deep. He had to keep command. It was, though he had no time to dwell on it, a strange reversal of roles.

Banks had for so long nursed, helped, protected him. Now all the decisions were his own.

He went back to his desk. "And that leaves the man Fenn," he said. "The number one problem."

He picked up the telephone and for the second time that day asked to be connected with Sir Robert Hollen.

CHAPTER 31

Hollen had been back from his second meeting of the day with the Prime Minister for just over half an hour.

It was 7:05 and he was waiting for Brighouse to answer his summons to return to the office.

He was also waiting for Sir Peter Chambers to return his call. He needed to tell him what had happened and to seek his advice and reassurance. The Secretary to the Cabinet, however, was deep in discussion with his French counterpart who was visiting London and he was taking no calls.

It still seemed unreal. He fetched a new bottle of sherry from the cupboard, broke the seal and poured a glass. It was his third since returning. It had been hard not to interrupt the Prime Minister, to ask questions. Two blows in one day. First, the explanations for Banks's handovers of material in Curzon Street. Now being asked to deal with a Russian agent—James Fenn!

There had been hints, not instructions. One thing was obvious—and that was the one piece of good news. The Prime Minister did not want publicity, not even a trial in a closed court. That gave them some time—if the Prime Minister had wanted Fenn arrested formally!

Without asking, he poured a sherry for Brighouse the moment the man arrived. Then he launched straight into the story. When he finished, he became silent and started drumming the desk with the fingers of his left hand, an annoying habit when under stress, as Brighouse had noted once before.

"The question," he said at last, "is what we do." His gaze prompted Brighouse to make a suggestion.

Brighouse resented it. It was Hollen's decision and both men knew it. Now, thought Brighouse, Hollen was trying to sidestep his responsibilities. God almighty, the man had taken the job. He knew what was involved. He should take command now.

"I should say it's obvious," he said. "Unfortunate but obvious."

Hollen hunched over the desk; his face was strained.

"I suppose you're right," he said. "Who? Mallahide?"

"He'd do it well . . . and he'd have no problems getting close to Fenn." A thought struck him. "Fenn doesn't know anything?"

"No. Just the P.M., Banks, you and me . . . and the girl, of course, but she's in a clinic under sedation. I've had the police put a guard on her door."

Brighouse finished his drink and waited to be dismissed. "You want me to arrange it?" Again, it was something Hollen should have handled. If you had to order a man's execution, at least have the guts to do so yourself. But once more Hollen refused to be decisive. Brighouse knew what it was: ten months to retirement. The man had already opted out.

He stood, anxious to be gone.

Halfway to the door, the thought suddenly came to him. "Banks's mission," he said, referring back to their earlier conversation, "when did it really get under way again?"

"I got the impression some contacts went on all the time, but more regular ones—around April, I gather, when it became pretty obvious an election was coming."

"And we were treated to a ringside seat at Suslov's interrogation in—when? May?"

Hollen nodded. He had already thought it all through.

"We've been set up, Andrew," he said. "Set up by our so-called friends."

Brighouse left without speaking. What was there to say? It was suddenly obvious. The Americans had somehow found out about Godwin's private talks with the Soviet doves, and had not liked it.

Their earlier suspicions of Godwin's negotiator, Banks, would have added to the disquiet.

Hence Suslov and all that had happened since.

Their pressures had not been to destroy a traitor. They had been to destroy Anglo-Soviet talks which they disliked and distrusted. Brighouse could understand. He and his MI5 colleagues—like them—did not believe in Kremlin "doves." Anyone who did was a naive fool, falling for a Soviet trick. But *that* was not the point now.

He unlocked his office and telephoned Mallahide. At least, he told himself with grim humor, Mallahide would enjoy the situation.

The sedatives had not worked.

Lying in the private room at the clinic, Jennifer looked peaceful enough, but her mind was still reeling.

There was some relief in knowing that she had not killed a man, but that was outweighed by the realization that she had ruined her father's life . . . and that Fenn had betrayed her.

At first that had been hard to accept. She had been set up from the very start. She herself had had many lovers, had left them—but had never done what Fenn had done.

She remembered his voice on that last telephone call. God, how could he even act like that! Even when her mother was dead, he had continued with his "work."

Jennifer slid gently out of bed and checked that her clothes were in the wardrobe. She listened at the door and heard the scrape of a chair. The policewoman was still there.

Jennifer dressed quickly and checked the telephone directory. No one had thought to disconnect the telephone—the room, after all, was a private, expensive one and merited such a facility. Jennifer lifted the receiver and made a call. The number she dialed was the clinic's second line. She asked the operator for the third floor—her floor.

A breathless nurse answered the telephone.

Jennifer made her voice brisk and officious.

"Scotland Yard. There's a policewoman outside Room 9. We must speak to her urgently. Would you fetch her to the telephone? Straight away, please."

The nurse did not argue. Jennifer heard the receiver being put down.

She climbed into bed, pulled the covers high and closed her eyes, feigning sleep. Moments later she heard the hurried conversation outside. Then the door was opened as the policewoman checked what Jennifer was doing.

Less than a minute later Jennifer was out of her room and halfway down the emergency exit. She knew the clinic. She had been there many times before.

They met outside the Notting Hill station.

Mallahide realized there must be an emergency but knew no more. Nevertheless nothing was said until the two men had descended underground and boarded a train. The compartment was almost empty. It was too late for people to be going out for the evening, too early for them to be returning home.

The two men stood at one end. No one was within hearing distance.

Brighouse hated conducting this briefing. It was something he had only had to do once before—and even though intelligence was often necessarily a dirty game in which people were sometimes destroyed or killed, actually ordering someone's murder coldly and dispassionately was not easy.

He outlined the situation. Mallahide had to strain not to miss any of the words above the clatter of the train. Whenever it stopped at the station, Brighouse became silent in case any passengers passed near. When he had finished, Mallahide asked, "And Fenn?"

"That's our problem now." He looked deep into Mallahide's eyes. "Yours specifically, unless you have qualms, having worked with him."

Mallahide shook his head. "No. No. It's necessary."

Although he was involved, Brighouse winced at the word. "Necessary." How many times in man's history had that word been used to justify such actions?

"You'll leave it to me?"

"Within reason, but there are guidelines."

Mallahide listened attentively while Brighouse listed them: It was not to happen in this country; it should either look like an accident or the body should not be found; backup facilities could be provided if necessary, but it was better if Mallahide could cope alone.

Mallahide nodded. All were obvious and sensible.

"Two questions," he said. "Does Fenn suspect anything, and is there a time limit?"

Brighouse answered the second question first. "No time limit, within reason, of course. A *sound* job is the first priority." He was reducing it to basics—the only way to handle it. Forget the flesh and blood.

"As for the other, no, he shouldn't suspect. He called the girl earlier, but nothing was said." Brighouse had checked the tape; Banks's telephone was still being tapped.

"And Banks's resignation? Fenn won't hear it on the radio before I reach him?"

"I gather it's been agreed that there's no rush. It will be a day or two. Time to prepare a neat job."

The train stopped at Embankment Station and a crowd of people got in and milled around Brighouse and Mallahide.

Mallahide caught Brighouse's eye to see whether they should

move. Brighouse shrugged. He had nothing more to say. They remained silent until Mallahide left the train by himself at Notting Hill Gate. Brighouse was glad to be alone.

Mallahide needed little time to prepare.

The overnight bag with the false passport—Donald Wenner-ham, international property consultant—was kept permanently packed and ready. The first priority was to get Fenn out of the country in case the Prime Minister changed his mind and or-dered Fenn's arrest.

Mallahide would have to travel with him—better not to use his own name, although he had already decided that the other would vanish without trace.

He was on his way less than a half hour after leaving Brig-house.

Chambers called Hollen on a safe line soon after nine-thirty. Hollen, still at his desk, had finally insisted that a priority message be passed to the Cabinet Secretary. He took the return call with a mixture of fear and relief.

Halfway through his brief summing up, he realized he was having to speak slowly in order not to slur his words: he was glad that the scrambler and the way it gave voices a metallic ring would help hide the fact he was half-drunk.

Chambers listened without comment until the MI5 man had finished. Then he asked, "And you are dealing with this man Fenn now?"

"Yes."

There was silence for several seconds and sweat began to break on Hollen's forehead.

At the other end of the line Chambers was silently cursing the Prime Minister for not telling him about Banks's mission—unprecedented behavior! He was also listing mentally everyone who knew anything about the operation to deal with Banks—

from his fellow department heads, whom he could deal with, to the MI5 men who had handled it. And, of course, not least, Hollen himself.

When he spoke finally, his voice was dismissive and held no comfort for Hollen. "I'll want to see you in the morning. At my flat. Say seven. You should know more then."

He put down the receiver without saying "Goodnight."

Hollen stared into space for a long time, and then made his way to the cupboard to fetch another drink.

Jennifer arrived at the flat just before ten.

Fenn was sprawled on the sofa, watching television and concentrating on getting quietly drunk. His relief when he opened the door and saw her was intense. He realized he had wanted to be with her, to hold her, more than anyone else in the world.

"Jen, my love," he said, "I've been so worried." He opened his arms to take her inside.

She did not move. Her face confused him. The expression was . . . he could not quite be sure. Then there was no mistaking it. Pure hate. She moved closer and spat full in his face.

"You shit," she hissed. "You unimaginable shit. I think I loved you and you used me and you've destroyed him."

He wrestled with her as she tried to claw his face. Her weight carried him into the hallway and they both fell. Suddenly she was no longer struggling, but was sobbing, hunched on the floor. He made the mistake of trying to help her to her feet.

"Don't touch me, you bastard." But she stood and walked into the living room.

"What is it?" He already knew, but he had to pretend.

"Oh, you lousy bastard. Making me think I'd killed someone . . . torturing me . . . just to get to him." The sobs drowned the rest of the words. Then her face twisted into an obscene grin. "I came here wanting to kill you, but I'll let them get you. They'll put you away for life."

She *had* talked.

Fenn checked the window. A number of people outside, but no one who looked as though he were watching the block.

Jennifer laughed. "Go on, check. They'll be here soon."

Fenn went into the bedroom and feverishly threw a few belongings into a small case. He turned. She was at the door. As he walked toward her, carrying the case, she reached for him again. He pushed her aside and she fell huddled on the floor, not hurt, but spent.

He looked down, listened to the sobs, wanted to touch her, to explain. But what could he say? Everything she thought was true.

He left by the fire escape, the only precaution he could take. There was a chance the police were already watching—waiting instead of arresting him in the hope he would lead them to the others. The girl had thwarted that.

On the street he decided he had to act quickly. No time for finesse. It was pointless trying to go to ground in Britain. Apart from his controllers, he had no contacts who would help or hide him.

He found a telephone box and tried Mallahide's number. There was no reply. He checked the time. 10:21.

Speed was his only hope. Before leaving the telephone box, he checked his wallet. It still contained over four hundred pounds—money that Mallahide had given him and which had remained unspent. At least that was not a problem.

He was lucky—finding a cab took less than five minutes. The roads were quiet and he was at the airport soon after eleven. Walking into the terminal building, he was nervous. The alarm might be out. But he knew he had to take the chance. It was folly to remain here.

He checked the departure board. There was a flight to Paris at midnight and, yes, said the girl, there was a seat.

He sweated until he was on board and the plane was airborne. Even then his mind kept echoing with the shock of what had happened.

The stewardess's voice pulled him back to the present. He looked out of the window. The lights of Charles de Gaulle

Airport twinkled below. Suddenly he felt better; he thought he had made it.

Mallahide found the girl still lying on the floor when he let himself into the flat. He was surprised to find anyone. His ring at the doorbell had not been answered.

It took a half hour to hear her story, arrange for an ambulance to get her back to the clinic—or, as he suggested, a more secure one—and to get Brighouse's decision that they should not put out a general alert on Fenn.

It was not a safe line, but they had to talk.

"What happens if he tries to get out and gets stopped?" said Brighouse at the other end of the line. "What I mean is, what in the Lord's name do we do with him then? The P.M. wants him questioned."

Mallahide endured the long silence.

"No," said Brighouse. "Let him go. We won't lose him. We know where he'll go. It's like turning loose a homing pigeon."

CHAPTER 32

Fenn took a room in a dingy hotel near the Terminus-Nord, left early and caught a train to Brussels.

The journey gave him time to think. British counterintelligence would probably track him on to the Paris flight if they hadn't done so already—he had traveled on his own passport. If they enlisted the aid of the French, it would be only a matter of time before they located the hotel at which he had stayed.

The best he could hope for was to muddy their search by moving on before making for home. He felt sure he would be safe from the British on Gozo—the Maltese authorities would not help them. If—and he thought this was an unlikely possibility—they tried to take him against his will, he could hardly be better placed to resist than on his home ground.

And, in any event, where else was there for him to run, even if Gemma and his daughters had not drawn him?

From Brussels he flew to Frankfurt and there he stayed two nights at an airport hotel. There was, he had realized, another problem. His Soviet masters.

As far as they were concerned, the operation had been aborted. Banks was no longer available as a target. They would have to accept the situation. But what would they do about him? Leave him alone? They would know he was a target for MI5, the only man the British could identify on Banks's and Jennifer's evidence. And he, of course, was the one lead who could identify the others if he was questioned.

They might, he concluded, be just as anxious to see him . . . and their aim would not be to question him like the British but, possibly, to silence him.

He had to protect against that.

In Frankfurt he bought a secondhand portable typewriter, a box of paper and carbons. It took the whole of a day and two nights before he was satisfied with what he had written.

Then he sealed the parcels and posted them.

"Why Paris?" asked Hollen.

"Availability of flights," said Brighouse. "He just wanted to get out as fast as he could."

"No sign of where he went after the hotel?"

"A booking clerk at the railway station thinks he recognizes the face, but can't remember to which destination he booked a ticket. But from the station, probably the Netherlands or Belgium."

"The French will keep looking?"

Brighouse shrugged his shoulders. "I suppose so, but I don't think we need worry. He'll go home soon. He's nowhere else to go. It's just a question of waiting."

Hollen raised his head. He was finding decision-making a strain. All he longed for was retirement and an end to the worries.

Nevertheless, he made an effort.

"You'll send Mallahide to wait?" he asked.

Again, an abdication of responsibility.

"I've already called him," said Brighouse. "He'll be on his way first flight in the morning."

* * *

Mallahide resisted the impulse until well after eleven.

The guns were under the floorboards in the bedroom. They had been hidden there since Ulster because it was expressly forbidden to keep a firearm. If it was considered that you needed one, you signed for it and returned it afterward. But they—the people making the rules—had never been in Northern Ireland . . . or been shot in the face. Besides, guns were ten for a penny there. Children were almost weaned on them.

This time he could have a gun issued to him or arrange to have one waiting for him . . . but he knew precisely the weapon he wanted for the operation.

Mallahide lifted the floorboard. There were two guns, both oiled, and carefully wrapped in toweling and plastic.

One was a .38 Smith and Wesson pistol. Mallahide disregarded that and lifted out the other. It was a North Korean–made 7.65 mm Type 64—a perfect weapon for his purposes. It was one of the two designs produced of the model—the one for use with a silencer.

He unwrapped it, screwed the silencer on and off and checked the seven-round magazines. Then very carefully he began to clean the gun, even though it had been so well stored.

His movements as he started to shine the barrel became quicker and quicker.

A series of words spun through his mind and became a mad refrain.

"Hit the bastards, hit the bastards, hit the bastards. . . ."

Like they had hit him.

CHAPTER 33

"He's returned," reported Brighouse three days after Fenn had last been traced, boarding a Brussels-Frankfurt flight.

"And Mallahide's there?"

"Yes."

"Then that's it." Hollen's voice was flat. He had not told Brighouse, but he was planning to ask the Prime Minister if he could retire early. He doubted the request would be opposed. Chambers had hinted gently that it might be the best action when the two men had talked. Operation cover-up was under way! Nothing would be rushed in case that aroused suspicions, but Hollen could smell it in the Whitehall air. He had bumped into one of the department heads who had been at that fateful meeting at Chambers's home—and there had been no mistaking the look he received. Crimpton, no doubt wanting to save his own skin, had already passed up a meeting. Once Fenn was dealt with and that end of things tidied, Hollen imagined he would be asked to reassign some of his staff. Or would that be left to his successor?

Brighouse's voice brought him back to the immediate problem.

"You're in contact?" Hollen asked.

"Yes, if need be. But I'll stay out of it if I can. Better he has time to do a good job."

Just as Brighouse had done days before, Hollen winced. A good job!

Mallahide found the ideal site on his second day in Malta—an area of wild ground, high above the sea, rarely visited. The kind of place where someone could vanish without trace.

Mallahide stared down at the sea as it swirled against the rocks hundreds of feet below. He picked up a stone and dropped it. The noise of the sea was too great, the distance too far, to hear it fall.

Yes, he thought, the perfect place. All he had to do was wait for Fenn's return to the island—and lure him here.

The answer to that second problem came to him over lunch, an hour after the relayed message that told him Fenn had returned.

Fenn and Gemma were nervous with each other for the first days after Fenn's unexpected return.

It was obvious from the way he looked and behaved—as though shocked—that something had happened. But he volunteered nothing and she forced herself not to ask.

Gradually they eased together again. Laughter became spontaneous, words could be spoken without having to consider them carefully first. The girls helped. Their joy at Fenn's return could not have been greater or more obvious. And his open feelings about the island helped. He felt as much in love with it as the first time they had arrived to live. Gemma noted it, and it was the most reassuring thing of·all. He wanted to be back, not just with her and the girls, but the way they had been.

Their bank account was swollen by the three thousand pounds that had been paid since Fenn had been in England. They made plans to finish the rebuilding and conversion work on the house.

By unspoken and mutual consent they did not try to make love. Both knew they had to work up to it, gently—a touch today, holding hands tomorrow, a hug, a kiss.

On the third night home Fenn awoke as dawn was lightening the room. Gemma was already awake, propped up.

"Can't you sleep?"

"Just thinking."

"Worries?" Was she wondering about London? Not making love had not been the only unspoken decision—there were no questions being asked about the previous weeks . . . yet.

"No . . . just thinking how nice it is."

And both of them knew that was the moment.

Afterward, they both cried, and she said, "We're fools. Oh, what fools."

Later in the day, as they sat on the rocks and watched the girls swim, he told her some of the story. Not details, just how he had been blackmailed from a long way back into getting close to a man to obtain information.

She took it well. The spying did not worry her very much. He had, she could persuade herself, done it to protect his family. The family was greater than the country. But she had to ask about the girl. "Was *she* part of it?"

"A way in."

"But she became more?"

He shrugged. It hurt.

Gemma reached for his hand and squeezed. "I won't ask any more."

The girls began yelling for them to join them in the sea. Fenn stood, took Gemma's hand and helped her to her feet.

Then, like children themselves, they ran laughing, hand in hand, to the water.

Mallahide found the man he wanted in one of the dockside bars.

The bar was dark, set back into the rock, a man-made cave. He was the third man Mallahide had singled out that day. Like the two others, whom Mallahide had discounted after striking up conversations, he looked Slavic and he looked villainous.

Mallahide moved from his corner seat to a bar stool and ordered another drink. "Thirsty work," he said.

The sailor turned, looked. Mallahide did not look like a man who wanted conversation. Someone wanting something carried? Discreetly?

"It is if you're sailing tonight."

Mallahide ordered two drinks and carried them to a booth. The sailor joined him moments later. The two men sparred for a while. Then Mallahide, satisfied, said, "I need someone to carry a message."

The sailor toyed with his empty glass and Mallahide pretended not to notice.

"That's all?"

"That's all. But I need someone who suffers an instant memory loss once it's done."

"How much?"

"Fifty. You'll be free by late afternoon."

"There's other things I need to do before I sail." He leered.

"You'll have time for that too. A hundred. No more. No bargaining."

He took the two glasses to the bar, returned with them full. "Well?"

"You've got a deal."

Mallahide watched the school exit from the other side of the street, just as he had for the previous three days.

It had been easy to pick out the girl from the copies of the photographs he had made after "borrowing" Fenn's wallet in London.

The timing was important.

The children who took the school bus began to gather in groups on the pavement. Mallahide picked her out, checked his watch. Good. Twenty minutes to get to the ferry and away. Just in case anything went wrong.

"The little girl in green, just to the right of that white post. See her?"

"The one just scratching her nose? Yes, I see her."

Mallahide handed the sailor an envelope.

"Just stroll over slowly. Don't frighten anyone. Hand the girl the envelope and say 'That's for your daddy.' Then walk away. Easy. That's all."

"You didn't tell me there was a kid."

Mallahide's expression did not change, but the voice was enough. "You back out now," he said, "and you'll float out of here. Face down."

The sailor took the envelope.

Mallahide checked his watch again. "Move now," he said. "Then straight back to the car. You'll be in time for the other, don't worry."

The bait was being laid.

"Daddy!" She bounded through the door, arms outstretched, so eager to tell him that the words ran together and were impossible to understand.

Fenn lifted her. "Easy now, easy," he said to Kate. "Tell me slowly."

"Careful," she said. "You'll bend it."

"Bend what?" He put her down and only then did he realize she was holding a letter.

"What is it? From school? For me?"

"A funny-looking man gave it to me outside school and said it was for you."

Gemma, who had been watching, amused, came over, suddenly concerned.

"What is it?"

Fenn tore open the envelope and read the single sheet of paper.

"Just a silly joke," he said. "Hey, you go and see what I've done in your playroom."

Kate bounded from the room.

Gemma took the message from his hand.

The message was short. In block letters it read, "How vulnerable are the children."

They decided against calling the police. There would be too many questions.

Carefully, trying hard not to alarm her, Fenn got a description of sorts from the girl. The blessing was that though the man obviously looked fearsome, the girl had not been frightened. Life on the island had isolated Kate from many of the fears of children in cities and other countries.

Fenn checked hotels by telephone. There was no one who answered the description.

He could do no more without leaving the house—something he would not do. He took unaccustomed care to lock doors and windows.

"Is there nothing else we can do?" said Gemma as he returned.

Fenn poured himself a drink and slumped down in a chair. He did not answer. He was thinking. Who was it? Who was behind it? The man who had given Kate the envelope was simply a messenger but for whom? The British—planning to try to frighten him into returning to England? It was possible. More likely, though, the Russians. The approach, he thought, had all the sadistic touches of Mallahide.

CHAPTER 34

On the orders of the Home Secretary, the Post Office had been intercepting Frederick Donovan's office and home mail for over a year.

The interception had been ordered after Donovan had written a particularly sensational and politically embarrassing story. It had detailed how British intelligence was feeding South Africa with information on their black neighbors. Attempts to stop the story after the newspaper's first edition had failed. So had later efforts to discredit the defense correspondent.

The interception had followed. That had had no greater success. Long before it began, Donovan had assumed that his post and telephone might be monitored. He had advised informants that they should hand over any sensitive material personally—or, if they had to post it, they should mail it to one of his friends or colleagues.

The "confession" was, therefore, an unexpected prize for Post Office Investigation who had not previously seen anything remotely exciting.

At first there was confusion over what to do with it. Finally it reached MI5 and, though it was a Saturday, Hollen himself, who was called back to his office.

He, in turn, summoned Brighouse.

Brighouse read it in Hollen's office. At the end, he said, "I suppose we might have expected this. The man's not a total fool."

Hollen took a cardboard box from his desk and handed it to Brighouse. It contained a carbon copy of the same manuscript.

"This only reached me an hour ago," he said. "After I was called back to the office. It was sent to the safe house in Charing Cross Road."

Brighouse said what Hollen was thinking. "He's trying to protect himself, saying that if anything happens to him. . . ."

"He couldn't know the one to Donovan would be intercepted."

"No. That's a bonus." It had been accompanied by a letter asking for the manuscript, unopened, to be locked away and opened only if anything happened to Fenn.

"But he meant his Soviet masters to receive the other one— a warning that it would be unwise to harm him."

"We may have all the copies."

"We may. The lab says there are carbon paper smears on the back of the copy. There could be a third. Even a fourth."

Hollen pushed himself to his feet and began pacing the floor. His head ached. So many twists, so many turns. Nearly retirement day, and then all this.

Until then, though, decisions still had to be made. "So," he said aloud, "we have two possible courses of action. We continue as planned and eliminate our friend, risking more copies of his confession surfacing, or we let Fenn live."

Brighouse's contribution to the discussion was as cautious as his chief's. Damn it! This time Hollen was going to have to make the decision. "If we kill him and there are more copies, we ought to bear in mind the next time they may go to people overseas—people we could do nothing about. But if we let Fenn live, we have him hanging over us for years."

Hollen started to bite at the nail of his right thumb: a new nervous habit, Brighouse noted.

"It *would* be cleaner to eliminate him," he said, and for a moment Brighouse thought he had reached a decision. But Hollen followed up with a question. "You know him by now," he said. "What would you say Fenn would do if we simply left him alone?"

Brighouse thought. "It's only guessing . . . but I'd say all he wants is to settle back to a normal life."

"A normal life." Hollen resumed pacing the floor. His letter of resignation was written and in a desk drawer. He had held back from the final step—actually sending it. Now he would do that, as soon as Brighouse had gone.

That helped him make his decision. "The P.M. seems happy to let things drop. Taking Fenn out is too risky. Leave him, let him be." If he was wrong, it would be a long time before anyone knew—and it would be his successor's problem.

"So you would like me to do what?" asked Brighouse.

Make as few ripples as possible.

"Get Mallahide," Hollen said. "Tell him it's off. Tell him to come home."

The only "safe" line was in the office of the High Commission. And because it was Saturday morning, Brighouse had to sweat and fume as the assistant he had called in worked through a series of home numbers to find someone to man it.

He had telephoned Mallahide's hotel but the younger man was not in his room. Nevertheless, the message Brighouse had left would alert him and send him to the High Commission office.

Now all he could do was wait—and curse the laziness of diplomats. They were probably all out in their boats.

Mallahide made the call from a bar.

Fenn took a long time to answer—he had been outside.

"Yes."

Mallahide allowed a silence before speaking.

"You know who this is? You received my message?"

"I received it." So it had been Mallahide.

"You and I should talk. I think you should come and see me."

"Where?"

"On the far side of Mellieha Bay, opposite the town, there's a holiday complex. You know it?"

Fenn did.

"Behind it, the cliffs follow the bay out toward the open sea. There are watchtowers. I'll be in the third one after you leave the road. At four. Are you listening?"

"I'm listening," said Fenn.

Mallahide continued. "Whatever you do, don't do anything silly. And come alone."

He slammed down the instrument. Fenn would come. He had no choice.

And when Fenn vanished? He would probably tell his wife who he was going to see.

But that did not matter. It helped things. Fenn still believed he was a Russian. Let them take the blame.

Fenn put down the telephone and turned to face Gemma.

"The people who made me go to London," he said. "The man I told you about—Mallahide."

"They're not trying to send you away again?"

"No." His voice was firm. "No one will send me anywhere." He flexed his fingers, touched the switch-blade that had been strapped to his wrist since the afternoon Kate had returned with the letter.

Gemma was waiting for him to continue.

"They want to see me later today. On Malta. Alone."

"You'll go?" She knew the answer.

"Yes. I'll go."

Later Mallahide wished he had not gone to the High Commission, had pretended not to receive the message until it was too late.

He might have guessed it would be something like this. The bloody fools. Didn't they know what the world was really like?

"It's off," Brighouse had said. "Come home."

Mallahide had already been tense, angry with the man who had been waiting at the High Commission to escort him to the telephone. He had left Mallahide in no doubt that he resented being brought in on a Saturday.

"Can I ask why?"

There was a pause while Brighouse considered the question. He decided Mallahide deserved an explantion. He told him about the manuscript.

He also made it clear that the decision came from the top— from Hollen himself. Even though Brighouse agreed with it and would have done the same, there was no reason to personally alienate Mallahide—the two men might have to work together again. Let Hollen incur the younger man's anger.

"I could persuade him to tell me whether there are more copies," volunteered Mallahide.

"No!" Brighouse voice had been harsh. "Come home."

Mallahide had had no chance to explain the situation. He tried. "He already knows I'm here. I've made contact. We're due to meet in less than three hours."

There was another long pause as Brighouse had struggled to make a decision. At last he spoke. "All right, keep the appointment. Use it to throw the fear of God into him. Warn him what might happen if he doesn't keep quiet. That can do no harm."

"But," he had added quietly, "don't forget, it's *off*."

Mallahide swept past the diplomat without thanks and walked back to his hotel.

They were sentimental, weak idiots.

Hollen was sealing the envelope containing his resignation when Brighouse reentered his room.

"You reached him?" asked Hollen.

"Yes, just in time." He explained about Mallahide's imminent meeting. "He didn't like it, though—I think he was really looking forward to killing Fenn."

Hollen nodded. His fingers began toying with the envelope. "Yes, he's been very . . . zealous lately." He began to smile. "Would have been funny, wouldn't it, if Fenn had turned the tables on Mallahide?"

He noted Brighouse's shocked expression and his voice became serious. "One day that man is going to cause someone great trouble. Watch him, Andrew."

Brighouse began to say, "Why don't you . . .?" And then his eyes focused on the envelope in Hollen's hand and he knew what it was.

In his hotel room Mallahide sat, watched the clock and downed whiskey with a hand that shook with anger.

That fool Hollen! Thank God the idiot was nearing retirement! Even Brighouse, cautious time-server that he was, obviously thought the decision was crazy—otherwise, he would not have made it so clear who was responsible. Nor would he have agreed so readily to Mallahide keeping his appointment with Fenn. He *knew* that leaving things as they were was not right.

Mallahide put down his glass and opened his bag. The pistol lay there, unwrapped, ready for use. He lifted it out, ran his fingers over it lovingly.

Brighouse knew what had to be done. Brighouse felt like him.

Mallahide reached for a magazine to load the pistol.

He had been given his orders. He would obey them . . . after a fashion. But what if Fenn attacked him? He would have to defend himself, wouldn't he?

Mallahide reached for the silencer.

And he had no doubt at all that that was exactly what would happen.

CHAPTER 3 5

Paul Grima was the archetypal Gozitan: short, barrel-chested, taciturn, slow-moving.

He was a semiretired builder who now let his men and his money work for him. He was also the grandfather of a girl in Gemma's class, an admirer of Fenn's wife and a keen sea fisherman. That was why Gemma was able on a Saturday afternoon to convince him that her husband needed his urgent help and his boat.

At this time of the year the channel was too dangerous for an inexperienced sailor like Fenn. Grima was experienced and he had the ideal boat—a Seaworker 22, fast, with a round bilge displacement, especially designed for offshore work.

As they cast off, the weather was idyllic: clear, blue skies, just the hint of a breeze. Then, out in the channel, the wind stiffened and the sky began to darken. From the distance there was a rumble of thunder.

"How will you get from Marfa?" It was the first time Grima had spoken, apart from the muttered greeting on the dock. He knew Fenn's destination was Mellieha.

"I'll walk," Fenn shouted.

The fact that Fenn would not take a taxi confirmed what Grima had already deduced from Gemma's words and the tone in her voice: There was trouble, and the fewer people who know what was happening the safer.

Grima had anticipated Fenn's problem. He had many building operations currently underway on Malta and all he had had to do was make one telephone call. "You'll find a dark blue Ford station wagon at the foot of the dock—there's a newspaper in the front window. Keys are in the ignition. Take it."

Fenn began to thank him, but Grima turned away, seemingly oblivious to the reply.

The waves began to rise and even under the cockpit Fenn was soon wet with spray.

Grima said nothing else about Fenn's mission until they reached shore. He throttled the engine right back and began his turn, coming to a standstill just a few yards from the dock. The boat drifted in.

"I'll wait for you," said Grima. He did not ask how long Fenn would be. Nothing. Just, "I'll wait."

"It could be some time."

"I'll wait."

Fenn found the car easily. The driver's door was unlocked and he slid inside. The car smelled of cement and there was a pair of overalls on the back seat. The engine started immediately and he began to drive across the point.

The thunder came nearer, but there was no rain. The land he passed through was barren. Occasional windmills pumped up brackish water from below the rock to make possible the growth of a few crops.

Fenn left the car in the parking lot of one of the hotels—it would excite no curiosity there. Few people were about—tourists were enjoying their afternoon siesta or had taken tour buses to other parts of the island.

Within ten minutes of leaving the car, Fenn could have been in a different world. The carefully tended gardens gave way to grass and weeds that ran riot. There were paths of a sort, but he still needed to fight through undergrowth. To his right there were sheer drops to the sea. In the cliffs there were giant gaps, and in the chasms created sea birds and sand martins wheeled.

The air was humid. That and the exertion made Fenn sweat but he did not dare remove his denim jacket. He needed the jacket's sleves to hide the knife attached to his wrist.

Three-forty. The watchtower that Mallahide had specified was in sight, perhaps a further ten minutes' walk away. Fenn found a large stone, sat and looked down at the angry sea.

He imagined, rightly, that he was being watched from the tower, probably through glasses. He made himself look more exhausted than he was. Fenn was still not sure what he would do. He was resigned to letting events dictate his actions, but if it came to a struggle, he wanted the edge this time. Mallahide might be overconfident after their previous encounters. Fenn's exhaustion could reinforce that.

As he pulled himself to his feet, he saw the glint of sun on glass. He had been right.

From thirty yards away he could see inside the doorway into the tower. The stone floor was overgrown with weeds and moss. There was no sign of Mallahide; he had probably retreated into the shadows.

Then Mallahide was in the entrance. He wore a pale gray safari suit, dark glasses. A real tourist. In his hand, though, the barrel resting across his chest, was a pistol. Fenn knew enough of guns to know that it was fitted with a silencer.

Fenn was smiling faintly. He was, Fenn realized, relishing what was happening. He *wanted* a confrontation.

Mallahide gestured with the gun and stepped aside to let Fenn enter the tower. It was about ten feet across and on one side there was a heap of rubble where one of the parapets had collapsed.

"There," directed Mallahide. "Sit!"

Fenn obeyed, taking care to keep his arms free.

"Now stretch your legs out straight." Fenn did so.

"Why don't you ask me what I want?" said Mallahide.

"All right. What do you want?"

"Personally," said Mallahide, smiling even more warmly, "I want to kill you. This would be a good place. A perfect place, I'd say."

Fenn tensed.

Mallahide centered the pistol barrel on Fenn's chest and felt good. He was going to kill him, but not for a few minutes. First, he would goad him. He would act it through. It *would* be self-defense.

"But," continued Mallahide, "those are not my orders. I'm supposed to let you live—to warn you of what will happen if you don't behave. A pity."

Fenn could tell something else, though, from Mallahide's tone. He realized why Mallahide had not insisted on searching him. The man wanted him to attack. He was so confident of his abilities, he was certain he was the one who would triumph.

Mallahide moved so that he was in shadow. Fenn, on the other hand, was held in a beam of light that shone through one of the observation slits.

"You did a rash thing the other day," said Mallahide. "We don't like being blackmailed."

They *had* received the manuscript he had sent to the safe house.

"We also," Mallahide went on, "don't think you realize the length of our arms. We *know* about the copy you sent to the journalist Donovan."

Fenn was still absorbing that shock when Mallahide continued. "And we doubt that you *really* understand what is at stake."

Mallahide smiled.

"Oh yes, we could kill you—and I would like to do that now. I personally would like to put one of these bullets into you. Or perhaps a few—each time in a slightly more vulnerable place." That's it, play with him, make him think he's off the hook.

He paused, widened his smile still more. God, thought Fenn, he really is enjoying it.

"But," Mallahide went on, "that's not really it, is it? If you are *not* a sensible man, many things can and will happen. We have shown you how vulnerable your daughters are. *Anything* untoward, anything we do not like, and we will not harm *you*— at first. Think of the possibilities." His voice was almost purring with pleasure. "Your wife—blinded perhaps . . . a daughter crippled . . . another killed. . . ."

A clap of thunder erupted outside, followed by the crash of torrential rain. Mallahide's eyes flicked to the window. Fenn broke.

His fingers touched the handle of his knife, activating the spring. Using all the leverage he could manage, he rolled and at the same time pressed the catch and threw.

Mallahide was rolling too. He had wondered why Fenn had failed to remove his jacket in such heat.

And when he saw Fenn's hand move, he moved too.

Nevertheless, the blade caught him in the bicep of his right arm, sinking deep into the muscle, bringing immediate pangs of nausea.

Almost miraculously he still held onto the gun and as his vision cleared for a brief moment, he saw that Fenn had toppled onto the rubble and was finding it difficult to rise to his feet.

He strained and the redness moved away. It was Northern Ireland again, but he could manage, he would survive.

Mallahide wriggled himself so that the wall supported him and he used both hands to raise the gun. He pointed it at Fenn's stomach—nothing clever, just the biggest target.

Fenn, half on to his feet, saw the gun and stopped. Mallahide's face was contorted with pain and rage and the corner of his mouth was twitching. A narrow line of blood was running down his arm.

Fenn knew that this was the moment. Perhaps all of his life should have flooded before him. But all he felt was regret. Sad to die.

Even now Mallahide took his time: the cat and the hopeless mouse.

He held the gun steady with one hand, and extracted the

blade from his arm. He smashed the blade against the wall, and pushed a handkerchief onto the wound.

It was a mistake. A second, sudden wave of nausea swept through him. His eyes clouded, his body shook.

Fenn knew it was his last chance. He pushed himself forward. The loose stones impeded him, but nevertheless he caught Mallahide in the stomach, rolling him backward.

The two men half lay, half crouched a yard apart, neither of them able to pull themselves erect on the slippery surface. The harsh grunts of their breath sounded against the backup sound of the rain.

Fenn managed to get to his knees. He raised his head and saw Mallahide again trying to raise the pistol, this time using both hands once more.

He tried to move forward but only slithered. Then he saw it—the handle half of the broken knife, nearly an inch of jagged blade still attached.

It was just within reach of his right hand. He grasped it and swung, falling flat on his face as he did so. The knife hit something and flew from his hand. When Fenn raised his head and looked, Mallahide was lying against the wall, the gun no longer in his hand. He was moaning and his hands, already red, were clutched at his thigh. Fenn had sliced into an artery.

There was time now, and he knew he had to do it. He dragged himself to his feet, took the pistol and began firing at close range. It jammed after three shots, but that was more than enough.

Surprisingly, he felt nothing, not even when Mallahide's body gave its last twitch.

He waited several minutes to regain some strength and then dragged Mallahide's body outside. It was harder than he had anticipated and, outside, he collapsed on his knees.

The rain helped him, its coolness refreshing him. The corpse was near the edge of the cliff and the rain had washed the blood away.

Something caught Fenn's eye, and he moved a few yards to

investigate. It was a small rucksack tucked against the tower. Fenn opened it. It was already filled with stones. Mallahide had not wasted his time while he had waited.

Fenn turned away and looked down at the sea below—waves crashed twenty feet high. He knew that *this* was the way Mallahide had intended Fenn would go. The body might surface and be found one day—when it was hardly recognizable as a human corpse. But what would the police think? A dockside killing—perhaps, even a Mafia murder carried out in adjoining Sicily and the body dumped out at sea.

Fenn turned Mallahide onto his stomach and strapped on the rucksack with difficulty. He added more stones, and then used his feet to roll the body to the very edge of the cliff. He pushed hard.

It bounced twice on the way down and was then lost to view.

Inside the tower Fenn gathered together blood-stained rocks and threw them over the cliff. He became manic, collecting stones long after no blood remained. Then he stopped, his heart pounding. There were still the broken pieces of knife and the gun and he disposed of those too.

Only then did he kneel and retch convulsively.

He was well on his way back toward the car before he realized he was moving. His body sobbed in great racking movements.

The rain, hiding him like a fog, was a blessing. So too was the memory of Mallahide's 'confession—that he was acting against orders in trying to kill Fenn. It meant that others would not follow.

No one was near when Fenn opened the door of the Ford and drove away.

Grima said nothing on the crossing. Nor would he ever talk about the trip. Fenn and his wife were part of the island, and they were a tight-knit people.

At home, Gemma had sent the children away overnight.

Fenn stumbled through the door. Gemma stared into his white face, at the wet on his cheeks that could have been rain or tears.

"Is it over?" she asked.

"It's over. All over."

She came into his arms, sobbing. "Thank God," she said. "Thank God."

P O S T S C R I P T

Moscow, December

It was a promising December day that early morning as Valentin Gogorin entered one of the six pedestrian gates into the unmarked headquarters building of the KGB two long blocks from the Kremlin.

It was not yet fully light, but there was a hint of sun, and the air was already crisp and dry. The snow, after a succession of mild winters, gave the skyline a special beauty.

It was Saturday—normally Gogorin's day off and his chance to sleep late. It was also indecently early—the building was not yet even officially open.

At the entrance, he showed his pass, entered the light green corridor, waited at the elevator and fought the temptation to travel up to the eighth floor and have breakfast. Even though he was working when he should have been at home—and was glad to because it was helpful to his career—he wanted to finish in time to accompany his son to the ice hockey match.

If there was time, he would breakfast afterward. It was his son's nineteenth birthday. There would be a party in the evening, but his son was ice hockey mad. Gogorin did not want to disappoint him.

It was particularly important this year—he had been working especially long hours in the past few weeks and had seen less of his family than he liked.

Still, that had been inevitable: So many strange reports had passed through his department and attempts to make some sense of them had often lasted long into the night.

Gogorin's office was on the fifth floor, but he took the elevator three levels down, deep into the bowels of the gray stone building, deeper even than where prisoners were interrogated.

He was expected. A file clerk tried to explain procedures, but Gogorin shrugged him away. Gogorin had been around the building for years, had worked his way up, had practical experience of most of the things his colleagues only knew from lectures and hearsay.

In theory, he could have made use of the computer, but for what he wanted it was only amateurishly programmed. What was needed, he reflected ruefully, was more American support and know-how. Pity that detente was at such a low ebb.

The files were in regimented rows, a vast area of green cabinets under neon lights. He soon forgot his desire for breakfast and drank imported instant coffee as he worked.

Gogorin was a desk officer in the Third Department of the First Chief Directorate, that part of the KGB responsible for clandestine activities abroad. The Department's area of responsibility included Great Britain.

At forty-one, he had reached his position late in life, but was rapidly making up for it. His knowledge, gained through practical experience, was finally paying off.

It was reports from that country that had kept him so busy so many nights recently. Over the recent weeks there had been a flurry of reports from London. As always, of course, there had been a temptation to link all the individual happenings, to create a pattern.

He thought that now at last his department was beginning to put it into the right perspective. Sir Joseph Banks had resigned for the obvious reasons—he had cracked under the strain of his wife's suicide and the recently confirmed mental breakdown of his adopted daughter.

Sir Robert Hollen's early retirement was an unrelated incident—no more than the man having burned himself out in what, Gogorin knew, was a self-destructive business.

And no doubt the movements within MI5 that they had heard about were related to that early retirement—Hollen's successor was moving out some dead wood. Gogorin found himself sympathizing with Brighouse, though—a worthy adversary, he had always thought. To end up in Belize!

There was more than a hint, too, that the *éminence grise* of the British Establishment, Sir Peter Chambers, was taking full advantage of the situation to move in his own men—why else should Crimpton, the SIS chief, be offered an ambassadorship he could hardly refuse?

Still, interesting though it was, *that* was not today's problem.

Gogorin slid one folder back into the cabinet and extracted another. There was an operation looming and he wanted to be ahead of the game when he attended the meeting with the head of his department on Monday.

At 11:20 he was satisfied. He held three folders. He signed them out of the archives, took them to his room, had himself locked in, and sat staring at them.

He read for several minutes, then walked to the window overlooking the courtyard. It was barred, but he had long ceased to see the bars.

The clock that his wife had given him when he was promoted chimed the hour. Twelve. He was lucky—lots of time to go home, have lunch, get to the match.

He returned to his desk, spread the files. It was a relatively straightforward job—to find someone who satisfied various specified requirements. The man would then undertake an assignment.

Gogorin glanced at the names on the covers of the folders.

All were English. All the men involved were in their forties—he had chosen them carefully. All, too, lived outside their country.

All were sleepers.

Gogorin continued thinking.

He glanced at his watch. Time to go to the KGB club in Building 12, buy some smoked salmon and some real Scotch whiskey.

He picked up two files. One of these men, he thought.

He opened his wall safe, placed the files inside.

The name on one was "Donaldson, Peter," on the other, "Jacobs, Frederick."

He placed the third file on the corner of his desk, ready to return it to archives.

About to close the safe, he reconsidered. Perhaps he was wrong. Let his chief make the final decision. Give him the three names.

Gogorin placed the third folder on top of the two already in the safe, closed the door, sealed it with wax according to regulations.

Beaming contentedly that things had worked out so well, he made for the elevator, the club and then home.

The top file in the safe had a number in the upper right hand corner.

It said, "File Number 14/97845/311."

Below it was the name of the subject.

"Fenn, James."

ERIC CLARK *was*
years a journalist for th
Manchester Guardian
server—*with articles a*
New Statesman, Lor
Times *and the* Wash
before turning to su
His *first novel,* Black
an immediate success
plished in seven c
Sleeper *is his secon*
career, Mr. Clark h
opportunity to learr
cloak-and-dagger, a
was himself approa
in intelligence worl
he declined. Mr. Cl
wife and two dau
ton, England, wher
ing on a third nove